SECOND STAGE: THE ALTERNATIVE THEATRE MOVEMENT IN CANADA

SECOND STAGE

The Alternative Theatre Movement in Canada

Renate Usmiani

UNIVERSITY OF BRITISH COLUMBIA PRESS
VANCOUVER

SECOND STAGE: THE ALTERNATIVE
THEATRE MOVEMENT IN CANADA

This book has been published with help of a grant from the Canadian Federation for the Humanities using funds provided by the Social Sciences and Humanities Research Council of Canada.

Canadian Cataloguing in Publication Data
Usmiani, Renate, 1931-
    Second stage

Includes index.
Bibliography: p.
ISBN 0-7748-0176-X

1. Experimental theatre — Canada — History.
I. Title.

PN2304.U86   792'.0971   C83-091150-2

40,760

International Standard Book Number 0-7748-0176-X
Printed in Canada

Contents

Illustrations

Plates 1-3 were supplied by Theatre Passe-Muraille, 4-7 by Tamahnous Theatre, and 8-10 by Théâtre d'Aujourd'hui. We gratefully acknowledge their co-operation.

Preface

In art, as in life, greatness is achieved in periods of maturity, growth in periods of rebellion. It may well be that critics of the future will fail to find "great" plays among the productions of the alternative theatre movement of Canada, which flourished in the decade of the 1970's; it is inconceivable that they should not canonize this movement as the major force which brought Canadian theatre into the mainstream of the international theatre scene. In an international context, the alternative theatre of Canada is only another, and somewhat belated, manifestation of the rebellious spirit of the 1960's: student revolts in Europe, the anti-Vietnam movement in the United States. Within Canada, the appearance of an alternative theatre was of enormous importance. It testified, once and for all, to the often-questioned existence of a national tradition in drama and theatre (as an antithesis, alternative theatre helped to confirm the existence of the corresponding thesis beyond the doubt of even the most cynical critics). While remaining aggressively nationalistic, it also helped to link up the Canadian theatrical scene with developments everywhere else in the Western world.

The alternative theatre movement has produced one of the most exciting phenomena ever to appear on the cultural scene of this country. It is the purpose of this book to provide the reader with an understanding of the phenomenon in general and to provide an overview of the alternative theatre scene of Canada: by providing a cultural/historical background, and setting Canadian alternative theatre into an international context; by outlining the historical evolution of alternative theatre and giving a brief survey of the major developments in both English and French Canada; and by selecting a number of representative companies, coast-to-coast, and subjecting their work to detailed analysis. I have not tried to be "complete"; this is not a reference work on the alternative theatre of Canada. Rather, I have sought to provide some useful insights, a broad overview, and a glimpse of the inner workings of this elusive, significant, and exciting cultural phenomenon.

This, of course, raises a major question: if the book does not aim to be all-inclusive, what are the main criteria used for selection? And selection there must be, in view of the vast amount of material which could potentially be part of such a study. Ideally, such a selection should be based on historical factors as well as aesthetic criteria; the author must seek to combine the function of cultural historian, with those of theatre and literary critic. In this kind of situation, a certain amount of arbitrary judgment and subjective preference is inevitable; I have, many times, followed nothing more scientific than my own critical instinct. Let me also admit at once that in an area where few records are kept the simple availability of a script or videotape may make a difference. Nevertheless, I have tried to follow in my selection process a number of basic, objective principles:

1. SELECTION OF COMPANIES

Because *Second Stage* examines the alternative theatre movement as a cultural phenomenon of Canada, I have tried, first and foremost, to focus on pioneering companies and companies representative of developments in the major cultural regions: East, West, Central, and French Canada. Also, I hope that a discussion of the alternative theatre companies included here will provide a good overview of the wide range of techniques and approaches of the movement. Comparisons could also yield some significant insights (for example, certain parallels which arise between Quebec and Newfoundland). Finally, the selection made here should provide the reader with some understanding of the evolution of alternative theatre in this country, its links with, and parallels to, alternative theatre in other parts of the Western world, and the socio-historic forces at work at its inception in different parts of the country.

Individual companies have also been singled out for detailed discussion because of their relative longevity on the cultural scene; their influence on other companies; and their development of a distinctive style of their own (it is now possible, for example, to speak of the "Passe-Muraille style of production"). Specific companies have been selected for the following reasons:

Passe-Muraille (Toronto)

One of the first (1969) alternative theatre companies of English Canada, Passe-Muraille has been both the most successful and the most influential. Passe-Muraille has produced commercially viable alternative theatre; created a distinctive style of its own; acted as a seeding agent for a number of similar smaller companies across the nation, especially in the Prairies; provided workshop facilities for aspiring playwrights, directors, and fledgling companies. With a number of its productions now available in print (*The Farm Show, 1837, Baby Blue*), its innovative production style much imitated, and its satellite companies becoming established, Theatre Passe-Muraille has made a definite and no doubt lasting mark on Canadian theatre history.

Tamahnous (Vancouver)

Like Passe-Muraille in Toronto, Tamahnous Theatre in Vancouver remains the only one of a large number of small underground companies whose operations have survived into the 1980's; and also like Passe-Muraille, Tamahnous has developed a distinctive style of its own. The influence of Tamahnous Theatre, however, remains limited. I have chosen to discuss its work briefly in the context of chapter four mainly because it illustrates so clearly the difference in approach between East and West. While alternative theatre companies in the East tend to emphasize their social commitment and aim at producing political theatre in the Brechtian sense, groups on the West coast have been heavily influenced by the more egocentric, introspective approach of the California counter-culture. Tamahnous provides a perfect example of a company with deep emotional roots in the hippie culture of the 1960's. A "family" rather than a professional "ensemble," Tamahnous evolved a style which reflects the group's experimentation with alternative lifestyles, their strong commitment to the communal enterprise, their interest in exploring dreams, fantasies and psychotherapies such as Gestalt as a basis for their theatrical work. It must be added, however, that this kind of commitment ended with the end of the alternative theatre decade; more recently, Tamahnous lacks a clear-cut orientation.

John Juliani and Savage God (Vancouver/York/Edmonton)

Juliani's Savage God does not fit the definition of an alternative theatre "company"; rather, one might describe Savage God as a multi-faceted cultural phenomenon on the alternative theatre scene, which revolves around the personality of John Juliani. In the programme notes to its first production, 1966, Savage God calls itself "an anthology of question marks," and this is exactly what it has been ever since: an attempt to question and challenge all established traditions and assumptions.

As far as it is possible to discern at this point, Savage God has not had the immediate impact and seeding effect on other groups which has made Passe-Muraille an institution on the alternative theatre scene (although certain lines of cross-fertilization can be seen, as with the work of Chris Brookes, director of the Newfoundland Mummers' Troupe, who served part of his theatrical apprenticeship with Juliani). I have chosen to devote a rather large amount of space to the discussion of Savage God because of their intrinsic and unique features, their wide scope of activities, and their sometimes intriguing underlying philosophy.

Savage God has done more than any other Canadian group in the area of exploring the potential of environmental theatre. Through its experimentation with new and different theatre spaces, it has pushed the search for new actor-audience relationships further than any other group has done in this country. Juliani has also attempted to revive the Romantic notion about the fusion of life and art, blending real life events and theatrical happenings into a holistic experience where the line between "performer" and "viewer" disappears in favour of a general process of participation. His ballet *Mosaic*, for example was built into a citizenship ceremony; his productions often come close to Performance art. Savage God repeatedly managed to create links between the university (his student companies at Simon Fraser and York Universities) and the community, and between different areas of artistic endeavour within the community. All of these, of course, echo the various manifestations of the modernistic revolution in European theatre more than fifty years earlier. Within Canada, Savage God provides the best illustration of the implementation of practically every aspect of the earlier European wave of theatrical renewal. Finally, with his PACET experiment, Juliani has created a blueprint for workable, alternative models to the existing establishment theatre. I have dealt at some length with the document describing this experiment, *The Free Theatre*, because it represents the most serious and complete "alternate" model to have emerged from the movement. Finally, the chapter on Savage God reflects my conviction that we are dealing here with a significant phenomenon on the Canadian cultural scene, which so far has not been given the recognition it merits.

The Mummers' Troupe (Newfoundland)

I have included a chapter on The Mummers, first of all, because they represent the most long-lived alternative theatre company in Eastern Canada (1971 to 1982). Also, although influenced by Passe-Muraille techniques, the Mummers have developed an original style which has grown out of their Newfoundland environment and reflects their strong community commitment. By reviving the traditional Mummers' Play, the company has firmly linked itself to an existing local, popular, and oral tradition; in their original work of collective creation, they combine their regional involvement with a strong sense of social commitment. They have also created some fine examples of political theatre.

Jean-Claude Germain and Le Théâtre d'Aujourd'hui (Montreal)

In the survey chapter on the evolution of alternative theatre in French Canada, I have tried to show parallels to, and obvious differences from, the alternative scene in the Anglophone regions and pointed to certain parallels, in the areas of militant nationalism and separatism, between Quebec and Newfoundland. I have singled out the work of Jean-Claude Germain for a number of reasons: although definitely anti-establishment, his Théâtre d'Aujourd'hui has become an institution on the Montreal theatre scene (much like Passe-Muraille in Toronto), and his productions, all scripted, are readily available for analysis. From a more philosophical and less pragmatic point of view, Germain has been included because his work represents a novel political, cultural, and theatrical approach to Quebec history. His productions represent a conscious attempt to link up, not with an existing literary tradition which has its roots in Europe, but with the native, oral tradition of Quebec: the tradition of the monologue and the satirical revue. With his popular approach, and through his choice of themes, Germain attempts to effect a transition from the folkloric stage to the cultural stage, bypassing any reliance on prefabricated colonial models. His alternative theatre thus goes beyond the models used by the *jeune théâtre* companies of Quebec; like the Mummers, more than the Mummers, he links his work to a little-known, popular tradition. The resulting play deserves critical analysis. Again, as with Tamahnous, this is a phenomenon of the 1970's, whose importance is rapidly fading.

It is not too hard to select a number of representative companies to demonstrate the scope of the alternative theatre scene in Canada; singling out individual plays, or productions, is considerably more difficult. I have tried to achieve a reasonable balance between the discussion of interesting, but unpublished material and the analysis of scripts available in print, which are accessible to the reader for further study. As a general principle, I have omitted discussion of plays by authors who have become mainstream dramatists, since such material is available elsewhere,[1] and focused on productions which have remained within the province of alternative theatre (for example, the book includes a discussion of Passe-Muraille's *Them Donnellys*, but not of the James Reaney trilogy on the same theme).

The first chapter, on backgrounds, influences, antecedents and definitions deals with the distinction between avant-garde (spearheading the mainstream) and alternative (antithetical, but parallel, to the mainstream) theatre, showing the connection between new approaches to theatre and modern communications theory. Three major areas, Canadian antecedents, American influences, and European backgrounds, are included.

Because there is little information available about either the Workers' Theatre movement of the 1930's or the anti-realistic, modernist theatre theories of Mitchell and Voaden, I have felt it imperative to include this material to correct the generally held view of the total and utter rootlessness of contemporary developments on the Canadian theatre scene. However, obviously, straight lines of influence lead from the American radical theatre groups in the 1960's to the work of the alternative theatre companies of Canada in the 1970's; and any study of the movement in Canada must necessarily take this connection into account. I have tried to emphasize the major aesthetic principles which have made their way into the Canadian scene (especially as developed by The Living Theatre, and Schechner's formulation of "environmental theatre").

In Europe, the transition from realism to modernism in the theatre occurred through a series of cultural shock waves from the late nineteenth century on; in Canada, a similar transition took place in the late 1960's and early 1970's — an accelerated parallel to the earlier European phenomenon and one which telescoped the cultural manifestations of many decades (Symbolism, Dada, Surrealism, Expressionism, and so forth) into a few short years. Although the influence of the earlier European movements reached Canada only indirectly, and in a much subtler form than the easily identifiable American influence of the 1960's, it is nonetheless essential to remain aware of this European background to the contemporary development. Canadians have a tendency to see themselves as isolated and utterly cut-off from other cultures and previous developments: having denied a colonial past, they feel they must necessarily start from a cultural zero point. As Germain has said in all sincerity with reference to the work of his company, "[nous] on a réinventé le théâtre." Yet in a period of cultural growth and national and regional pride, it is essential not to lose sight of the general cultural and historical context of contemporary developments. As T. S. Eliot has emphasized, "originality" does not mean a denial of one's cultural origins, but on the contrary, an awareness of them. There is much in the current Canadian alternative theatre movement which is indeed unique, brought about by a combination of circumstances entirely our own. However, this "original" development also forms part of a cultural process of which we are a part. Many of the cultural phenomena which we experience as totally "new" have clear antecedents in an earlier stage of the evolutionary process. They are not simply imitations; rather, similar situations (revolt against the cultural and social status quo) bring about similar reactions. In order to evaluate the current Canadian phenomenon of alternative theatre as objectively as possible, it is absolutely necessary to keep in mind the earlier developments. Only thus can we see the regional and national pattern in an international and historical context, evaluate its uniqueness, and make meaningful value judgments. It is the purpose of this book to enable the reader to do just that.

1

Canadian Alternative Theatre in an International Context: Backgrounds, Influences, Definitions

What is "alternative theatre"? How does the concept of an "alternative" art form differ from that of "avant-garde" art, with which it is often confused? A clarification of terms is in order before any specific discussion can take place.

"Avant-garde" refers to the spear-head of the mainstream development within a cultural evolution process (for example, the Storm and Stress movement which spearheaded Romanticism); "alternative," on the other hand, defines itself as a consciously posited parallel to this mainstream, which it does not seek to replace. It may, of course, exhibit avant-garde features; it may also run parallel to an avant-garde movement. To give a Canadian example: the *nouveau théâtre québécois* as practised by Tremblay, Loranger, Barbeau, and others is definitely avant-garde; the *jeune théâtre québécois* is an alternative parallel development. Both avant-garde and alternative movements arise in opposition to an established tradition as a result of the dialectic pattern of cultural history. But whereas "avant-garde" usually refers to a strictly aesthetic concern, alternative movements set themselves up in opposition to institutions and social patterns, as well as artistic conventions. While the existence of an avant-garde has always been part of the historical evolution, alternative theatre must be seen as a modern development (non-mainstream theatrical forms of the past, such as puppet shows, folk theatre, clown and mime shows differ from modern alternative theatre in the sense that they were not specifically set up as a counter-movement or alternative; they were simply minor genres within the general context of theatre). Also, in alternative theatre the emphasis is shifted from the play itself as a work of art to the audience and its involvement in the theatrical process. It is this reciprocal/communicative aspect which is seen as the central function of theatre by alternative companies.[1]

Although the alternative theatre movement varies greatly from country to country and encompasses a multiplicity of forms and ideologies even within each country, it is nevertheless possible to identify the most basic criteria shared by the movement as a whole.

1. Alternative theatre is produced by companies operating outside the theatrical establishment, either without outside subsidy or with minimal grants. This implies freedom of expression; it also implies poverty of means.

2. Alternative theatre is revolutionary and experimental in its aesthetics. Here, of course, there is a clear point of overlap with avant-garde theatre.

3. Alternative theatre is revolutionary in its social and political ideology.

4. Alternative theatre takes a different approach from that of traditional theatre to its audience. It eschews the bourgeoisie, and aims at producing "popular" theatre, that is, theatre physically and financially accessible to the masses, the ideal being free theatre. It also often aims at audience involvement at some level.

5. Alternative theatre is not necessarily based on the traditional author-director-script triangle; it often uses techniques of collective creation and improvisation, with or without co-operation by a writer.

6. In the Canadian context, one further, and essential, criterion must be added: alternative theatre here is definitely nationalistic. Its emphasis on original works and the need to support Canadian playwrights constitutes a strong protest against cultural colonialism. The goal of alternative theatre in this country, then, would seem to be implementation, at last, of the demand made already in the 1940's by Gratien Gélinas, when he called for a "national and popular" theatre[2] — with a considerably more radical interpretation of those terms than the one given to them thirty years earlier.

To gain a more specific understanding of the principles underlying alternative theatre movements internationally, we must turn to modern media theory. The "mobilizing power" of the mass media was recognized very early, and leftist critics were especially quick to denounce the one-way communication systems they developed, leaving the public in a totally passive role. This critical attitude then extended from media theory to the philosophy of theatre. The link here is Bertold Brecht, who, as early as 1932, demanded that radio should be changed from a "means of distribution" to a "means of communication."[3] Modern German media theory has developed this idea a good deal further. Hans Magnus Enzensberger, for example, sets up a model of "repressive" vs. "emancipatory" media use which evokes instantly the parallel of traditional vs. alternative theatre. In his *Baukasten zu einer Theorie der Medien* (*A Building Block Set For a Media Theory*), he makes the following points:[4]

Repressive use of media:	**Emancipatory use of media:**
Centrally controlled programme	Decentralized programme
One transmitter, many receivers	Each receiver a potential transmitter
Immobilization of isolated individuals	Mobilization of the masses

Depoliticization	A political learning process
Control by property owners of bureaucracy	Social control by self-organization

Enzensberger sees the "emancipatory" use of the media as a cultural revolution, a means to release the masses from the bonds of ignorance and tutelage. He also points out the decreasing role of the written word as a means of mass communication.

The ideology of alternative theatre parallels Enzensberger's ideas closely. Contained within his media theory are the concepts of audience involvement and participation in production, the democratic collective of creation, and the non-literary emphasis. The parallel becomes fully apparent in the work of Richard Schechner in America, who has attempted to set into specific counterpoint the distinction between "traditional" and "new" (alternative) theatre. In his essay on "Happenings," Schechner develops the following list of opposites:[5]

Traditional theatre:	**New theatre:**
Plot	Images, events
Action	Activity
Resolution	Open-ended
Roles	Tasks
Themes/thesis	No pre-set meaning
Stage distinct from house	One area for all
Script	Scenario or free-form
Flow	Compartments
Single focus	Multi-focus
Audience watches	Audience participates, sometimes doesn't exist
Product	Process

The list provides a good illustration of Schechner's own concept of "environmental" theatre. Alternative theatre generally, then, rejects traditional theatre techniques and theatre space in favour of environmental theatre and collective creation. Collective creation echoes back to the *commedia dell'arte* in its lack of scripted dialogue and emphasis on improvisation; however, in its contemporary form, it is definitely a phenomenon of the alternative theatre. How exactly does it work, and how well does it work?

To provide some understanding of these two questions, there is the testimony of the first Canadian theatre artist to engage actively in collective creation, George Luscombe, of Toronto Workshop Productions. Luscombe's *Hey, Rube!* of 1961 was, in fact, the first collective creation staged in Canada. Although a pioneer in the technique, Luscombe occupies a middle-of-the-road, rather than a radical, position in his attitude towards collective creation.[6] Toronto Workshop Productions uses the services of a writer-in-residence, and the director exercises a great deal of control over what is happening. The process of collective creation starts with a consultation between the director and the writer-in-residence, following which certain broad lines of theme, character, and situation are discussed with the actors and technicians. Then only, improvisations begin. Some may lead nowhere and are therefore dropped; some lead to useful insights and are further built upon. Slowly, through constant analysis of what seems "right," characterizations deepen, relationships develop meanings, and a pattern of scenes and narrative lines begins to emerge. At this point, light, set, and costume design begins, changing and progressing along with the improvisations. Eventually, dialogue is written, at first based closely upon the actors' improvisations, then gradually freer and wider until the script begins to suggest scenes and characters which have not yet been introduced on the stage. Luscombe quotes Brecht in describing the final result, the play itself: "the most frequently repeated of what has not been rejected."

Co-operation and division of labour, then, are the fundamental principles of collective creation in the case of Toronto Workshop Productions. Unlike later, more extreme proponents of the new techniques, their director rejects the notion that everyone involved in the production of a play must necessarily also be involved in the creation process:

> Language is the province of the writer, and the actor no more creates language than the writer creates movement or the technician creates music. But the actor can, and should, create characterization. The actor who merely interprets a fixed character is doing half his job. . . . That most actors do half their job is no more unusual than the fact that most dramatists write outside the theatre.

A more radical approach to collective creation rejects the concept of "scripted" dialogue altogether: such productions are based entirely on the work of the actors themselves, who research their proposed material, and their characters, and then develop a play, again by a process of trial and error through improvisation. Depending on the company, the director may exert more or less influence and control over the production.

As for the ultimate results of the collective creation technique: it is difficult to establish how well the method really works. For one thing, the concept of "results" would have to be clarified before any evaluation is made. Most of the politically oriented companies would certainly reject any purely aesthetic criteria for measuring the success of their work, which aims at achieving practical results, or at least, a definite raising of consciousness. Nevertheless, an objective critic cannot (and must not) lose sight of the artistic merit of any production. A further problem is created by the fact that collective creation is the most ephemeral type within an already ephemeral genre. Because of the large proportion of improvisational work within a production, the quality of performance varies widely from one performance date to the next, making it difficult to pass judgment on anything more than any one particular show. And since there is often no official script, it becomes impossible to preserve the production for critical analysis at a later date. Some collective creations, which were particularly successful, have found their way into print, such as Passe-Muraille's *The Farm Show*. Quite clearly, the very best specimens of the genre also make interesting "reading," and can thus pass into the general body of dramatic literature. Some have been preserved on videotape and thus remain accessible for further study. But the bulk of collective creations has simply exercised a subtle influence on subsequent dramatic development through its emphasis on the role of the actor, and on the generally co-operative, as opposed to hierarchical, nature of any theatrical effort. Theatre artists, both French and English, now consider the period of collective creation as a necessary stage which Canadian theatre had to go through, for ideological and aesthetic reasons; but it is a stage which is coming to a close, at least in its more extreme form.

The alternative approach to creation implies an alternative approach to theatre space in order to create a new basis upon which to build the actor-audience relationship. Schechner's "environmental" approach, favoured by alternative theatre companies, implements ideas developed as early as the late 1920's with the experiments of Piscator and Gropius. In fact, the manifold manifestations of Canadian alternative theatre can be linked, indirectly or directly, to practically all the European avant-garde movements since the late 19th century, the cultural upheaval often summed up as "modernism."

Modernism was itself influenced to a large extent by a new awareness of the conventions of Oriental theatre, which came as a revelation to Western playwrights steeped in 19th century realism. From Oriental theatre, the West learned a stylized, as opposed to a naturalistic, approach, and techniques of alienated acting. Japanese Noh theatre became known in Europe through Ezra Pound, who obtained Ernest Fenollosa's studies on the subject from his widow in 1902 and passed them on to Yeats. Noh techniques influenced the work of most major reformers of the modern stage, most importantly, Meyerhold and Brecht; the latter's technique of alienated acting is partly based on the Noh style. Reinhardt and Meyerhold both adapted the Japanese Kabuki system of a *Hanamiche* ("flower path") to their stage design. Originally a path from the back of the hall to the stage through which actors made their entrance (and which fans covered with flowers, hence the name), this Japanese feature found its Western counterpart in the use of elevated paths, or scaffolding. Artaud was decisively influenced in his views about the theatre as image and spectacle by his experience of Balinese theatre. And Grotowski's work, which has affected alternative theatre throughout the West, consciously repeats some of the techniques of Noh, Kathkali, and the

Peking Opera. This Oriental influence, then, has come to Canadian theatre thrice removed; nevertheless, it is a factor to be borne in mind.

Looking more specifically at the evolution of "modernism" as a series of cultural revolutions beginning in the late 19th century, we can determine two major lines of development: one mainly introspective, with its origins in Romanticism; the other "committed" or socially concerned, originating in Naturalism;[7] with forms and directions such as Expressionism and the post-naturalism Russian theatre combining both. Although it is quite easy to demonstrate the existence of these two separate streams, it must also be emphasized that here as with any other cultural categories, the lines of demarcation are often blurred, and a lot of overlapping occurs. Chronologically, the two movements run parallel (1857 marks the date of Flaubert's *Madame Bovary* as well as Beaudelaire's *Les Fleurs du Mal!*). The two divergent streams often go back to a common basis: thus, the work of Freud has been essential for both, with its emphasis on the importance of the dream life and the unconscious marking the introspective movement, his psychological determinism, naturalism, and the socially committed stream. The great dramatists of the period often move from one to the other — Ibsen and Strindberg provide cases in point. Other biographical facts confirm the essential indissolubility between the aesthetic and the political factors: most French Surrealists, although dedicated to formal experimentation, also belonged to the Communist party, while proponents of political theatre such as Piscator and Brecht were equally fascinated with formal experimentation and often formulated aesthetics of their own.

For purposes of this study, however, and with this *caveat* in mind, it will be easier to keep the distinction clear. The introspective stream in modern drama is essentially anti-illusionistic. It rejects the recreation of surface reality through realism/naturalism, its justification summed up by Schopenhauer's dictum that "A work of art can have its effect only through the imagination, and therefore must stimulate it constantly"; or, as Voltaire put it more unceremoniously, "le secret d'être ennuyeux, c'est de tout dire" ("the secret for being boring is to say it all"). From its roots in Romanticism and the idealistic philosphy that accompanied it, this movement developed via Jarry and French Symbolism to Dada and Surrealism; from there to Artaud's Theatre of Cruelty and the modern Theatre of the Absurd. Postmodern alternative theatre often provides a synthesis of all of these antecedents.

From Romanticism, subsequent movements took the revolutionary spirit; the cult of the individual; and the emphasis on the irrational, the mysterious, the occult, or subconscious as sources of inspiration and enlightenment. These attitudes combined with a demand for the abolition of all traditions and conventions in favour of total freedom of artistic expression (Victor Hugo defined romanticism as "liberalism in the arts"). This demand for freedom of expression has since taken on more and more radical proportions.

Meanwhile, German idealistic philosophy laid the theoretical groundwork for modernism, starting with Kant's distinction between "Verstand" and "Vernunft" (logical vs. intuitive reason) and his postulate of art as an end to itself. Idealism, then, proclaimed the emancipation of aesthetics from the bonds of logic and rationalism. It also postulated the freedom of genius to find and apply its own laws, regardless of convention. The aesthetics of German idealism found their final embodiment in the work of Richard Wagner, whose concept of "total theatre" left a strong mark on modern dramaturgy through its adaptation by Adolphe Appia and Gordon Craig. Margaret Croyden has effectively summarized the link between the aspirations of the Romantic artists and the contemporary theatre: "The elevation of felt experience over a rationalistic approach to life resulted in an idiosyncratic aesthetic through which the Romantic artist sought first to expand his consciousness, then to transform the world."[8]

From Romanticism, the French Symbolists took over the emphasis on self. They also developed to a high degree the ability to fuse art and life (a goal also in the more contemporary happening, and in certain experiments of alternative theatre). They often consciously chose a life of decadence, drug addiction, and sexual aberration in an attempt to achieve mysticism, dreams, and subconscious states that could then be given artistic expression. Evil exercised a special fascination for them as in Beaudelaire's *Les Fleurs du mal*, or Alfred Jarry's real-life involvement in vice. Jarry's revolutionary Ubu plays illustrated a particularly influential aspect of anti-naturalism. Unlike the highly poetic tone of the Symbolists, Jarry's plays carry their message through verbal and physical violence, shock tactics and grotesque exaggeration. When *Ubu Roi* opened in 1896 with the first "merde" ever pronounced on stage, the event marked the beginning of a new era in theatre. Jarry's techniques influenced the development of both Dada and Surrealism. Antonin Artaud was fully aware of Jarry's relevance to much subsequent drama when he named his own theatre "Théâtre Alfred Jarry." Symbolist theatre, on the other hand, emphasizes dream-like states of consciousness and images as opposed to character and action; Maurice Maeterlinck with his highly evocative "static theatre" is probably the most successful dramatist in the genre. The Symbolist poet Paul Fort introduced his plays to Paris audiences at his Théâtre Mixte (the later Théâtre d'Art).

The gentle, dream-like quality of the Symbolist approach was rudely shattered by the nightmare experience of World War I, which brought about a re-examination of all traditional moral and political values — so obviously bankrupt — and of the cultural system that went with them. A violent, anarchistic, nihilistic, iconoclastic, and irrational protest movement arose: Dada. Dada was a totally negativistic, primeval scream of protest against the outrages of Western civilization, with its capitalist system and middle-class culture. Because of its extreme negativism, it could not outlast the first passionate impetus. Eventually, it led to the more purposeful approach of Surrealism.

Dada had been founded in 1916, in Zurich, by two poets, Tristan Tsara and Hans Arp, and a painter, Richard Huelsenback. Tsara summed up the dadaistic creed in his 1918 manifesto: "every product of disgust capable of becoming a negation of the family is dada; [so is the] abolition of logic; a social hierarchy; memory; archaeology; Prophets."⁹ All of these attitudes have left their mark on the later alternative theatre; the negation of the family plays a particularly important role in the nouveau and jeune théâtre of Quebec.

By the early 1920's, many of the participating artists had become disenchanted with Dada's excessive and sterile iconoclasm. One of these, André Breton, initiated a new movement of his own in 1923: Surrealism. Actually, the term was not new. it had been used by Guillaume Apollinaire with reference to Jean Cocteau's *Parade* as well as his own play, *Les Mamelles de Tiresias*, in 1917. Breton took over from the Symbolists the ideal of fusing life and art (he favoured eccentric behaviour and role playing in his private life). His main concern, however, was the expansion of consciousness, which he tried to achieve through trance, hypnosis, and induced hallucinations. He felt that a work of art should come straight from the subconscious mind without rational control. This process of writing, which was intended to lead to a literature of dream, he termed "automatism." This attempt to give concrete form, on stage, to the images of the subconscious was repeated in the contemporary avant-garde and alternative theatre. Breton formulated his theories in a number of manifestoes. The first Surrealist manifesto (1924) emphasizes the importance of the dream process, with credit given to the work of Freud. The opening statement reflects Breton's disenchantment with post-Enlightenment technological society: "We are still living under the reign of logic, but the logical processes of our time apply only to problems of secondary interest."¹⁰ He advocates automatic writing, with thought freed from rational control, and working quickly, instinctively, allowing chance to become a major factor. This means a fusion of two states considered incompatible till then, dream reality and higher reality: "I believe in the future resolution of these two states . . . which are dream and reality, into a sort of absolute reality, a surreality, so to speak."¹¹ The manifesto also provides a useful definition of Surrealism, which is worth quoting *in toto*.

> SURREALISM: Pure, psychic automatism by which it is intended to express, either verbally or in writing, the true function of thought. Thought dictated in the absence of all control exerted by reason, and outside all aesthetic and moral preoccupations.
>
> SURREALISM is based on the belief in the superior reality of certain forms of association hitherto neglected, in the omnipotence of the dream, and in the disinterested play of thought. It leads to the permanent destruction of all other psychic mechanisms and to its substitution for them in the solution of the principal problems of life.¹²

While Surrealism has probably left its most significant mark on modern cinema, it is easy to see its effect on many of the themes and techniques of the contemporary stage. As a movement, it lost its impetus with the depression of the 1930's. But the underlying ideology continued with the work of Antonin Artaud, a former Surrealist himself, whose major book, *The Theatre And Its Double*, appeared in 1938. Although never able to put his ideas into practice on stage, Artaud was without doubt the most influential champion of the anti-naturalistic, imagination-oriented movement from the 1930's on; his influence persists to this day.

Artaud's essential roots in the anti-rationalism of the Romantic movement appear clearly in the Preface to *The Theatre And Its Double*, where he states that "far from believing that man has invented the divine, I think it is man's age-old intervention which has corrupted the divine within him."[13] Like his Polish contemporary Witkiewicz who also saw theatre as a means to bring back to man a metaphysical experience, Artaud wanted to "restore to the theatre a passionate and convulsive sense of life."[14] This would be accomplished through his "theatre of cruelty," which was to effect change in the human being, not through didacticism or propaganda, but rather through ritual and exorcism. Man's true nature must be revealed ruthlessly:

> The essential theatre is like the plague . . . because it is the revelation, the bringing forth, the exteriorization of a depth of latent cruelty by means of which all the perverse possibilities of the mind, whether of an individual or of a people, are localized . . . like the plague, the theatre has been created to drain abscesses collectively.[15]

The concept of a theatre of "cruelty" has often been misinterpreted or used as an excuse to show excessive physical violence on stage. This is far from the intentions of Artaud, who uses the term in a metaphorical sense: "[Cruelty] is not equivalent with bloodshed, but the much more necessary and terrible cruelty which things can exercise against us. We are not free. And the sky can still fall on our heads. And the theatre has been created to teach us that, first of all."[16] Shock effects in the spectacle must never be used as an end in themselves; however, "Without an element of cruelty at the root of every spectacle, the theatre is not possible. In our present state of degeneration, it is through the skin that metaphysics must be made to re-enter the minds."[17]

As for the production itself, Artaud advocates a "total theatre" in which all the elements work together equally, rather than the highly literary, dialogue-oriented theatre traditionally produced in the West: "I say that the stage is a concrete physical place which asks to be filled, and to be given its own concrete language to speak . . . it has first to satisfy the senses. There is a poetry of the senses as there is a poetry of language." He goes on to describe the "poetry of space," made up of "music, dance, plastic art, pantomime, mimicry, gesticulation, intonation, architecture, lighting, scenery."[18] Language, of course, is not to be discarded, but its relative importance should be no greater than the one it carries in dreams; also, it should be used in an incantatory manner, rather than to express logical thought. In this way, Artaud believes, theatre will truly fulfill its function as a "double" of reality — "not of this direct, everyday reality of which it is gradually being reduced to a mere inert replica — as empty as it is sugar-coated — but of another, archetypal and dangerous reality."[19]

Artaud cites Balinese theatre, which he had an opportunity to see in Paris, as the most perfect example of "pure" theatre, based upon stylized signs, rather than words. Instead of subjecting the spectator to a text, theatre should provide a total experience, in which "the truthful precipitates of dreams, his taste for crime, his erotic obsessions, his savagery, his chimeras, his utopian sense of life and matter, even his cannibalism, pour out, on a level not counterfeit or illusory, but interior."[20] Obviously, such an attitude leads to the rejection of the masterpieces of the past and a call for total renewal. Alternative theatre everywhere has taken up Artaud's challenge.

Just as World War I produced the nihilistic approach to art exemplified by Dada, World War II produced the Theatre of the Absurd. Although rooted in the same tradition of irrationality (and paradox), the Theatre of the Absurd differs from Dada in having solid foundations in a clearly formulated worldview, the philosophy of Existentialism, and in its production of a significant corpus of dramatic works. Like anti-naturalistic theatre in general, the Absurd is not concerned with psychological realism, character development, or logical plot situations. Instead, it aims at expressing the human condition through a series of stage metaphors with the non-verbal element at least equal in importance to the spoken dialogue. Canadian theatre artists have had direct contact with practitioners of the Theatre of the Absurd, and its major representatives, especially Beckett and Pinter, have been frequently produced in this country. Thus, there is a direct link between the Canadian theatre scene and the last stage in the long evolutionary line of the introspective theatre tradition.

As for political/committed theatre, it can be traced back to the social concerns already present in the realistic/naturalistic tradition of the late 19th century. It is a development heavily influenced by other than literary, or even cultural, aspects of society: the growth of the Socialist movement; modern, and especially Freudian, psychology; the popularization of Darwin's theory of evolution. The new school of naturalism looked upon man as a product of his heredity and environment, with little scope for free will (as opposed to the extreme emphasis on the self in Romanticism and post-Romanticism!). The only hope seemed to lie in working towards a change in man's environment — a radical reform of his conditions of existence. This way of thinking led directly to the development of political theatre, of cause. Emile Zola spearheaded the movement, in his novels as well as his theoretical writings on the theatre. His ideas were taken up in France by André Antoine, who founded the Théâtre libre, and by the Freie Buehne (Free Stage), later Freie Volksbuehne (People's Free Stage) concept in Germany. Probably the most radical implementation of the concept of naturalism on stage was realized in Russia, with the work of the Moscow Art Theatre under Stanislavsky. However, with the first of a series of revolutions beginning in 1905, this style, which was purely aesthetic, seemed somewhat dated. With the establishment of the Studio Theatre under Vsevelod Meyerhold, Russian theatre moved into the age of experimentation. Meyerhold's contribution will be discussed in detail later.

The first theoretician of a political theatre to grow out of naturalism was a German, Erwin Piscator. His work eventually led to the internationally effective renewal of theatrical styles effected by Bertold Brecht. Brecht was present at many of Piscator's experiments and took a large number of his revolutionary ideas from the older man. The fact that it is now Brecht, rather than Piscator, who has come to be acknowledged as the leading spirit of political theatre is a result of Brecht's formulation of two key concepts, "epic theatre" and "alienation effect." As well, he was able to put his ideas into practice in the form of highly successful plays, while Piscator remained a theoretician and director.

In his basic approach, as well as some of his techniques, Piscator laid the foundation for the modern activist, committed theatre. He rejected both excessive aestheticism and psychological realism with its emphasis on individual destiny, in favour of a larger view, more appropriate to modern mass society, which he saw governed by the facts of politics and economy: "Our destiny lies in economy and politics, and as a result of both, society, the social factor. Only if we recognize these three facts . . . can we relate our life to the 'historical' aspect of the 20th century."[21] He fully realized the need to introduce new themes to the theatre, if it was to retain its relevance for modern man: "It was a case of coming to terms on stage with the great contemporary thematic units, the battle for oil, the war, the revolution, justice, the racial question, etc."[22] This ideology clearly prefigures the concerns of all contemporary alternative theatre companies with a political orientation. Piscator in fact looked upon the theatre as a moral institution, linking up with a view that goes from Plato to Schiller and Tolstoy; but his emphasis was political/activist rather than religious/moralistic. Actually, Piscator had started out in a more romantic vein as a member of the Dada movement; but he soon came to the conclusion that active participation in the class struggle was to be preferred to theoretical nihilism. He founded a number of theatres, all based on the proposition that art should be carried out largely by the proletariat (he favoured amateur working men's groups) and should serve the cause of the proletariat. Piscator thus continued in the earlier tradition of the Volksbuehne, theatres dedicated to providing suitable entertainment at a low price for the working classes; establishment theatre was unaffordable to them, of course. To illustrate just how far removed traditional theatre was from the needs and consciousness of the people, Piscator cites the example of the controversy which surrounded the performance of Hauptmann's naturalistic/revolutionary drama *The Weavers* at the Deutsches Theater in Berlin. To objections that the work might prove subversive, the director countered with the unassailable argument that anyone who might feel personally involved and therefore react violently to the play, could not possibly afford the cost of a ticket — and he pronounced the production quite safe! (Experience later proved him wrong after all.)

Piscator's theatres all followed one basic programme: to speed proletarian culture and to raise the consciousness of the masses. To this effect, he reformed both staging techniques and theatre space. His was the first documentary drama, *Trotz Allem (In Spite of All)*, 1925, a montage of speeches, essays, leaflets, newspaper clippings, and so forth performed on a plain, functional stage and making use of modern technology (war episodes, for example, were documented by film footage from the national archives). The entire work was based on close co-operation, a "Gemeinschaft," or collective, as Piscator called it, made up of the writer, director, technicians, musicians and actors. Beside the documentary, Piscator introduced the revue style (for example, *Roter Rummel, Red Upheaval*, 1924), which became the foundation for Brecht's "epic," that is, episodic method of dramatic structure. It has remained a favourite style and can be clearly seen in the structure by "units" of most collective creations. Piscator's views on how to approach historical drama also prefigure exactly the approach taken by contemporary companies: "Historical drama . . . not as the personal tragedy of some hero, but as the political document of an era."[23]

With such a radical view of theatre went a new view of theatre architecture: the attempt to abolish the "psychological wall" between the performers and the audience which had been the trademark of Western theatre from court theatre to the bourgeois institutions of the 19th century. Piscator's views laid the foundations for the 20th century concept of "environmental" theatre, elaborated by Schechner. Piscator envisioned a "total" or "universal" theatre structure, with a fully flexible audience space and an adaptable staging area equipped for the use of all modern technical equipment, with film projections possible all around, including at the back of the audience. Walter Gropius, the famous architect, made an attempt to realize Piscator's vision in actual designs for a building. These designs are preserved, although they were never executed. Gropius explains the goals of his revolutionary design as follows:

The aim of this theatre is . . . that the spectator should be pulled right into the midst of the goings-on on stage, that he should be a part of the space of these events, and unable to escape behind a curtain. Besides this, the theatre architect has the task to make the instrument of the stage so impersonal, functional and flexible that it imposes no limitations on the director in any specific case, and allows divergent artistic interpretations to develop.[24]

Because of the historical developments in Germany, Piscator eventually emigrated to the United States and founded a school for actors in New York. In this way, he established a direct link between the beginnings of political theatre in Germany in the 1930's and the modern alternative, or "radical," theatre movement in America. Among his students were Judith Malina and Julian Beck, who eventually founded the Living Theatre; based, no doubt, upon concepts originally formulated by Piscator, but carrying these concepts to much more radical extremes. Piscator's most important contribution, however, is the influence he exerted on the young Brecht. From Piscator, Brecht learned many of his staging techniques; for he was able to see political theatre in action. Modern dramaturgy is of course heavily influenced by the dramatic theories eventually evolved by Brecht, his concept of "epic theatre" (which spelled the end of Aristotelian theatre), and the idea of alienation, "Verfremdung," a distancing process brought about by a combination of script, setting, and acting techniques and calculated to increase the social awareness of the audience. Because of his dramatic genius and the sheer power of his best plays, such as *Mother Courage*, Brecht was able to popularize his ideas much more than Piscator had. Although performed in Canada relatively late, and relatively rarely (this is true of both English Canada and Quebec), Brecht has nevertheless exercised an enormous influence on the alternative theatre movement in this country — as the discussion of individual companies will show.

Modernism has been defined as a series of revolutionary movements along two main streams, introspection and commitment. However, there also developed certain approaches which do not fit either of the two main categories, but which still exercised a considerable influence on subsequent developments: German Expressionism, and the experiments in Russia from Meyerhold on. Expressionism, for example, had a specific variant in Canada with Herman Voaden's "Symphonic Expressionism" of the 1930's.

Expressionism actually aimed at a combination of the two antithetical forms of modernism: it tried to be both poetic and social/revolutionary. A good example would be Ernst Toller's *Masse Mensch (Man and the Masses)*, of 1921, in which he shows social revolution, dramatized in the form of a dream. Three of the seven scenes which comprise the play are actually dream sequences. The shifting among levels of reality creates a definite disharmony in the tone of the play.[25] The combination which the Expressionists sought did not work, and the movement eventually failed — not before it had made some significant contributions, however. In fact, the passionate commitment of Expressionists left its mark not only on subsequent literary approaches, but also on the major political movements of the period, Communism as well as Nazism.

Although Expressionism as a literary genre is considered mainly a German phenomenon with writers such as Brecht, Hermann Bahr and Franz Werfel, it originated in France, as a movement in the fine arts. The term itself was coined by the painter Hervé, and later used to characterize the work of Matisse, Van Gogh, and Cézanne. Expressionism never achieved stylistic unity, but rather was characterized, in the words of its proponent Kurt Pinthus, by "the intensity and radicalism of feeling, world-view, expression and form."[26] In his manifesto of Expressionism, Kasimir Edschmidt described his confreres as follows:

> They did not look.
> They envisioned.
> They did not photograph.
> They had visions.
> Instead of the rocket
> They created the perpetual state of excitement.[27]

Expressionism took its inspiration from both Surrealism and Cubism. From Surrealism, it adopted the emphasis on dreams, visions, hallucinations; from Cubism, a tendency towards abstraction and intellectualism. A basic dichotomy, then, seems to run through the entire movement. Expressionism reflected the trend of reacting against "establishment" art in any form and favouring styles and techniques borrowed from the cabaret, the beer cellar, and the musical improvisations of jazz. Plots were disjointed, bizarre, and irrational; language ran the gamut from the rhapsodic to the crudely vulgar; the style was often telegraphic and attempted to render the "telescopic" nature of inner experience. Extremes in theme, language, and stage craft were often calculated to shock the audience. Extreme subjectivism and the replacement of conceptual language by the impact of a single word, a silence, or pantomime as in silent film often make expressionistic plays difficult to apprehend; but at their best, they can provide their audience with a powerful experience. Hermann Bahr singled out the "Schrei," the "shriek," as the one most characteristic feature of expressionistic theatre. Walter Sokel, a specialist on German Expressionist theatre, sums up its basic features as "the projection of abstract ideas and psychic situations into symbolic images and happenings."[28] The characters tend to be soulless, often expressed by masks or by the exteriorizations of a single main character, usually a projection of the author. It achieves a dream-like or nightmarish quality through exaggeration and distortion.

An important aspect of Expressionism for modern contemporary art was the typical Expressionist's sense of alienation, of being isolated from the community of man (a feeling not unrelated to the *Weltschmerz* of the Romantic poet, but experienced with considerably greater harshness in the modern age). Art was seen as a negative influence, destroying, rather than creating, bonds between humans. Expressionists therefore developed a theory of "Wandlung," or "regeneration," a renewal of spirit through which the artist would ultimately achieve identification and union with the rest of mankind. This attitude was strongly influenced by the more subjective plays of Strindberg, such as *The Road to Damascus* and *The*

Dream Play; Strindberg, in fact, can be viewed as a precursor of Expressionism in many ways. The desire for spiritual regeneration is illustrated, for example, in Reinhard Sorge's *The Beggar*, with the begger/poet's dream of a new, communal kind of theatre which would provide a religious experience, rather than entertainment. A less spiritual interpretation of "Wandlung" called for revolt against the political and social order. This led to the conflict of generations theme, prefigured in Wedekind's pre-expressionist "childhood tragedy," *Fruehlingserwachen (Spring's Awakening)*. One response to World War I was an emphasis on pacifism, often coupled with anarchistic attitudes (the parallel with the radical theatre of America at the time of the Vietnam War here imposes itself). Examples of these attitudes would be Ernst Toller's *Die Wandlung (Regeneration)*, or Georg Kaiser's *Die Buerger von Calais (The Citizens of Calais)*; in the latter, the central character defies the traditional ideal of national honour and sacrifices his life to the cause of peace instead. Idealism was, of course, a difficult attitude to maintain in the wake of World War I. A sense of utter futility soon replaced the activist enthusiasm of Expressionist art. The later dramas, such as Kaiser's *Gas* in 1920, are imbued with a deep pessimism, and the movement soon died out. The techniques of Expressionism, however, have remained an integral part of avant-garde drama world-wide.

Another important group which tried to achieve a synthesis of the two theatrical mainstreams of the period were the practitioners and theorists of Russian theatre in the early 20th century. The naturalistic style of production had reached its greatest heights with the Moscow Art Theatre, from 1898 on. However, a counter-movement soon arose under the leadership of Meyerhold, who, influenced by the French Symbolists, rejected extreme naturalism in favour of a theatre of the imagination. His work, centred on the Studio Theatre in Moscow from 1905, has become extremely influential for contemporary theatre, both in Europe and on the North American continent. Although he believed that a renewal of the theatre must first come from literature, Meyerhold also strongly emphasized the non-literary aspects of production, especially the role of the actor. To make the actor's body into the versatile instrument he envisaged, Meyerhold experimented with gymnastics, boxing, fencing, and the techniques of Oriental dance and Roman mime. He eventually developed his system of "bio-mechanics" based on the proposition that the entire body must be involved in each individual movement. He invented a series of exercises to that end, of which the most famous, "the cat," is still frequently used today. Meyerhold also believed in the need for active involvement on the part of the audience, and he experimented with new uses of theatrical space, such as scaffolding and ramps, and the free mingling of actors and audience, and the use of "found spaces," such as public squares. Perhaps most interesting from the point of view of contemporary alternative theatre with its rejection of traditional hierarchies is Meyerhold's 1906 graphic representation of the "old," triangular, vs. a new, "linear," system:[29]

OLD SYSTEM (rejected):

NEW SYSTEM (recommended):

author ——— director ——— actor ——— audience

Meyerhold's totally democratic, linear system obviously foreshadows the rationale of the collective creation companies of the 1960's and 1970's. His pioneering work remains a central influence on contemporary alternative theatre.

Other Russian theoreticians of the period also deserve mention; especially Mayakowski, and Tairov. Mayakowski first saw the importance of art as "process," rather than "product" only — an essential distinction for contemporary theatre; he was also the first to implement the concept of "disposable" art. His *Mysterium buffo* of 1917 was designed to change from one performance date to the other in order to keep up with historical changes.

Alexander Tairov, although elitist/reactionary in his view of theatre space and the function of the audience ("creative receptivity," but no participation), must be recognized as one of the prophets of the collective creation movement. He saw the actor as the key to theatrical renewal: "This new, genuine theatre which we aim for . . . will be brought about, not by literature, but by the new master actor."[30] Tairov actually envisaged a day when theatre would be able to get away from the use of scripts altogether, with a director creating the production in co-operation with his actors! Until this happened, Tairov suggested using the services, not of a dramatist, but of a poet to assist in the finalizing of the performance — a system which was effectively implemented by alternative theatre groups some fifty years after his prophetic statements of 1921.

These, then, sketched very broadly, are the major lines of the European modernistic developments which led up to the contemporary avant-garde; all of these have filtered through, mostly in an indirect way, to the Canadian theatre scene. There have, however, also been more recent developments, which have had a more direct influence. The European avant-garde of the 1960's was connected immediately to the local political and social unrest of the period (for example, the student revolts of 1968) and to the Vietnam War, under the impact of the Living Theatre, which had left New York for Europe in 1964. The new theatre revolution took up the old battle cry, often in the same terms: Dada's crude motto "Kunst ist Scheisse" ("art is shit") was reiterated by John Cage in New York, and inscribed on the curtain of the venerable Odéon Theatre in Paris. Traditional playwrights viewed the new developments philosophically. Max Frisch's reaction is typical:

> Thank God! It was more than necessary. If you think of Living Theatre, of the non-literary theatre. We were in a phase, a terminal period, where theatre consisted of illustrating a literary text on stage . . . this iconoclasm was absolutely necessary . . . I assume that what we are living now is a very regenerative in-between stage. . . . It was the end of the literary theatre, a temporary end, anyway, and it is a good thing that it came about.[31]

The iconoclasm of which Frisch speaks was particularly apparent in France following the events of May 1968. Commenting on this new cultural revolution, Gilles Sandier uses terms which characterize the attitudes of alternative theatre everywhere:

> L'imposture a croulé, avec la singerie de la grandeur. Toute une culture mise en question, radicalement dénoncée . . . culture d'ossuaire, dérisoire et abjecte, quand on pense à l'usage qu'on en a fait et aux crimes qu'elle a couverts.[32] ("Imposture has been destroyed, together with the monkeying of greatness. A whole culture put in question, radically denounced . . . a culture of the mortuary. Laughable and abject, when you think of the use it was put to, and of the crimes it served to cover up.")

In the absence of a central cause around which to rally, the alternative theatre movement in Europe lost a good deal of its impetus in the 1970's. However, the influence of the new approach remained, both in playwriting and directing. Several directors have been especially influential from a Canadian point of view. Peter Brook in England aimed at a synthesis between the approaches of Brecht and Artaud; his production of *Marat-Sade*, which caused a considerable stir in New York, has left a mark on much subsequent dramaturgy. Jerzi Grotowski in Poland originated the concept of "poor theatre," which remains one of the central elements in Canadian alternative theatre; his mystical/religious views and his most recent use of theatre as therapy have had less influence, though there are traces of these approaches in the work of Canadian John Juliani. A number of young Canadian theatre artists were able to participate in the work of Grotowski's Theatre Lab in the early 1970's and thus brought their experience back to their respective companies: Claude Larouche of Dansepartout, Gabriel Arcand, from the Groupe de la Veillée, Richard Nicocym, of Actor's Lab. Grotowski's contribution has also been popularized in English Canada through the direct research of Don Rubin, editor of the *Canadian Theatre Review*.

Other important direct links between European and Canadian companies were established by George Luscombe, of Toronto Workshop Productions, and Paul Thompson, of Theatre Passe-Muraille. Luscombe worked with Joan Littlewood in England; Thompson, with Roger Planchon in France. Both of these directors were actively engaged in experimentation on the basis of Brechtian techniques. Thompson also familiarized himself with the work of Peter Cheeseman, director of the regional/experimental Victoria Theatre at Stoke-on-Trent. Finally, exchange programmes and guest appearances at some of the international avant-garde festivals (Nancy, Avignon) brought at least a small number of Canadian alternative theatre companies into direct contact with their European counterparts during the 1970's.

In spite of these contacts, the direct European influence remained marginal in comparison with that of the radical theatre movement which developed in the States during the 1960's: its sheer proximity created a strong impact. All the major American groups left their mark on the Canadian theatre scene: The Living Theatre; The Performance Group; The Open Theatre; The San Francisco Mime Company; The Bread and Puppet Theatre; and Teatro Campesino. However, the two single most important factors in the evolution of the Canadian movement were The Living Theatre and the concept of "environmental theatre" as developed by Richard Schechner, founder of the Performance Group.

The Living Theatre has come to be considered almost as an embodiment of the entire radical theatre movement. Its work was itself influenced by the appearance of the "happening," America's major contribution to the international alternative theatre scene. The first happening took place in October 1959 in a loft in Greenwich Village when painter Alan Kaprow invited a selected audience to participate in "Eighteen Happenings in Six Parts," combining a show of paintings and photography with various activities. The term "happening," chosen almost accidentally by Kaprow, soon became widespread, and the "happening" as an event came to be a popular form of participatory theatre. Although happenings took a variety of forms, with no two alike, they all shared certain common features: a rejection of art in the conventional sense; non-verbal expression; an emotional, rather than rational, approach; an emphasis on spontaneity and the subconscious, often achieved through the use of drugs or other stimulants; and a total abolition of the concept of the actor as "performer." Margaret Croyden defines the happening as "a juxtaposition of diverse elements and occurrences, performed in an environment by an audience who are at once spectators and participants."[33] The happening, then, can be seen as a form of anti-theatre: an attempt to abolish fully the distinction between life and art. It achieves a degree of social commitment through the use of everyday objects which are revealed in all their crudeness and vulgarity.

The happening was an international genre. In America, the Living Theatre used it as the basis for a theatrical style. Led by Julian Beck and Judith Malina, the Living Theatre combined the principles of Piscator with those of Artaud to develop a new concept of didactic theatre. The group was as strongly committed to its social ideology as it was to the development of new theatrical forms. Its philosophy has been called "pacifist anarchism": the Living Theatre advocated the abolition of all institutions of capitalist society, from money to war — but through peaceful means only. Its technique is based on Artaud's view of the stage as primarily spectacle: Living Theatre productions make their point through stage images, rather than logical discourse. Silence, non-action, and the eloquence of the human body itself are the main elements used. According to Julian Beck, even speech must serve a new function:

> Theatrical speech . . . is something artificial, a kind of regality. That is, the way an actor generally speaks is very closely related to the ancien régime idea of the way a king speaks. . . . We, The Living Theatre, are trying to reach toward some kind of communication of feeling and idea that push toward some other area, that is beneath words, or beyond words, or in addition to words. The object is not to destroy language . . . but to deepen it and amplify it and to make the communication real rather than a series of lies.[34]

This statement sums up perfectly the general approach of alternative theatre companies to the problem of language on stage and its relative importance within a production.

The Living Theatre carried out its creed of fusing life and art quite radically. Members of the company lived a communal life and regularly used drugs to heighten their state of consciousness. Beck and Malina chose the members of the company carefully on the basis of thorough interviews; but the major criterion for becoming a member of the group was suitable personality, rather than acting talent. The company was probably the most conspicuous embodiment of the hippie movement of the 1960's on the American theatrical scene. Between 1964 and 1968, they travelled throughout Europe, participating in political and social uprisings and spreading the gospel of a new theatre. By 1970, the group had spent its collective energy, and The Living Theatre disbanded after the final performance of their last production, *Paradise Now*. However, the Living Theatre concept remained an ideal for many of the alternative theatre companies of the 1970's, who tried to emulate its theatrical style as well as the lifestyle of its members.

Richard Schechner's Performance Group, organized in 1968, did not achieve success as a theatrical enterprise. However, the concept of "environmental theatre" developed by Schechner has become one of the central elements of alternative theatre productions internationally. Like Meyerhold and Piscator before him, Schechner seeks to abolish the traditional distinction between performance space and audience space. He considers his performance theory a social science, rather than part of any aesthetics. To create a new actor-audience relationship, he calls for open architecture that would allow the actors to see the audience, just as the audience is able to see the actors. This should result in the kind of contact that is "continuous, subtle, fluid, pervasive, unconscious. Lovely."[35] This kind of contact must be created also by a new, and different, approach of the actor towards his role. Schechner emphasizes the importance of modern psychotherapies on performance styles: rather than going through the "mechanical" motions of the traditional rehearsal, the actor should go through a stage of "preparation" for his part. With the help of various psychotherapies, the modern actor is at last able to exteriorize inner states — an achievement which Schechner feels was not possible before. Environmental theatre, then, means not only a new approach to theatre design and the use of space, but a whole new concept of the relationships involved in a production. Schechner has elaborated on this aspect of his theatrical theory in an essay entitled "Six Axioms For Environmental Theatre."[36] His axioms provide some excellent insights into the principles underlying alternative theatre:

1. "The theatrical event is a set of related transactions." Schechner first analyses all of the relationships involved in the theatre experience, going beyond the traditional actor/audience juxtaposition to include each one of the elements of the production; their relations to each other and to the production as a whole; and the relationship between the production and the space in which it takes place. He thus introduces a new awareness of the holistic nature of the theatre event.

2. "All the space is used for performance; all the space is used for audience." This basic principle has been applied, in varying degrees, by the majority of alternative theatre companies. Flexible space abolished the traditional separation between performer and public and thus helps to achieve a sense of communal and collective experience.

3. "The theatrical event can take place either in a totally transformed space or in a 'found' space." Alternative theatre companies, as a rule, do not perform in conventional theatres. If they have a permanent home at all, it is usually a reconverted warehouse (Passe-Muraille), a church (Tamahnous), or a union hall (The Mummers); otherwise they take their productions to whatever space becomes available. "Found" space, like found art, is simply any existing space whose potential for artistic use has been suddenly discovered: performances have been held in cafes, shopping malls, outdoor parks, even in buses and streetcars in motion. The physical trappings of the found space become ready-made settings and props for the production.

4. "The focus is flexible and variable." This allows for multiple-focus productions, where a number of events take place simultaneously, with the audience moving about from scene to scene. The now classical model for this approach was Ariane Mnouchkine's interpretation of the French Revolution in her *1789*, staged at the Théâtre du Soleil near Vincennes (itself a "found" space — a former armoury, la cartoucherie de Vincennes).

5. "All production elements speak in their own language. There is no fixed

hierarchy among the elements." Like the text, the performer is considered only one, and not necessarily or at all times the most important element in the production; he may be replaced by a puppet, de-emphasized with the use of a mask, or even totally eliminated.

6. "The text need not be the starting point nor the goal of a production. There may be no text at all." In alternative theatre, improvisation on a theme, and the subsequent collective creation of a play, often replace the traditional, authored script.

Canadian alternative theatre thus had strong models to base itself on: a long tradition of avant-garde experimentation in Europe, and definite patterns of performance style in the United States. How about Canadian antecedents? Is there any evidence at all in Canadian theatre history of developments which would prefigure the alternative theatre developments of the 1970's? The answer is definitely affirmative.

2

In the Beginning was Toronto — The Emergence of an Alternative Theatre Movement in English Canada

Canadian theatre history offers evidence for the existence of antecedents to the alternative theatre movement, along the lines of both introspective/poetic and committed/political theatre; however, there is as yet no demonstrable influence of these developments, which mostly took place in the 1930's, upon the new wave. Only now, at a time when the alternative theatre movement itself is already on the decline, are these antecedents being discovered by historians of the theatre. And there is no evidence that the leaders of the movement were aware of these antecedents at all. Nevertheless, it is interesting to glance briefly at just what sort of a Canadian background there was for alternative theatre, even if a definite hiatus separates the past from the more recent developments.

On the side of political theatre, a militant workers' theatre existed in French Canada as early as the nineteenth century, and in English Canada, from the 1930's on. The French Canadian workers' theatre operated in conjunction with the Typographical Association of Quebec City, Canada's first labour organization, from the 1830's on. These labour union plays were either contemporary satires and plays of social criticism or classical plays which carried a subversive message: for example, a production of Voltaire's *The Death of Caesar* in 1839, which led to violent audience reaction and the arrest of the man responsible for the production, a newspaper editor by the name of Napoléon Aubain.

In English Canada, workers' theatre began with the rise of the Progressive Arts Clubs in the major cities; the first such club was founded in Toronto in 1931. From 1932 on, the Workers' Experimental Theatre (later known simply as The Workers' Theatre) set itself up as a deliberate antithesis to bourgeois theatre. Its slogan was "Art is a weapon," and its goal, as described in the socialist newspaper, *Masses*, was to produce "plays that would fill a deep need in the hearts of a working class audience and etch there the fundamental ideas of a revolutionary philosophy of life."¹ The plays themselves followed the pattern of *agitprop* everywhere, ranging from mass recitation to socialist realism. Rehearsal and performance took place wherever a space could be found — in parks, labour halls, on the backs of trucks, or even on street corners. A minimum of props and costumes was used, a frequent uniform being a black sateen shirt with a red kerchief. The most ambitious of these productions was a six-act play collectively produced by four authors and entitled *Eight Men Speak*.² Besides its social and political goals, the Workers' Theatre also served as a form of protest against the regular fare of British West End comedies served up by the mainstream Canadian theatres — the same protest that was repeated forty years later with the members of alternative theatre groups.

On the side of introspective, or poetic theatre, two pioneers deserve mention: Roy Mitchell, whose almost unknown theories proved truly prophetic; and Herman Voaden's plays of symphonic expressionism. Voaden, playwright and visionary, fought a losing battle throughout the 1930's to make his Canadian contemporaries aware of the backward state of theatre in this country. A violent opponent of naturalism, Voaden developed a highly poetic style which he termed "symphonic expressionism" and which incorporated choral recitation, music, and choreography into the drama. His principles of total theatre were close to Wagner's. As he wrote in a manifesto of 1929 "If our stage is to save itself, it must no longer be the scene for the actor and the producer in the narrow sense . . . it must . . . embrace the playwright, the student, the thinker, the poet, the musician, the designer and the artist."³ Voaden, it turned out, was a prophet who was sadly ahead of his time; in response to his manifesto, the British dramatist Harold Brighouse published a note, which appeared in the *Toronto Globe*, in which he suggested Canadians would do better to stick to a volume of plays for amateurs, rather than follow Voaden's ambitious theories. Roy Mitchell did not fare much better. In 1929, he published a book entitled *Creative Theatre*, in which he developed his ideas of theatre as a mystical experience. Although much of his work sounds excessively romantic and somewhat naive to a contemporary reader, his basic ideas are surprisingly modern. He realized the deadly effect of American commercialism upon the theatre, and he insisted that another way must be found if theatre was to fulfill its essential function. He saw the importance of the link between a theatre and the community within which it operates and he realized the significant part played by the audience within the total theatre experience. His evocation of the ideal theatre of the future sounds exactly like the goals described by alternative theatre leaders forty years later:

Not a state theatre with its burden of high-salaried incompetents . . . not a civic theatre to be tossed about by politicians. Not a coterie theatre to be the vehicle of literati and esthetes. Just a forthright, ingenious, native, friendly theatre, living for and by a wide enough circle of friends to support it, rather as a church lives, or a club. . . . Such a house, then, will be built in the expectation that people may come to the theatre to spend the evening, may possibly arrive early, may stay late, may like to eat or perhaps dance after the play.[4]

From the vantage point of the 1980's, the prophetic character of Mitchell's work is indeed striking; and it is a sad comment on the cultural scene of Canada that the importance of his ideas was never realized, not even by the proponents of alternative theatre some forty years later, who followed in his footsteps without being aware of the fact. Alternative theatre in Canada is definitely a phenomenon of the 1970's, a movement of protest and rebellion against the newly arisen theatre establishment. Its emergence reflects the development of a new type of theatre consciousness, largely influenced by the European and American precedents. The new attitude can be seen in the text of an anonymous manifesto, passionate and somewhat romantic, which was read on the occasion of the premiere performance of Sauvageau's machinerie-revue *WoufWouf* at the Gesù theatre in Montreal on November 1, 1974:

> Le fait d'être assis sur un siège de théâtre numéroté ne fait pas partie intégrante d'un jeu, d'un divertissement, d'un hasard ou d'un certain snobisme, mais . . . plutôt partie d'un acte social, politique, spirituel et magique, posé en toute conscience et en toute acceptation.''[5] (Sitting on a numbered seat in a theatre is not part of a game, an entertainment, an accidental occurrence or a certain snobbishness, but . . . rather it means taking part in a social, political, spiritual and magical act, performed with full consciousness and fully accepted.)

Somewhat ironically, the rise of an alternative movement confirms beyond a doubt that Canada had indeed developed both a theatrical tradition and a theatre establishment strong enough to bring about a vigorous opposition movement. The period between 1950 and 1970 had been one of enormously accelerated development, in dramaturgy as well as in the setting up of theatre centres; this was largely the result of a newly arisen sense of nationalism, spurred on even more by the centennial celebration of 1967. By 1970, Canada could boast a national theatre of its own, Stratford; a national Art Centre; and a series of regional theatre and art centres across the nation. Canadian theatre, finally, had arrived.

However, for the young artists who grew up during this period of cultural progress, the ultimate results seemed anything but satisfying. They attributed the emergence of art centres from coast to coast to a kind of collective "edifice complex,"[6] rather than to a genuine understanding of the cultural needs of the country, and they soon rose up in rebellion against this newly created "concrete establishment" and the social and cultural value system which it represented. The main accusation was that cultural colonialism not only persisted, but was even being reinforced, by these new developments. Nationalists pointed out the irony of placing Canada's "national theatre" in a town named Stratford, rather than in the nation's capital, and of running that theatre as a Shakespearean company, rather than as a showcase for Canadian playwrights, directors, and actors. Regional theatres were accused of being unduly under foreign influence and totally unreceptive to Canadian work. In 1970, Jean-Claude Germain created the following witty satire of the typical theatre establishment director:

> Les gens de théâtre tolèrent les auteurs dramatiques québécois comme un mal nécessaire, tout en se gardant bien de faire quoi que ce soit pour que le mal se propage. . . Molière dans une main et Beckett dans l'autre, le cul posé sur une pile de Shakespeare et la tête appuyée sur Brecht ou Tchekov ou Pirandello ou Sacha Guitry ou Anouilh ou Pinter ou Albee ou Maeterlinck ou j'sais plus qui, une citation de Racine à la boutonnière et un coup de Corneille dans le nez, repus de culture universelle, pétant de bonne volonté et de modestie, l'homme de théâtre québécois attend la pièce québécoise . . . en attendant, il se fait la main en montant des chefs d'oeuvre.[7] (Theatre people tolerate quebecois playwrights as a necessary evil, while taking great care the evil should not spread. . . Molière in one hand and Beckett in the other, his behind on a stack of Shakespeare and leaning his head on Brecht or Chekhov or Pirandello or Sacha Guitry or Anouilh or Pinter or Albee or I don't know who, a quotation from Racine in his buttonhole and his nose full of Corneille, stuffed with universal culture, farting with good will and modesty, the typical quebecois theatre director waits for the quebecois play . . . meanwhile, he keeps in practice by putting on masterpieces.)

English Canadians are no less acerbic in their views. Ken Gass, founder of Factory Theatre Lab, justified his policy of showing only Canadian works as follows: "I do not feel unusually nationalistic. I am simply trying to relate to the world around me. . . . The major theatres of the country have reneged on their commitment to Canadian plays."[8] Jim Garrard, who started Theatre Passe-Muraille, also emphasized the need for an approach more clearly directed at the Canadian people than that of the elitist theatre establishment and its classically educated leaders: "Theatre must be indigenous. It must be organic. . . . The professional artist is ruining the theatre. It's important to get out . . . into the streets, into schools and parks, into prisons and apartment buildings. We need a guerilla theatre front."[9]

Ironically, if not entirely surprisingly, the anti-Stratford movement was partly started in Stratford itself: Jean Gascon, artistic director of the festival, brought in a number of young, aspiring directors to assist him (John Juliani, Paul Thompson); instead of falling into the pattern of Stratford as expected, these young rebels took the Festival as a negative role model and went off to found companies of their own in protest. Some of these emphasized the need to provide a workshop and showcase for local artists; others stressed a socio-political or aesthetic and experimental orientation; but all were based on the premise that their work must be original, national, and popular. In John Juliani's words, to the "exorbitance, elitism and museum theatre" of the establishment they opposed an alternative of "poverty, democratization, contemporaneity."[10]

In 1976, the grievances of young Canadian theatre artists were summed up in the form of a brief play — the satirical monologue *Henrik Ibsen: On the Necessity of Producing Norwegian Theatre*, written by John Palmer as a curtain raiser for Factory Theatre Lab. This witty speech, delivered by "Ibsen" dressed in period costume ca. 1900, deserves to be quoted at length, since it exposes all the flaws and inadequacies of the Canadian cultural scene as they are viewed by the young generation of frustrated artists:

> I . . . find myself in the untenable position of trying to address something vital to a gathering of no one, for no equitable reward, to no apparent purpose. . . .
>
> It seems to me that we in Norway are having difficulty with the definition of a nation. This is not surprising, as we have been part of first Denmark, then Sweden, up until the present year. While art in general is an international commodity, it is produced by an artist of a particular culture and there is, in fact, no such thing as an international work of art. . . . A nation that emulates all but itself is the true homeland of decadence and dictatorship.

At this point in the lecture, the actor produces a national flag from behind his pulpit and waves it tauntingly at the audience; he then folds it up again, with a reassuring "That wasn't so bad now, was it?"

He then goes on to discuss the problems of native dramaturgy, specifically, the arguments that there are no Norwegian plays in the first place and that producing new plays would cause the demise of the classics, a cultural catastrophe. Countering these arguments which he considers patently false, he launches into a vigorous attack on the theatre establishment and the state of theatre criticism:

> Why is our largest theatre controlled by a foreigner? Why are many regional theatres, all subsidized as well by Norwegian tax payers, equally manacled? Why do these aliens overwhelmingly produce drama originating in any nation other than Norway?. . . Why is government condoning this state of affairs with subsidy and indifference? What is suicide?

And he goes on to denounce the offerings of the concrete establishment as:

> this eternal soirée given by an obsequious Norwegian government and Boards

of Governors as culturally lobotomized as they are impressed and grovelling at the sound of a foreign title. . . .

The state of criticism here is even more unhealthy than that of the theatre to which it owes its keep. It is a sad fact that Norwegian criticism is irrelevant to Norwegian theatre because the critics themselves are yearning after something they will inevitably not see on the Norwegian stage since it is not the English stage or the German stage. . . . Why this tautology should cause them so much anguish and confusion is beyond my modest powers of comprehension . . . the criteria these critics use in diagnosing our indigenous drama are from other times and other places. You cannot find a liver ailment if you are looking for a broken heart.

Norwegian art is abundant, and at this very moment, it is clearly defining Norwegian existence. "We have embarked on nothing less than a fight for our own culture. I can think of nothing sadder than inaction. . . . We will produce well and badly, but we must produce."[11]

It has sometimes been said that unlike the American alternative groups who had the passion-rousing cause of the Vietnam war, the Canadian alternative theatre did not have a real "cause" to rally around, and that because of this difference, Canadian productions lack both dynamism and originality. It is true that the Canadian alternative phenomenon followed a decade after the American and was obviously heavily influenced by this precedent, becoming at times exceedingly imitative. Nevertheless, the distinguishing mark of Canadian theatre, and the feature which gives it a certain uniqueness in spirit if not necessarily in style, remains its nationalistic commitment. If there is a "cause" common to Canadian alternative theatre groups from coast to coast, it is this commitment to indigenous talent. A cultural and local cause, as opposed to the social, political, and universal implications of the Vietnam war, it obviously could not arouse the same tempestuous feelings. However, within the context of Canadian theatrical evolution, it served as a significant catalyst to bring about new and original productions.

Three different dates could be given to indicate the formal beginning of an alternative theatre movement in English Canada: 1959, the founding of Toronto Workshop Productions by George Luscombe; 1970, the year of the first Underground Theatre Festival and also the year when the term "alternate theatre" was first used; 1971, the year of the Gaspé and Niagara-on-the-Lake Playwrights Conference.

The founding of Toronto Workshop Productions by George Luscombe meant the creation of a model for much of the "underground" or "off-Yonge Street" theatre which was soon to follow, as small, unsubsidized companies set up highly idealistic, if shoestring, operations in warehouses, basements and lofts (John Herbert's Garret Theatre was one of these).

The Toronto Underground Theatre Festival of 1970 led to a greater sense of cohesion and common purpose among the participating groups; with the adoption of the term "alternate theatre" coined by Tom Hendry, the underground or "off-off-Yonge" theatre groups proclaimed themselves, in an indirect manner, a "movement" within the Canadian theatre scene. "Alternate" remained the Toronto expression; however, I shall continue to use the wider term "alternative" to designate the movement in general and in the international sense.

The Playwrights' Conferences of 1971 were instrumental in instilling a sense of urgency about the need for greater support for Canadian dramatists in Canadian theatre. As has been noted earlier, a concern for the development of a genuine native dramaturgy became one of the major features of Canadian alternative theatres; this concern was the result, in a large part, of the growing discontent of Canadian playwrights which was expressed at the Gaspé and Niagara-on-the-Lake conferences. The Gaspé conference, sponsored by the Canada Council, resulted in a manifesto by the playwrights in which they demanded that the Council provide a 50 per cent Canadian content requirement for all subsidized theatres; the second conference repeated the demand. The playwrights' requests met with violent protest from the directors of the traditional theatres, most of whom felt that such a policy was highly unrealistic in terms of audience demands. They did not consider the support of Canadian writers an important priority within their mandate. Alternative theatre companies stepped into the breach. With the creation of the LIP (Local Initiative Projects) and OFY (Opportunity for Youth) grants by the federal government, these small companies became viable, and local playwrights turned to them to have their work workshopped or performed, on a small scale at least.

Not all playwrights looked upon this development favourably, of course. George Ryga, for example, expressed his dismay at the rise of what he termed a "beggars' theatre," and he refused to have anything to do with it, suggesting that Canadian dramatists should attempt to take over the administration of the state-funded theatres themselves rather than accept the humiliations perpetrated upon them by the regional theatres.[12] Nevertheless, the movement gained momentum rapidly: by 1975, *Canada on Stage* lists no less than twenty alternate theatres in Toronto alone;[13] and similar movements occurred, on a smaller scale, all across the country. With the government money freeze of 1978, a gradual decline set in, as well as a noticeable change in attitude: companies had to adopt a more commercial viewpoint in order to survive. Also, by the end of the decade, several of the "alternative" theatres had become successful enough to attract a "mainstream" audience and thus lost some of their rebellious and experimental thrust. Many did not survive. Others, like the Tarragon Theatre in Toronto, became fully mainstream: the Tarragon now presents only the works of well-established Canadian writers, such as James Reaney, Michel Tremblay, David Freeman, and David French. Ken Gass is probably correct when he suggests that "alternate" (with reference to Toronto, anyway) should now be considered a historical term, applicable essentially to the decade 1969–1979. He himself resigned from the Factory Theatre Lab in 1979, declaring that (at that point), "Toronto . . . is simply not a conducive environment for serious theatrical experimentation."[14] He suggests that the avant-garde of the future is to be found in the cabaret scene, rather than in theatre.

If the alternative theatre movement in Canada had run its course by the end of the decade, it is justifiable to look upon it from a historical point of view, even if the vantage point of the 1980's does not afford much distance. Going back to the beginnings of alternate theatre in Toronto, then, I will discuss here Toronto Workshop Productions, as the earliest example and model for future developments; the Factory Theatre Lab, as a prime example of concern with native dramaturgy; and, briefly, Toronto Free Theatre, as an example of extreme attitudes, both in its popular approach and shock tactics. Together with Theatre Passe-Muraille, these provide a representative cross-section of the alternate theatre scene in Toronto. Because of its enormous impact across the country, and the overall success of its operations, Theatre Passe-Muraille will be dealt with in detail in the following chapter.

Toronto Workshop Productions set the pattern for alternative theatre groups in both its political orientation and its experimentation with new performance styles. Definitely leftist from the start, the company aimed at producing social drama for a "popular" audience; to this end, it evolved a documentary style of performance, often based on collective creation, which incorporated such traditional techniques of popular theatre as improvisation, mime, and puppets. This approach was partly influenced by George Luscombe's apprenticeship years in England from 1952 to 1957, when he was exposed to Brechtian techniques through his work with Joan Littlewood.

Toronto Workshop Productions was the result of an amalgamation of two groups, both of which started out in 1959: the Arts Theatre Club, founded by Basaya Hunter, which had an ambitious programme calling for the development of a professional company, a theatre school, and workshops; and Workshop Productions, founded by George Luscombe. In 1961, Luscombe was appointed permanent director of the combined operation. Although still on the amateur level, the first show, *Hey Rube!*, a collective creation, proved a great success. From 1963 on, Toronto Workshop Productions became a professional company: actors were now able to work eight hours a day and submit to the rigid standards set by the director. To build his company, Luscombe auditioned some ninety aspiring actors and actresses, from whose number he selected twenty for further training without pay during a two-month period. At the end of that time, he chose nine promising candidates to form a high-powered ensemble. By 1976, some fifty original works had been produced in three different genres: collective creation; free adaptation of classics; and original scripted plays. For the first eight years, the company performed in the basement of an old factory in Toronto's West End, with a seating capacity of 100 on bleachers around an open stage. In 1967, the company moved to a permanent home at 12 Alexander Street, in downtown Toronto; the new house could seat 300 and still kept the open stage arrangement.

A disciple of Brecht, Luscombe feels that the theatre's most important function is to "say something,"[15] to make a social statement. He defines the purpose of the company as "popular theatre:"

> Popular theatre . . . means bypassing existing audiences, going into areas where people are totally unconverted and thereby creating new awareness. . . . The aim of popular theatre is not only to entertain, but to show that entertainment is, above all, saying something worthwhile, and saying it well.[16]

In order to achieve the high standard he aimed for, Luscombe emphasized actor training and the ensemble idea. He developed a special approach to prepare his actors for working in the collective creation genre which, he realized, made greater demands than the more traditional approach on both actors and director. His workshops aimed at developing actors along three major lines, all calculated to achieve maximum expressiveness: to be "witty in mind and body;" to "achieve voice," and to be "wise enough to be alert to poetry."[17] Luscombe also felt that the presence of a director "strong in knowledge and discipline" was essential for the new genre, both to give a sense of cohesion and direction to the group and to assure a proper balance between the more timid actors and those aggressive enough to take over in that particular setting. His "group theatre" workshops for actors soon became known beyond the confines of the theatrical world, and he had to turn away candidates sent to him by well-meaning physicians, eager to use the workshops as therapy groups for their patients.

Toronto Workshop Productions performed on the basis of all three of the techniques adopted by alternative theatre: collective creation; free use and adaptation of classics; and original scripted plays, with variants and combinations of these techniques. The collective creations were usually built around a current social or political problem. *Hey, Rube!*, for example, dealt with the immediate urban problem of people (in this case, the artists themselves) being evicted from the building they occupy; it was given the framework of a circus setting. More wide-ranging political themes were carefully researched and documented, and the documentary style Luscombe used for these productions came close to the Living Newspaper technique used by the American workers' theatre in the thirties. These included productions such as *Chicago 70*, a comment on the Chicago crisis of that year, and *You Can't Get Here from There*, on the Allende crisis in Chile. Another typical production was *Mister Bones*, a play based on writing contributions by five members of the company and performed by a cast of nine. These nine actors divided all the parts among themselves, with as many as nine parts being played by one actor — the aim here being broadly sketched outlines rather than in-depth characterization, since the emphasis is on the social message of the play, rather than psychological analysis. Although the practice of having each actor take on a number of different parts is obviously based on simple economics (large casts are expensive), it also serves a definite aesthetic purpose: because the audience is unable to identify an actor with any one character, an alienation occurs which draws the attention of the audience away from the character to the over-all message of the play as a whole. *Mister Bones* dealt with the race problem in America and used the framework of a mock minstrel show, with satirical scenes ranging from a parody of Abraham Lincoln to one of contemporary Harlem. Although the play exhibits many of the weaknesses inherent in political theatre, such as too much undisguised propaganda and excesses in language, it also contains a number of lively theatrical scenes which help to make its statement both forceful and enjoyable.

Toronto Workshop Productions also pioneered the utilization of classical works for what Brecht calls their "Materialwert," or raw material, for contemporary, original productions. Their adaptation of Buechner's *Woyzek*, an early production, used about 50 per cent original material and 50 per cent of Buechner's play to create a freely adapted version. A variant of this technique is the montage: a combination of texts from various authors are combined to form a new work. A brilliant example of that genre was exemplified in the satirical *King Richard Third-String* (1973), which was advertised as "A Tragical-Comical-Historical Theatre Thing, lifted from Shakespeare, Macchiavelli and others." Brecht himself felt no compunction about "lifting" texts from appropriate sources and incorporating them into his own work; he did not feel that such a use of a canonized text as a building block within a new script took away from the originality of his own work.[18] *King Richard Third-String* was a violent satire on Richard Nixon and the Watergate Scandal. The montage, created by Steven Bush and Richard McKenna, owed much of its satirical punch to the wide range of texts (from Renaissance to contemporary) it employed and to its stylistic alternation of blank verse and contemporary idiomatic speech.

Original scripts came mostly from Jack Winter, writer-in-residence at Toronto Workshop Productions for most of the period between 1961 and 1976; occasionally, the company and the resident playwright worked on a production together, as they did for *Summer of '76*, a history of the Olympics. Some plays resulted from co-operation between the director and a writer, such as *Ain't Looking* (1980), another treatment of the racial problem in the U.S. This play is particularly effective because of its simple, straightforward story line and characterization. It presents the case of a white man who, having disguised himself with the use of shoe polish, joins a black baseball team and finds out for himself the difficulties, restrictions, and humiliations which black athletes have to accept in order to survive. Occasionally, Toronto Workshop Productions also commissioned scripts from, and produced the work of, better known Canadian dramatists such as Len Petersen or Rick Salutin (their production of Rick Salutin's *Les Canadiens* won the 1977 Chalmers Playwriting Award).

While Toronto Workshop Productions emphasized its political and social commitment and pioneered in the area of collective creation, Factory Theatre Lab was dedicated from its inception to supporting the new Canadian playwright. We have seen its basic philosophy illustrated in John Palmer's satire *Henrik Ibsen: On the Necessity of Producing Norwegian Drama*. This monologue expressed exactly the attitude of Ken Gass, founder of Factory Theatre Lab, who wanted to provide a training ground for actors, directors, and most especially, writers who, he felt, had no chance of gaining access to the regional theatre establishment. In this way, the Factory Theatre Lab functioned as an essential catalyst within the alternative theatre movement.

The theatre began in 1970, through the efforts of Ken Gass, assisted by Frank Trotz. It originally opened in a makeshift complex on top of a garage on Dupont Street in Toronto, but eventually it found more suitable quarters downtown on Adelaide Street. Its youthful founders proclaimed their enthusiastic creed with a sign over the door which read "Don't wait for the Yanks to discover Canada." Gass and Trotz realized the urgent need for a laboratory set-up in which new, original material could be given a first chance at discussion, criticism, and development; and they saw the need for a showcase in which to present the eventual products of these efforts. In keeping with these ideas, they began operations with a series of playwriting contests, followed by workshops. The result was that within a year, eight full-length plays and nine one-acters were produced. Among the new authors discovered were David Freeman, with *Creeps*, and George Walker, with *The Prince of Naples*. Freeman very quickly moved on to the wider recognition of Tarragon Theatre; Walker, whose ironic/absurdist plays carried less appeal for the mainstream audience, remained the unofficial house writer for Factory Theatre Lab for many years to come. Soon many of the other small theatres were putting on plays by new Canadian authors. Gass's policy proved highly successful: within four years, in 1974, an anthology of representative Factory Lab Productions came out in print;[19] by 1979, Factory Theatre Lab had premièred fifty new Canadian plays. Gass's introduction to the anthology reiterated the rationale and philosophy of Factory Theatre Lab:

> [the founding of the theatre] was a simple and arbitrary way of escaping the Canadian theatrical rut of following fashion. Regional playhouses were (and largely still are) shaping their seasons to reflect fashions of Broadway and the West End, and young directors like myself in Studio or University companies were modelling our work after the Tulane Drama Review descriptions of Off-Off-Broadway and Eastern Europe. By limiting the Factory to only new Canadian plays, we were forced to abandon the security blanket of our

colonial upbringing. We found ourselves in a vacuum without roots and, indeed, without playwrights. The plays soon surfaced.[20]

It is interesting to note that while Gass's remarks were quite correct with regard to English Canada, by 1971 French Canada had developed a flourishing dramaturgy, and major writers such as Gratien Gélinas, Marcel Dubé and Michel Tremblay were well established. By 1980, of course, the same is true for English Canada, and Factory Theatre Lab now continues as a training ground for the second generation of young Canadian playwrights.

Probably the two most successful productions at Factory Theatre Lab during the period of Ken Gass's administration were Herschel Hardin's *Esker Mike and His Wife Agiluk* and Gass's own *The Boy Bishop*. These two plays will be examined here, as well as some of the early work of other important Factory Lab writers, especially George Walker and Hrant Alianak.

The production and publishing history of *Esker Mike* provides a good illustration of the reasons for the disillusionment of many young Canadian dramatists and their subsequent demand for an alternative theatre outlet. In his introduction to the published version of the play, Peter Hay describes Hardin as one of Canada's "lost playwrights," unable to find an audience in spite of their talent "because they were or are not British, American, French, or anything — except what they are, Canadian."[21] Hardin wrote *Esker Mike and His Wife Agiluk* in 1967. The play was published in the prestigious *Drama Review* of New York in 1969, but it was not brought before a Canadian public until Factory Theatre Lab premièred it in 1971; it was not published here until 1973. According to Hay, the reason given for its rejection by establishment theatre directors was its "epic scope" and "large cast of characters," which made it expensive to perform. These features, typical of Hardin's plays generally, are a result of his themes — he gives a social panorama rather than focusing in on the psychology of one central character — and a strong Brechtian influence. However, the cast of *Esker Mike* numbers only fifteen — certainly not an excessive demand for a reasonably well-funded theatre.

Esker Mike and His Wife Agiluk is subtitled "Scenes from Life in the Mackenzie River Delta"; it attempts to provide the audience or reader with some insight into the atmosphere and specific problems of life in a small community of the Northwest Territories, ca. 1960. It is a short play (some seventy-five printed pages), structured along epic lines in a sequence of fourteen scenes. The three central characters, Esker Mike, a white Northerner, Agiluk, his native wife, and William, his best friend, also an Eskimo, provide unity and a central axis for the plot. Although the play contains no overt social criticism or propaganda, it is an inflammatory work, revealing the depth of degradation and despair of native people, especially the women, in the face of a well-meaning, but totally ineffectual white administration.

The play centres upon Agiluk, who, after "four men and ten children," none of whom she is able to provide for, decides she will have no more babies and refuses to have any further sexual relations with Esker Mike. When she eventually gives in to a visiting friend, the mate off the boat, she knows that not only will she have conceived again, but that she will also be duty bound to give yet one more child to her husband to restore a proper balance. Her solution to the problem reflects the pitiless and uncompromising logic of the far North: she decides to kill two of her already living children to make up for the impending arrival of the next two.

While *Esker Mike and His Wife Agiluk* is a play in the rather straightforward tradition of Brechtian political theatre, Ken Gass's *The Boy Bishop* of 1976[22] is a much more complex work. Set in 17th-century New France, this historical play on a Canadian theme operates on a number of levels simultaneously, some obvious, others exceedingly subtle. The structure is epic, with many scenes grouped into three acts. *The Boy Bishop* is a combination of historical play and medieval pageant, but it also contains some rather acidic comments on the English Canadian situation under the guise of French Canadian history. It provides a personal catharsis for the author and enables him to voice his disillusionment with the Canadian theatre scene. In an interview which accompanies the version of the play published by *Canadian Theatre Review*, the author explains his social and artistic goals in this particular production:[23]

> It's a history play about English Canada, not about New France . . . the history of my perceptions of living in the Canadian reality . . . [a metaphor] for the malaise of here and now in English Canada.

The character of the Boy Bishop becomes a metaphor for the frustrations of the pioneer theatre in Canada: "He struggles to create a world which he doesn't understand," and, expressing his own pessimism, "he has learned that the art of effecting change is futile." Gass's description of the production itself reveal an experimental and environmentalist approach:

> The key to the production, although it was big and spectacular, was its immediacy — the very close personal contact with the audience. At times the audience members were face to face with the actors, and at other times were further away, watching it from oblique angles. Integral to the play is the feeling that something is being created, something is happening right then and there. . . . We worked with the idea of creating a spontaneous event.

The action is set in 17th-century Quebec. Governor Montcalm, Intendant Bigot, and Bishop Laval, all three corrupt to the core, represent authority and the establishment. Aware that they might have gone too far in their oppression and exploitation of the people, they decide to give the populace a Boy Bishop ceremony to prevent a revolution. The masses are represented by a crowd of teenagers, beggars, and half-wits, among whom a few special characters stand out.

The third act describes the eventual demise of the Boy, who had managed to seize power, and the final take-over by the "legitimate" reactionary authorities. In his disillusionment, the Boy becomes exceedingly bitter. His speech at this point obviously reflects the views of the author on his own society, both general and theatrical:

> The people of this colony don't need liberation. They liberated themselves long ago. Their freedom is not in the mastery of their destiny, however. They have willed themselves into perpetual serfdom, where there is no need for thinking, no need for moral consideration. Reaction, menial reaction, has become a way of life.[24]

The pessimism of this play, and its claim that it is the people themselves who are to blame for their wretched condition because of their inability to achieve inner liberation, strongly echoes earlier and contemporary French Canadian drama, especially the views expressed in the plays of Marcel Dubé.

Probably the most interesting work produced at Factory Theatre Lab came from George Walker, who experiments with grotesque and absurdist techniques in his heavily satirical plays. As Gass points out, Walker has been widely misunderstood in Canada:

> Even English-speaking audiences have no difficulty translating Michel Trem-blay's kitchen-sink squabbles into political realities. But when George Walker writes about living in a cultural desert and banging one's head against an increasingly grotesque wall, English Canada thinks he's writing a fantasy.[25]

In his first play, produced at Factory Theatre Lab, *The Prince of Naples*,[26] Walker deals with the theme of re-education to the real needs and facts of life through the characters of Oak, a fifty-two-year old student, and his instructor, Sayer, a man in his twenties. Among other things, the play comments on the conflict between different generations, pointing out both the arrogance of the young (Oak is referred to as "the old man" throughout) and the need for the old to continually review and readapt their understanding of the world. Through the dialogue between pupil and teacher, and particularly in the long monologues of the instructor, Walker brings out the young generation's enthusiasm for new learning and new approaches, as well as the eventual futility of it all. In the process, specific contemporary issues, such as the excessive optimism of the hippie period in the 1960's and the state of contemporary theatre, come in for some scathing criticism. Sayer's instruction begins with an admonition to the old man to discard all of his traditional knowledge, especially the classics: "Forget Thackeray. Forget

Henry James. Forget them all . . . empty your mind and follow me."[27] The goal, of course, is "to bridge the gap from then to now."[28] The impact of the play comes mainly from Walker's dynamic use of language in the long monologues; words pour out in torrential fashion, carrying the listener along. The development of the speeches is based, not on logic, but on the association of ideas or sounds; words are often used for their rhyme and rhythmic effects, rather than their meaning. Definitely, Walker is using language here in the manner suggested by Artaud; there are also echoes of music-hall dialogue and an alternation between brief exchanges and long monologues, both of which are typical of the Theatre of the Absurd. Here is an example of a typical "torrential" monologue, which is recited at an accelerating tempo and eventually emphasized by the sound of foot stomping:

> Sayer: "We've got a lot of ground to cover. Psychic resources, surrealistic causes, social corpses . . . the casting out of demons, the enticement of the truth.
>
> Conventions and pretensions, contemplation and deviation, humanity, divinity, and human and divine proclivity . . . casual perception . . . political perception . . . the new left, the new right . . . walking in the rain at night. Sensuality, logicality . . . art without form, the form in the formlessness. Reason, chaos, order, dissemination, impregnation.
>
> Understanding Mohammed, selling Jesus, sympathizing with Judas. . . . We've got to blend optimism with pessimism, overestimate the occult, utilize apathy, serenade the young and pacify the old. . . . We have to pierce the great minds in our history and then discard them in favor of the great minds of the present."[29]

The absurdity of the proposed programme, greater in scope than the giant-scale educational system devised for Gargantua by his tutor Ponocrates, becomes apparent instantly in spite of the hypnotic effect of the flow of words. Also in the tradition of Artaud, Walker builds into his plays exorcism through religious ritual. Thus, a long monologue on the glories of the "sixth decade" is followed by an admonition to his student to rise and "praise the sixth decade"; when the endless, litany-like list of praises produces fatigue and chest pains rather than enthusiasm in the reluctant Oak, Sayers bites his arm fiercely to bring him back to alertness.

Eventually the old man is promoted to "teacher and lecturer" himself, but he panics at the sound of thousands of students flocking to his door — only to be informed by Sayer that it was all a hoax, the noise having been produced by a record player to test the old man's reaction. Obviously, he has failed the test and must return for a further course of study. Sayer offers philosophical comfort: "Don't be disheartened, old fellow. It's not unusual to have to go through the whole process three or four times. Remember, this was just your second time around."[30] Like absurdist plays in general, *The Prince of Naples* makes a negative statement about the human condition and it also comments on a specific local and contemporary issue. *The Prince of Naples* set the tone for Walker's subsequent and more ambitious plays, such as *Zastrozzi* or *Bagdad Saloon*. Although still not a mainstream author, George Walker is probably English Canada's most innovative and controversial playwright at this time.

Hrant Alianak, whose work has been premièred at Theatre Passe-Muraille as well as the Factory Theatre Lab (he will be examined in that context later) has also produced some highly avant-garde work. One particularly unusual example is his short playlet *Mathematics*, produced in 1972.[31] This is a "comedy in one act," but a comedy without words or actors. The action consists entirely of a series of objects being thrown on stage at carefully timed intervals by invisible hands, to a musical accompaniment with a constant, methodical beat. The author gives exact instructions for the timing of the work: it consists of six sections of five objects each; a ten-second pause is required between sections, a five-second pause between each object within a section. The total duration of the performance should come to three minutes and ten seconds exactly. The six sections consist of the following series of objects:

Section one:	A duster; a dust pan; a pail; a bottle of detergent; a jar of coffee.
Section two:	A briefcase; an umbrella; a hat; a raincoat; a bunch of flowers.
Section three:	A glass; a plate; a spoon; a packet of spaghetti; a roll of toilet paper.
Section four:	A newspaper; a shoe; a t.v. guide; a beer can; a box of Ritz crackers.
Section five:	A dress; a pair of trousers; a sock; a brassiere; a tooth brush.
Section six:	A pillow; a Playboy magazine; a pair of pyjama bottoms; a packet of cigarettes; an alarm clock.

Quite clearly, this brief work for the stage (one hesitates to call it a play) is related to the techniques of Beckett's *Act without Words*, but it carries the abstraction a step further, to the point of doing away with the actor altogether. Although it does not make a clear-cut statement, it is a highly suggestive work, which evokes human sexual roles; the defining of the human being through material objects; the clichéd approach to life in modern society; and the perils of consumer societies. *Mathematics* represents an extreme realization of the idea of anti-theatre. It works very effectively because of its very small scale. Of course, like many of the absurdist techniques, it could hardly be extended to serve as the basis for a full-length play.

This overview of Factory Theatre Lab's contribution to the Canadian theatre scene can be completed by a brief examination of the plays represented in the

Factory Lab Anthology since they provide a good cross-section of the type of work produced at the theatre. The anthology includes George Walker's *Ambush at Tether's End*, Bill Greenland's *We Three, You and I*; *Strawberry Fields*, by Michael Hollingworth, and Larry Kardish's *Brussels Sprouts*. In *Ambush at Tether's End*, Walker employs his usual absurdist/grotesque/surrealistic technique to create a witty, if pessimistic, metaphor for the human condition in general and the state of Canadian society in particular. This play comes close to the grotesque tradition of "plays with corpses," which originated with Witkiewicz and was later carried on by Tadeusz Kantor and Friedrich Duerrenmatt. The central character is a corpse: Max, an intellectual who has demonstrated his superiority to his two best friends, Galt and Bush, through his rationally arranged suicide. He continues to manipulate them after his death, through a series of notes which are placed in every part of his clothes and anatomy, and which give the two characters instructions. The situation is complicated by the brief appearance of Max's parents (who enter and exit via the closet) and Max's rival, a truly dangerous character with the suggestive name of Jobeo. Jobeo tries to outdo Max by manipulating the two innocents — they are stereotypical Canadian businessmen — into homicide, but he fails. After a lengthy discussion of the validity of Rimbaud's principle that "it is better to suffer than to sleep," a view Max once held but obviously abandoned later, the two friends decide to do the only right and noble thing and commit simultaneous suicide using the double-ended noose provided by the thoughtful deceased for that pupose. At the last minute, of course, neither has the courage to go through with it, and the venture is a total failure. Galt and Bush, representatives of vulgar and unsophisticated ordinary man, go on living. This short play about philosophical one-upmanship may be interpreted as a caustic comment on the intellectual suicide of Canadian society. Yet aside from its social implications, it is also a highly diverting exercise in black humour and absurdism which is kept lively throughout by a kind of music-hall dialogue and the witticism of the short repartees.

Bill Greenland's *We Three, You and I* combines a social consciousness-in-reverse theme (the manipulation of the public by fund-raising agencies) with a theatre-in-the-making approach. The entire play consists of a put-on for the audience: as the public enters the theatre, they are given programmes stating that there will be a brief appeal for "Children International" before the play. Eventually, it becomes clear that the appeal *is* the play; there is nothing else. As the members of the audience gradually catch on to what is happening, they often take part in the action, walking up to the stage, questioning the actors, and generally interrupting the proceedings, which means that the actors must be prepared for a good deal of improvisation. Because of its unconventional theme — the de-mythification of the "noble" activity of raising money for a worthy cause — the play often arouses violent audience reactions; this happened in 1973 when it was performed in England, where audiences seemed to be more shocked than those in

Canada about the implied message. Frequently, heated discussion would take place following the performance.

The technique of the play is based on a gradual change from a naturalistic style, which deceives the audience into believing they see "the real thing," rather than a performance, to documentary, to expressionistic distortion and exaggeration. All of the action takes place in front of the closed curtain. The characters are the Matron, an Aide, and Cathy, a young girl in a wheelchair. The play is divided into two parts. The Matron first steps before the audience and makes her appeal for the cause of Children International; she uses all the customary clichés of charitable fund-raising, and the audience remains unsuspecting. This is followed by an appearance by Cathy, who has obviously been coached in each word and gesture by the Matron. Her every movement and utterance are calculated to tug at the heartstrings of the audience and loosen the strings of their purses: slowly and painfully, she gets herself free of the wheelchair, and manages to walk a few steps, demonstrating the miraculous benefits of the braces she received through the generosity of kind donors. She then appeals for further donations. The second part of the performance starts in the documentary style, with slide projections of children from third world countries; however, as the show progresses, the tempo of the slide projections rapidly accelerates until it reaches a point of absurdity and the audience can no longer make out individual pictures. The slides are accompanied by a taped speech, which also accelerates to a frantic rhythm. Above the din of this grotesque slide show rises the voice of the Matron, becoming louder and more insistent.

> Voices are now so loud they are not distinguishable. The Matron is now almost yelling. The slides become more rapid and the voices louder until the sound system quickly jams. The jam warbles in intensity and continues thus for several seconds. Then there is abrupt silence and darkness except for the last words from the Matron, screaming, 'GIVE!'

With this screeching finale, the curtain finally lifts, revealing a bare stage. The play is over.

Michael Hollingworth is one of the most controversial contemporary playwrights. Where *We Three, You and I*, provoked audiences into heated arguments, Hollingworth's *Strawberry Fields* shocked and repelled them to the point where many members of the audience simply walked out. A naturalistic vignette of the rock and acid scene, *Strawberry Fields* is set on a "field of garbage" covered with feces and swarms of flies left over after a three-day rock festival. The language matches the rawness of the scene, and there is a great deal of violence. Above and beyond this naturalistic picture of hippie life in the 1960's, the play also makes a political statement on the relationship between Canada and the United States and the need for Canadians to overcome their oppression by the giant to the South. The giant image is transferred to the stage literally in the character of Harry, an American bully of enormous proportions; confronting him are two young Canadians, Larry and Danny. The two Canadians find themselves in a pretty sore state, with no food to eat or water to wash in. Harry appears on the scene, shares his bread and cheese with them, and offers to prepare a rabbit feast. When he returns, however, his appearance is somewhat menacing: he is wearing a machete in his belt and a skirt of bulrushes, and the "rabbit" he pulls out of his bag turns out to be a pet dachshund he has killed. Danny and Larry are horrified by this show of brutality and decide to attack Harry. After a violent battle, they eventually manage to overcome the giant.

In a rather primitive way, this short play comes close to the tradition of the theatre of cruelty; it certainly aims at "exorcising" some of the "collective abscesses" of contemporary society. In his introduction to the play, Gass gives his own evaluation of Hollingworth and the "message" of *Strawberry Fields*:

> Hollingworth is a romantic nihilist exploring the aftermath of civilization, curious about the composition of the shit and the leftovers. The circus is over. . . . Two young Canadians get mindfucked by a giant American, but they kill him in the end and then start in on each other. Action is at last possible! We will arrive though it seems we will lose our humanity in the process.[33]

Fascination with, and disappointment about the 1960's scene forms a major part of the themes of the alternative theatre of the 1970's — naturally so, as the young playwrights of that decade were close enough to the sixties to look back with both nostalgia and amazement. *Brussels Sprouts*, by Larry Kardish, looks at this period in the context of the obligatory hippie grand tour of Europe by hitchhiking or motorbike. In the process, it presents the things which the traditional hippie values: friendship, sex of every possible type; the motorbike mystique. The brief play is naturalistic with some excursions into fantasy. It is followed, however, by a "curtain raiser" which suddenly creates doubts about the reality of the earlier action. In the first play, two young male lovers relax in a cheap hotel room in Brussels after a strenuous motorcycle ride. They are joined by a young girl, Charlotte, and an orgiastic weekend *à trois* follows. The "curtain raiser," which paradoxically follows the play (one wonders about the dramaturgical usefulness of this gimmick), again presents three characters, two men and a woman, now called Bernice, many years later, back in the "reality" of home, kitchen, and typewriter. This second part raises the question: are Bernice and Charlotte the same person? Also, one wonders whether the entire Brussels episode really occurred; is it presented filtered through the characters' memory, and thus transformed; or is it simply a fantasy which never happened? Although the play is intriguing, Kardish is not successful in handling the multiple levels of reality; the audience is left confused, rather than stimulated.

The efforts of Factory Theatre Lab to create a home and showcase for new Canadian playwrights in the 1970's thus made it possible for young dramatists to experiment widely, to learn the potential of the instrument which is the stage, and to see their work exposed to audiences, occasionally even published. The existence of Factory Lab and other alternative theatres also enabled Canadian dramatists to break with the realistic tradition — fail-safe from the commercial point of view — and finally to join the modern avant-garde in all its theatrical manifestations.

Of all the alternate groups that arose in Toronto in the seventies, the Toronto Free Theatre was perhaps the one most openly dedicated to avant-garde productions — like Dada earlier in the century enjoying nothing more than a good chance to "épater les bourgeois." Toronto Free Theatre deserves brief mention here also because its founders, playwright/directors Tom Hendry, Martin Kinch, and John Palmer, attempted to take seriously the concept of the popular theatre in the sense of theatre for the masses: they started out operations on the basis of free admission. This system had to be changed when their original LIP grant ran out, and "Free" theatre now refers more to artistic freedom than financial. Toronto Free Theatre occupies a renovated Victorian building on Berkely Street, combining the preservation of a historical site with theatrical performance.

The theatre has aroused a great deal of controversy because of the kind of productions it presents. Some are simply bold statements, such as Carol Bolt's *Red Emma*, or Michael Ondaatje's *The Collected Works of Billy The Kid*. But when the theatre staged *Clear Light* by Michael Hollingworth in 1973, it was closed down by the police morality squad. The founding playwrights have all been accused of sensationalism; their plays do indeed exhibit such controversial themes as incest, homosexuality, lesbianism, nymphomania, and alcoholism, alone and in various combinations. Their rationale for such controversial fare is the theatre's dedication to "psychodynamics," that is, "dramas of psyche and mind in which passions and neurotic conflicts are given physical and often surrealistic expression."[34] Again, this seems to be a rather primitive and unsophisticated realization of the principles enunciated earlier by Artaud; the arguments in defence of the company's often excessive shock tactics do not appear entirely convincing:

> Martin Kinch has described this 'narcissistic' theatre, confronting the audience with familiar personal obsessions and strong visual images that carry ambiguous messages of danger and eroticism. Sex, violence, blood or guts have often helped form the scenario, but as realization of our darker selves rather than as unmotivated sensationalism.[35]

A wide range in style, theme, and technique evolved on the Toronto alternate theatre scene during the 1970's. While all of the theatres discussed here remained within the local sphere of influence, Theatre Passe-Muraille exerted its impact on communities and new, small groups across the nation.

3

A Success Story: Theatre Passe-Muraille

Theatre Passe-Muraille first appeared, with a bang, on the Toronto underground theatre scene in 1969. Its premiere production, *Futz*, the story of the relationship between a man and his sow, caused a public scandal and brought the morality squad down upon the young company. Truly a taboo-shattering show, *Futz* not only dealt with an unacceptable theme, but also featured such theatrical and verbal explosives as bare breasts and expressions like "shit" and "fucking pigs." One might look upon the uproar caused by *Futz* as a repetition — Canadian-style and with the usual "Canadian delay" of a little over a century — of the scandal created by *Ubu Roi* in 1896 France. In spite of this unconventional beginning, Passe-Muraille eventually turned out to be the only one of all the groups participating in the Underground Theatre Festival of 1970 to survive commercially. It is now well established in a spacious permanent home on Ryerson Avenue; it has a faithful following in Toronto; and its impact has been felt nationwide over the years. Success stories such as this are not common on the alternative theatre scene: how did it all come about?

Passe-Muraille owes its existence and philosophy to the energy and vision of two men, James Garrard and Paul Thompson. Garrard founded the company and gave it its initial direction; Thompson developed the now famous Passe-Muraille style. It is interesting to note that both men came to the theatre from academic backgrounds. Garrard, a graduate of Queens University and a former school principal, had become disillusioned with education and decided to study theatre in England. In the late 1960's, he attended the London Academy of Music and Dramatic Art. Returning to Canada in 1968, he quickly became a part of the growing cultural and nationalistic protest movement of the period. Part of that protest movement was Rochdale College, an experimental school set up in antithesis to traditional educational institutions. Garrard joined the Rochdale

Theatre Project, which used the college population as a "laboratory" for exploring the relationships between theatre and society. In 1969, he founded an independent company, which he called "Passe-Muraille." The name carried implications of his visions of a truly popular theatre: theatre "without walls," a theatre which would "pass beyond" all the conventional barriers. His first Passe-Muraille manifesto, written in 1969, reflects very clearly the influence of the hippie movement of the 1960's, the ideology of the Living Theatre, and the happening as a kind of theatrical event: "The renaissance of the theatre as experience, as event, demands that contact be made, first, among the actors, who must work together as a continuing ensemble; second, between the actors and those individuals termed 'the audience'; third, because theatre is a human event, between people and people."[1] Like American radical theatre, Garrard included in his ideology a strong social and political concern; as a Canadian, he also felt it his duty to open up his theatre to new, unknown dramatists, since the regional theatres were obviously not taking up the challenge of creating Canadian drama. Passe-Muraille, then, would be experimental, national and popular: "I'd like to make theatre as popular as bowling,"[2] Garrard said, in the true spirit of Brecht, who had envisioned theatre for the masses, preferably performed in large sports arenas.

Passe-Muraille started humbly. From the basement of Rochdale College, it moved to a variety of locations in the city, playing wherever cheap space was available. Often, the lack of a permanent space led to imaginative, environmental experiments: the *Immigrant Show*, for example, was performed in a streetcar hired for the purpose, which travelled through the city as the show progressed, stopping at relevant locations to create a sense of real authenticity. By 1978, however, the company was able to acquire a permanent home, a large old warehouse which provided enough space for a main stage as well as two smaller performance areas. In fact, within ten years, the company had fulfilled most of its founder's dreams. It had produced an astounding number of shows: twenty-two collective creations (ten pure collectives, twelve in co-operation with a writer) as well as a large number of scripted works, many of them new Canadian plays. Throughout that period Passe-Muraille was also actively engaged in a nationwide "seeding programme" which led to the establishment of such "parallel" alternative theatre groups as Codco, in St. John's; 25th Street House, in Saskatoon; and Theatre Network, in Edmonton. In Toronto itself, the theatre offered the "New Works Program" — a workshopping programme for individuals and groups, offering its own facilities, financial assistance, and counselling. Passe-Muraille views this activity not only as assistance given to junior artists, but as a means of stimulating and renewing the company itself and safeguarding against complacency and stagnation.

Although Garrard had set the ideological pattern for Passe-Muraille, it remained for his successor, Paul Thompson, to develop the specific Passe-Muraille style of collective creation. This style reached full maturity with *The Farm Show* of

1974. With this production, Passe-Muraille achieved its artistic identity — an achievement largely due to the vision and labour of its director.

Paul Thompson had studied English and French at the University of Western Ontario and spent some time studying French in Paris. He was one of Jean Gascon's assistant directors in Stratford; but the major influence on his artistic approach was the result of his stay in France, where he worked with Roger Planchon at the Théâtre de la Cité at Villeurbanne. Planchon's work descends in a straight line from the political theatre of Piscator and Brecht and, in France, the work of Jean Vilar. His productions, like all political theatre, concentrate on the social and political behaviour of the characters, rather than on psychology; this is true also of Planchon's versions of the classics, where he stresses social class through costume and interpretation. Although a dramatist himself, Planchon always emphasizes the importance of the non-literary aspect of theatre. Describing his own work, he insists "Notre action n'a rien de littéraire."[3] Planchon also favours process over product in the sense that he never sees any one production as a final effort, but rather as a basis for further improvement.

Paul Thompson's approach to his work at Passe-Muraille was equally dynamic ("dynamic" here meaning the antithesis to static). In fact, if one were to look for a single attribute to describe the essential quality of Theatre Passe-Muraille, it would be "dynamism" — a constant flow of energy directed at finding new and better forms of expression, a total refusal to be locked into any tradition or convention, absolute openness and adaptability to new experiences. This dynamism is apparent on every level of the operations of Passe-Muraille. It lies at the base of Thompson's use of collective creation, rather than the "closed" text of a finished script for most of his productions. It is equally evident in the variety of performance spaces used by the company, calculated to expose the actors to new audience reactions and relationships. As Thompson says, "We need the unexpected meeting place."[4] The same principle is at work in the company's encouragement of experimentation by other groups under their own roof. Passe-Muraille productions usually go through a number of versions, none of them considered definitive, on the basis of the Planchon principle that "if an idea is good it only gets better by reworking."[5] It is for this reason that the published versions of the company's collective creations are usually released with a strong *caveat* to the reader: the printed text captures only one fixed moment in an ongoing, dynamic creation process. Thompson captures the essential philosophy of the group when he says: "We are defined by energy and a vital definition of what we are doing. When we run out of ideas we'll close down or die."[6]

More specifically, Thompson's work is oriented towards two major goals: actor development and the invention of new and effective methods of collective creation. Although he does call on the services of writers quite frequently, his shows are conceived with the actors, rather than the script, in mind. This approach builds on the pattern set earlier by George Luscombe at Toronto Workshop Productions;

but Thompson goes a great deal further than Luscombe in emphasizing the importance of the actor's contribution, especially in the context of collective creation:

> Part of the concept of doing collective plays is saying that the actor has more to give than often is required or demanded of him in traditional plays. I think . . . he should be more than a puppet. In the kind of work we're doing, we like the actor to really put some of himself in the play. We also work through the skills an actor has. If an actor could yodel, e.g., then I'd really like to put his yodel in a play.[7]

Actors in the traditional theatre would be quick to point out that their work indeed demands far more than being a "puppet," and that they, too, put a lot of themselves into their role; and it could reasonably be argued that it may be more difficult to "be" Phaedra, Hamlet, or Lady Macbeth than a character you have created yourself and tailored to your own strengths and limitations. There are directors working in the area of collective creation who admit that they use the technique mainly because it can be adapted to actors with little professional training and limited skills.[8] Thompson, however, firmly believes in the validity of collective creation as the most effective instrument to bring out actors' maximum potential. The success of a large number of his shows indicates that his method, if not superior to that of traditional theatre, at least represents a valid alternative, with interesting results.

Thompson's original contribution to the technique of collective creation was to put the onus for research and documentation entirely on the actors themselves. He discovered that, by forcing the actor into a first-hand relationship with his material he could achieve considerably greater immediacy and a sense of commitment, which would then be communicated to the audience. Critics have often commented on the strong sense of authenticity of Passe-Muraille shows; it is a result of the actors' direct involvement with their material.

The technique was applied to two major lines of investigation: sociological and historical. The sociological shows attempt to create authentic mirror images of a specific community: *The Farm Show, The West Show, The Immigrant Show, Under the Greywacke*. To produce these, the actors and the director move into the community themselves. Through personal contact, sharing experiences and observations, the actors assemble the necessary documentation to serve as basis for the show. Improvisations follow, and gradually through the use of acting techniques, to which are added mime, song, and poetry, an image of the community emerges. As Thompson has pointed out,[9] this type of creation depends on strength and self-confidence on the part of the actors; they must be confident enough to be able to submerge their own personality and to approach the experience with openness, compassion, and love. If successful, the truthfulness of the production can be striking. Sociological shows were usually first presented to the community where they originated; although members of the community could instantly identify themselves with the characters and situations on stage, nobody complained; no one's feeling were ever hurt in the mirroring process — a testimony to the actors' serious desire to understand the workings of the community and to give a sympathetic picture of it. While the actors are on their own to research and develop the parts they will play in this type of show, the director acts as a necessary "outside eye," helps to shape the final product, and also arbitrates in case of disagreement among the actors.

Although the collective creation movement forms part of the general anti-naturalistic trend of the modern era, the type of sociological show developed by Passe-Muraille really represents the ultimate in naturalism — an imitation of life in the most literal sense. Although Thompson maintains that his productions go beyond imitation to capture the "real spirit," the "essence" of the community portrayed,[10] his technique amounts to the kind of photographic reproduction of reality for which modernists condemned the naturalists. The success of his shows testifies to the enduring appeal of the realistic/naturalistic mode, which has here undergone a change of style and emphasis — from authored play to collective creation, from psychological theme to sociological concern. Thompson's naturalism does not belong in the school of Ibsen; it is a post-Brechtian version of that mode, with a strong local and contemporary flavour.

The historical shows, on the other hand, do not aim at simply recreating historical events or characters; rather, they try to demonstrate the political significance of past events in relation to the present and, above all, to discover a national mythology within the material provided by Canadian history. The creation of myths which can be shared by all and provide Canadians with a sense of national identity has long been the goal of poets and novelists — largely under the influence of the teaching of Northrop Frye. Passe-Muraille took up the challenge in the dramatic genre. This type of show, then, went considerably beyond the scope of the sociological shows. Beyond the need to portray individuals and communities at certain points in time, it also required the structuring of action into plotline and the interpretation of the significance of historical events. Because of the complexity of the historical shows, writers were usually called in to assist the company, but the basis for the work remained collective creation. The writers' main task was shaping the final product and helping with the structuring of scenes and plotline as the show developed. While some writers find the experience of working with a collective stimulating, others describe it as "an exercise in frustration."[11] As in the case of the actor, certain special qualities are required for a writer to work in this particular genre: self-confidence, flexibility, the capacity for self-abnegation, and above all, as Rick Salutin, who has worked successfully with Passe-Muraille many times, points out, the ability to be "interested more in the general statement made by the play than in details."[12] The difficulties inherent in working with a collective can be seen in the genesis of individual productions. *The Farm Show* (1972;1974) is generally considered the best and most typical example of Passe-Muraille style in the sociological genre; it will be discussed in detail here, along with two other representative productions, *I Love You, Baby Blue* (1975), and *Far As the Eye Can See* (1977).

The Farm Show was originally created in and for a small farming community near Clinton, Ontario, with first production in a local barn. However, the success of the show was such that the company took it to Toronto, and from there on tour, performing in Ottawa and various Saskatchewan communities. It was also performed on radio and its creation documented on film by Michael Ondaatje. The enormous appeal of *The Farm Show* to audiences everywhere was truly astounding. John Coulter gave a partial explanation when he compared it to the impact of Irish theatre in the 1920's, based on self-discovery and identification. But while this theory may be correct for rural areas, it surely does not hold for big cities like Toronto and Ottawa. To urban audiences, *The Farm Show* appealed by its simplicity, its spontaneity, and its authentic characters and situations.

The Farm Show was published in 1976,[13] in a version prepared by Ted Johns, a member of the company and occasional dramatist in his own right. The text is prefaced by two notes, one by Paul Thompson, the other by Ted Johns. Together they provide an excellent explanation of Passe-Muraille philosophy and methods; both include a *caveat* to the reader. Thompson writes:

> This is a record of our version of "grassroots" theatre. The idea was to take a group of actors out to a farming community and build a play of what we could see and learn. There is no "story" or "plot" as such. The form of the play is more like a Canadian Sunday School or Christmas Concert, where one person does a recitation, another sings a song, a third acts out a skit, etc. . . . a picture of a complex and living community.
>
> The play was not written down; it developed out of interviews, visits and improvisations. Most of the words were given to us by the community along with the stories. We spent a great deal of time trying to imitate those people both in the way they move and the way they speak. We wanted to capture the fibre of what they were and this seemed to be the best way to do it . . . I'm not sure how much of this will come through in the printed word.

The Farm Show, in other words, was to be a mosaic of scenes literally "recorded" within the community. The list of characters is followed by a note to the effect that "All characters in this play are non-fictional. Any resemblance to living people is purely intentional." The success of the undertaking seems to invalidate the usual critical view that to be effective no dramatic idiom can be taken "raw" from life, that instead it must be carefully shaped to create the illusion of realism. On the other hand, it is quite obvious that although the company used the words "given" to them by the people of Clinton themselves, a process of selection took place which no doubt heightened the effectiveness of those words; the selection and arrangement of the scenes was also carefully planned, as we shall see.

Ted Johns gives some further details about the way the production process took place:

> Usually a script is the first hint of a play's existence. In this case, it is the last. . . . In the early days of that summer of '72, the actors had no idea what they were doing. The dramatic techniques, and the songs, grew out of the actors' attempts to dramatize their discoveries in daily improvisations. At first the result did not seem like a play: no lights, no costumes, no set, a barn for a theatre, haybales for seats. Simply pure performance.

The published text is based on the 1974 version of *The Farm Show*, performed in Toronto. It is divided into two acts of ten scenes each. As the audience enter, they are greeted by fiddle music, and a member of the cast helps to make them feel at ease, chatting and helping people find their seats: the friendliness of the small town is thus recreated. The informal atmosphere continues with the first scene, when an actor casually introduces the play: "Last summer, we visited a farming community in Clinton, Ontario"; he goes on to give some general information about the town and ends with "people there enjoyed the show, so we brought it back to see if we could brighten up the dull lives of the people in Toronto." The actors have also "brought back" some authentic pieces of farm equipment to show to their city audience: a bean dryer, crates, a cream can, and bales of straw. A lively "Auction Song" concludes the first scene, and the audience already feels part of Clinton.

The scenes that follow present a cross-section of life on the farm, from vignettes of ordinary daily life to serious social problems; interspersed are poeticized views of rural life ("The Winter Scene") as well as scenes designed to shatter the romantic and naive myths which city dwellers harbour about life in the country. The second scene "Miles meets Mr. Merrill" is a tongue-in-cheek dig at city folk; it presents Miles, a member of the company, introducing himself to one of the farmers and offering to help with the chores. His big-city enthusiasm leaves the farmer gaping; he cannot see why Miles would want to make a coffee table out of the old boards of his barn, nor why he expects "organic vegetables from your garden and all, far out!" when he's told that it is supper time. The "Bale Scene" (act one, scene five) deals with a similar theme. Here, we find one of the actors who has spent a day helping to bring in the hay recounting his experience in a long monologue. It appears that haying is a somewhat less exhilarating activity than city folk tend to believe (and we should remember the impact of Tolstoy's famous haying scene in *Anna Karenina* on generations of urban novel readers!). The monologue describes the strain of lifting the heavy bales, the stifling heat of the barn, and the sore muscles and skin torn by the rough material. It ends in a passionate outburst to the audience:

> Now I ask you, why? Why would any human being choose, for the better part of his life, twice a year, to put himself through that total and utter hell? I didn't understand it then . . . and I don't understand it now.

Excellent vignettes of everyday life are given in "Round the Bend" (act one, scene three), "Washing Woman" (act one, scene ten), and "Jean Lobb" (act two, scene one). "Round the Bend" presents a series of images of the daily routines of the people who live around the bend of the road. The actors impersonate themselves, as well as the farmers; they recreate the setting through mime (chickens being fed and a yucca tree) and sound (farm equipment and a dog barking). As in most collective creations, there is room for improvisation and audience involvement: in this scene, for example, the actor portraying a young boy throws the ball he is playing with into the audience; interaction between performers and the public may or may not develop, depending on the mood of the evening. "Washing Woman" gives a sympathetic account of the unending round of chores a harrassed farm wife goes through, from the time she gets up at 5:30 to collect the eggs until late at night. The washing machine, like most stage props, is mimed by one of the actors. The naturalism of this scene is lightened by a song and dance routine interspersed with the woman's monologue. The final portion of the speech and the last verse of the song establish a fine balance in mood. The woman's monologue ends with a gentle hint at sexual frustration:

> My husband is out *working* in the fields for ten, twelve, maybe sixteen hours a day. And of course it keeps him in good condition. But he's *tired* when he gets home. Now it's not as if I don't have a lot to *do* around the house, with the kids and the house and all, but well I *miss* him.

The understated pathos of this speech is counterpointed by the last verse of the song, which concludes the scene on a humorous tone:

> Well, she had her cake and she had her man
> And she had ten kids and a frying pan.
> And now old Maisy she is 84
> But she ain't looking for a man no more.

"Jean Lobb," the opening scene of the second act, is designed to draw the audience back into the spirit of the community as they return from intermission.

They find the actress impersonating Jean Lobb sitting stage centre on a milk can, reminiscing about wedding parties. The tone is chatty and light; her speech captures the flow of images as memories and associations follow each other in her mind. The technique is the same as that used by Michel Tremblay in *Les Belles-Soeurs* for some of the monologues, especially those of Yvette: both Yvette and Jean take the wedding party as a point of departure; both go off into long speeches filled with trivia and long lists of names. However, there is an essential difference in the effect created: whereas Yvette's monologue conveys the emptiness of her life (the "maudite vie plate" motif), Jean Lobb's speech exhibits a genuine *joie de vivre*, a capacity for enjoying the small and trivial events of daily life. As it starts out, her monologue is very close to the *Belles-Soeurs* style:

> Now Patty Tebbutt's wedding was last year and . . . this is a group of girls that have been married in the last two years. Jeannette started the ball rolling in February. And then there was Patty — no, Lois, and then Patty and then Marilyn. Four girls in the community. And this year there was Fay, and then there's Karen Oakes.

But whereas the Yvette monologues never go beyond the enumeration level, Jean Lobb also recalls all the fun that was had at these wedding parties: "Well, we laughed till we died. . . . It was simple, you know, but it was so funny." Again, the scene concludes on a happy tone, with the "Lobb Song," a folksy hymn in praise of that fertile clan:

> Mobs of Lobbs, Lobb-in-laws, ready-on-the job Lobbs
> All along the Maitland and the 16th line.
> If you go out driving there, any time
> Looking out your window you will see
> That ever-spreading, farming, Lobb dynasty, dynasty.

The most lyrical and poetic scene of *The Farm Show* occurs quite early in the play, "Winter Scene" (act one, scene four). This scene conveys the experience of a day of snowstorm in the country, from morning till night. It is structured into three parts, with a poetry-and-mime section at the beginning and end framing the central portion. The winter setting is simply indicated by the use of a large white sheet to cover the crates left on stage from the previous scene. Two lines of the "winter poem" open the scene:

> The middle of winter.
> Inside, everything is cosy, and warm, and small

"Window," "Frost," "Icicles," and "Snow" are then portrayed by mime. This introduction is followed by a highly complex recreation of all the multiple activities of a blustery day, with two actors taking on a dozen parts of men, women, and children at work and play. The dialogue is written in the form of a voice score; actors not only speak their parts but also create all the necessary sound effects for a car, a snowmobile, and animal sounds. The scene ends with the rousing finale of a square dance party before returning to the lyrical tone of the beginning, with the two characters miming "Moon" ("Bright") and "Snow" ("Stretches, for miles"). In terms of skill, versatility, and especially the timing of the voice score, this scene probably puts the greatest demands on the actors.

Although Thompson's introductory note to *The Farm Show* describes its structure as "like that of a Christmas Concert" and suggests that the play consists simply of a series of episodes put together casually, careful analysis reveals a definite design in its inner structure. The episodes of the second act deal with the more serious issues of farm life and, therefore, have a greater dramatic impact on the audience. There is a definite heightening of tension and emotion as the play progresses, a heightening which leads up to a climactic final scene. The style of *The Farm Show* may be that of photographic reproduction, but the arrangement of these reproductions is carefully calculated to achieve the desired effect on the audience. The subtle emotional manipulation of the public through the inner structure of the play is one of the reasons for its success.

The two most serious themes developed in the second act are, first, the physical dangers of farming — the ever-present farm accident; and second, the economic difficulties and ensuing generation conflicts, with young people eager to leave the land.

The accident theme is introduced in the first act with "Man on a Tractor" (act one, scene nine). Three actors mime the tractor, a fourth, sitting on the middle actor's shoulders, "steers" and delivers a long monologue on the central role of the tractor in a farmer's life:

> Now the thing about a farmer and his tractor is that he's gotta spend so much time on it. . . . It's like my friend Bill Lobb used to say . . . sometimes a man gets to taking better care of his tractor than he does his wife! Haw, haw. But you know, depending on what you're cropping, you may have to go over the same area, five, six, seven times in one season, and that can be pretty boring. But you can't let the boredom get to you. No, you gotta be awake, you gotta be alert, you gotta be watching . . . there's always a bit of danger involved. I don't know anybody on this line hasn't turned his tractor or come pretty near to it one time or another. Now you can see — I got a bugger of a hill right over there — every time I go up there, I think well, this could be it! It's a steep hill, loose earth, and a heavy tractor. It could just flip over and come crashing down! But you can't think about that. It's all part of being a farmer — it's all part of being a tractor.

With this monologue, the theme is introduced to the audience, and they are made aware of the fact, little thought about by city people, that farming can indeed be a dangerous occupation. Act two further develops this idea in several scenes, with the tractor remaining the central image. "Daisy" (act two, scene two) gives us one woman's recollections of a whole string of farm accidents, from a child falling into a well to a man killed while cutting trees and of course the common tractor mishaps:

> because there's been a good many people around here that's been killed on them. Especially going around these hills, they'll just flip over . . . they're not safe, they're not!"

The following scene, "Accident" (act two, scene three) focuses more specifically on one particular accident recounted from two points of view: first by a man who was present at the scene, then by the victim's wife. In spite of the tragedy and pathos implicit in this scene, it ends on a tone of hope, as the woman tearfully records the immediate reaction of her friends and neighbours: "The day after the accident, you could see about twelve tractors out in that field, and they had the whole thing done in a day."

The central social problem of rural areas — how to keep young people on the land when life is hard and financial rewards are few — is dealt with in several scenes of the second act. "Picture Frame" (act two, scene eight) creates a highly imaginative stage metaphor to illustrate the situation. Five actors, representing a husband, his wife, and their three children, stand in a row, framed by a large picture frame. The husband and wife remain in the frame throughout the scene, their lines stressing their sense of belonging to the land and their commitment. The three children, however, step out of the frame one by one and present rebellious statements against their parents' lifestyle: one girl takes a job with an insurance company in town, the second marries and moves to Toronto, the boy goes to university to become a teacher. At the end of the scene, the entire "picture" is auctioned off — an effective comment on the attrition of farming communities. The following scene (act two, scene nine) picks up the same theme in the form of a monologue, "Bruce Pallett." While scene eight gave a poetic interpretation of a social and economic problem, nine presents hard figures as Bruce confronts the audience with the real facts of life in agriculture; the problem is here taken beyond the local level and shown with its national implications:

> Y'see, we're losing agricultural land in Ontario at the rate of forty-three acres an hour. You look at this map of Canada on the back wall. This shows all the areas in Canada that'll ever produce food. Ever. Not very many, is it? Now, look at this narrow strip of land from Windsor to around Montreal. That varies in depth from ten to around seventy miles, and that strip of land provides food

for almost forty percent of the nation, and that land is disappearing at the rate of forty-three acres an hour. Now, arithmetic was never my strong point, but by rapid calculation that's about a million acres a year.

And that's pretty fast, y'know! Pretty damn fast! . . . .

In 1971, we sold $73,000 dollars worth of stuff off this farm. But it took $73,006.40 to do it! And that's allowing $6,000 for management — that's to keep three families, for one year . . . each of my kids got three thousand bucks a piece. I didn't get a red cent.

Y'know, I just want my kids to make a living at it, I got grandchildren I want to make a living at it.

So what else can I do? Y'know, how else do you build a nation?

Clearly, this penultimate scene is calculated to raise the audience's awareness; political theatre without Brechtian alienation, it is simple and direct. With the final scene, however, the play returns to a fully theatrical approach: *The Farm Show* ends most appropriately with a rousing song, "The Ballad of John Deere," celebrating the symbiotic relationship of man and tractor. In the process, John Deere is raised to the level of a folk hero who sacrifices his own life as he rides his tractor into a flash flood to rescue two stranded boys and a little girl's pet kitten.

In spite of its deceptive surface simplicity, *The Farm Show* is a highly complex production; it is clearly the most successful in its genre produced by Passe-Muraille. The same basic technique is applied to the big city scene in *I Love You, Baby Blue*, an attempt to render the essence, the very "soul" of Toronto through an examination of the city's sex scene.

Unlike *The Farm Show*, which was universally popular, *Baby Blue* aroused a great deal of controversy. In fact, the show was closed down by the police morality squad after its twelve-week run from January to April 1975; during that period, however, it was seen by more than 26,000 people. The script was eventually published by Press Porcépic in 1977. The title of the show is based on Toronto's City-T.V. Friday night showings of the pornographic "Baby Blue" movies, a programme which, according to research done by Passe-Muraille, captures 48 per cent of the city's television audience. *I Love You, Baby Blue*, then, was meant to be a spoof of television pornography as well as a serious analysis of the sexual mores of Torontonians. It is loosely structured into individual episodes, and, much like *The Farm Show*, builds up eventually to a climactic finale. As in most collective creations, all of the actors took on multiple roles (from four to nine each); the entire cast consisted of eight people. Because of the controversial nature of the show, Passe-Muraille found itself forced to go outside the company itself to find actors, since most of the regular actors were unprepared to do nude scenes or feared negative reactions from their family if they took part in *Baby Blue*. In his introduction to the printed version of the play, Thompson defends his sociological approach against accusations of sensationalism:

The experiences we were relating were mainstream. . . . in the sense that they were currently visible activities or they were attitudes that you could find in the households of many people. Characters were chosen not because of their exceptional nature, but because they reflected a number of people with the same attitude.[14]

The published version of the play certainly comes across as a very human and sympathetic look at the problems of sexuality, with a definite emphasis on the role of sex as a shield against the loneliness and isolation of life in a big city.

The show itself is preceded by a prologue which parodies the "Baby Blue" television programme: a young woman dressed only in a blue diaper streaks across the stage, whereupon a Narrator announces "our version of the Baby Blue movie." The parody which follows consists of several short scenes. The most outrageous of them presents a couple, Harry and Babs, who drug a young woman, Gloria, in preparation for group sex; the two women, however, change their minds, kill Harry with a kitchen knife and happily proceed to make love to each other. End of "film." The Narrator then announces the play itself, a play which will deal with

the force that brings so many people from so many situations together on the same night, to watch the same thing. We suspect that force is sex. And so, Ladies and Gentlemen, "I Love You, Baby Blue."

The majority of the scenes in the play deal with some psychological implication of sex; some remain on the level of pure physiology. The opening scene presents a parody and demythification of commercial sex. It is set at "Hungry Harold's Burlesque Emporium," where an MC announces a torrid act but produces only a tired stripper who goes listlessly through her motions and then "shlumps off stage." "Toronto At Night" is probably the most moving scene of the show. It captures the loneliness of the big city through a highly poetic monologue, spoken by a woman:

Toronto at night.
Cold.
Black.
Hard, grey steel.

On Saturday night there's a half a million people out there on those streets. All jacked up. All plugged in. Mainlined into that great whirring motor of the city . . . and these people are crying out, they're crying out, "Oh Lord, from the highrises deliver us." "Oh Lord, from the windy streets deliver us," "Oh Lord, from the moonless night and the lonely bed deliver us." And the Lord

looks down on all his children and he says, "I give you neon signs! Neon signs
to guide your way in all that darkness!"

The tone of despair set by this speech is further reinforced with the tavern scene
that follows: it is the last call before closing, and patrons frantically make dates for
the night, regardless of partner, to shut out loneliness and isolation.

Scenes between couples tend to be equally pessimistic: "Gene and Chick"
shows a typical young executive on the rise who comes to Chick's apartment at
regular intervals, strictly for therapeutic reasons. Even during these brief interrup-
tions of his professional life, he is unable to stay away from the telephone. Finally,
Chick, humiliated and angry, sends him away for good. "Larry and Margaret," in
a lighter vein, makes fun of the new "liberated" attitudes toward sex: Margaret
tells Larry there is no need for him to use the clichéd "I love you" formula just
because he wants to have sexual relations with her. Harry is much relieved — but
eventually finds he is unable to perform in this liberated atmosphere. The most
explicit intercourse-cum-orgasm scene is handled very wittily, with the man and
woman escalating to the tune of the list of stops on the Toronto subway; they
simultaneously climax as they "reach" Union Station. "Human levitation" combines humour with extreme boldness: a girl in a black suit and top hat, standing in
front of a black curtain, announces she will perform an act of levitation — which
may or may not succeed. The object of the enterprise, it turns out, is not a human
body, but a penis pushed through a hole in the curtain.

As in *The Farm Show*, the two final scenes are designed to make the audience
think seriously about the implications of the play. Xaviera Hollander, the notorious
madam, appears as a mother figure and sexual guru. Her method is to solve
everyone's problem by way of a mass orgy. Standing behind the bed used for the
purpose like some latter-day saint, she looks upon her sex worshippers with
approval: "This is how it should be. This is good sex, good people. Toronto the
Good."[15] Her message, however, is invalidated by the last scene, a direct counterpoint to the orgy theory, and the play ends on a serious note. Again, a stage
metaphor is used: an actor centre stage holds up two chairs, trying to balance them
against each other — an image of the difficulties of human relationships:

> But when you really get down to it, you're ultimately dealing with only two
> people. Two people in a relationship (he tries to balance the chairs). And I
> think you'd all agree, it's a very difficult thing to achieve . . . it takes a lot of
> give and take, push and pull . . . and just when you think you have it . . . you
> have to try again . . . (but) when you find it . . . it's unmistakeable!

In spite of this obviously simplistic and clichéd ending, *Baby Blue* succeeds in
its basic purpose. The play does convey a sense of big city life through its cross
section of sexual behaviour; the parodies are highly entertaining, and in the more

serious scenes, the show does achieve odd moments of poignancy. In 1976, Passe-Muraille members made yet another attempt to capture the elusive spirit of their city. Ten actors went out to explore the daily lives and attitudes of Torontonians. The result was *City: The Toronto Show*, an account of their investigations and experiences. The image of the big city which emerged from *The Toronto Show* turned out to be just as pessimistic as that created earlier by *I Love You, Baby Blue*. The actors found Torontonians a joyless lot, "materialistic, emotionally uptight, isolated from one another." They concluded there was more *joie de vivre* to be found among immigrants, in spite of their relative poverty and isolation.

Although most of the sociological shows of Passe-Muraille are based on pure collective creation, writers were occasionally called upon to collaborate with the production. An example in point is *Far As the Eye Can See*, which portrays the controversy surrounding the Dodds-Round Hill community in Alberta, whose residents were threatened with eviction so the land could be used for strip mining. This play was developed with the help of Rudy Wiebe, Alberta novelist and short-story writer. It is interesting to follow the genesis of the collaborative process.[16] It began with a meeting between Wiebe and Thompson, when the general concepts of place, subject, and characters were developed. Following this, their ideas were presented to a group of four actors, who went through an intensive four-week course of "jamming" sessions to explore the dramatic possibilities of the material. Wiebe was present throughout these improvisational sessions, collecting some 350 pages of notes in the process. On the basis of these notes, he wrote a first version of the play — a task which took eleven days. This first version was then presented to the actors and thoroughly reworked in three weeks of rehearsals before its eventual premiere in Edmonton's Theatre Three. Before its Toronto showing, the play underwent yet another revision. The published text is based on the final, Toronto version.

The history of *Far As the Eye Can See* clearly illustrates the large part played by the actors themselves even in the case of a production involving a writer and the need for "flexibility" on the writer's part. However, the writer's contribution is immediately apparent if we look at the finished product. Unlike the episodic structure of pure collective creation, this play follows the traditional three-act pattern, with well-developed plotline. The carefully worked-out alternation of realistic scenes and fantasy (appearances by the three "Regal Dead") also testifies to the organizing influence of a single mind. Yet, *Far As the Eye Can See* is not one of Passe-Muraille's most successful ventures. The dialogue often appears stilted and the device of the Regal Dead (Crowfoot, William Aberhart and Princess Louise Alberta) artificial and quite unnecessary. The most interesting portion of the play occurs in the second act, which portrays the confrontation of the opposed parties with careful documentation of both sides of the argument.

Passe-Muraille was more successful in its collaboration with writers in the area of historical plays: *1837: The Farmers' Revolt*, with Rick Salutin, *Buffalo Jump*, with Carol Bolt, and *Them Donnellys*, with Frank MacEnaney, are all excellent examples of the potential of the genre.

1837: The Farmers' Revolt, is a good example of Passe-Muraille's general approach to historical topics. While describing events of the past, it very clearly reflects the contemporary issues of nationalism as opposed to colonial dependence on the mother country; the revolt of 1837 becomes the archetypal Canadian insurrection against oppression from outside forces as well as from within the country itself. In the process, an attempt is also made to create hero figures of sufficient status to become national legends, especially in the characters of Mackenzie and Van Egmond.

Like *The Farm Show, 1837* went through two successive, distinct versions. It was first produced under the title *1837* at Theatre Passe-Muraille in Toronto in 1972; in 1974, a revised version went on tour, playing in auction barns in Southwestern Ontario, as well as at the Victoria Playhouse in Petrolia. It was published in 1976.[17] The production process in this case began with collective creation, with the script finalized by the collaborating writer, Rick Salutin, after the actors had gone through the basic outline. This system proved more successful than the one used for *Far As the Eye Can See*.

The play is divided into two acts, each consisting of a number of loosely connected scenes; there is no direct plotline. The large number of characters are played by a small cast of five — three men and two women — who take turns playing all the parts. There is a clear thematic differentiation between the two acts: the episodes in act one provide the background for the revolution; act two presents a selection of scenes from the revolution itself. The play is particularly effective in its mixture of fact and fiction — documentary passages, such as authentic speeches by some of the historical figures, stand next to freely invented characters and situations. Act one excels in several satirical scenes, while the second act, more sombre in tone, contains a number of truly gripping episodes.

Several scenes of act one combine to give a clear picture of the frustrations suffered by the farmers which eventually led up to the revolution. The first two scenes, "Walking" and "Clearing," show the enormous effort the homesteaders put into the land and the depth of their despair when they were ruthlessly evicted after years of hard labour because they could not show a deed to the land. In "The Tavern," a play-within-a-play, the people act out the common experience of one among their number, Fred Bench, who returns, furious and humiliated, after many days of waiting to see the commissioner of crown lands: he was not only unable to see the commissioner to purchase land for twenty dollars (as promised in the papers), but he was approached by a private land agent, obviously in league with the commissioner, who offered him land at a price he cannot afford — two dollars an acre. This type of oppression is made possible by "The Family Compact": a small number of families hold all the power in Upper Canada, as demonstrated by Mackenzie through the metaphor of a conjuring trick.

This grim background is rounded out by small vignettes of the daily life of the period, such as "Mary MacDonald," the arrival of a farmer's new bride from Scotland. The couple have never laid eyes on each other before, and the scene of their first meeting is treated with gentle sympathy and humour. Three scenes of political satire — "Lady in the Coach," "The Head," and "The Dummy" — add punch to the historical panorama evoked in this first act. "Lady in the Coach"[18] presents "Lady Backwash, an English gentlewoman of the memoir-writing ilk" — an obvious parody of Susanna Moodie. She is on her way to a dinner party in Niagara Falls when the coach she is travelling in becomes stuck in the mud. When the driver asks her to get out to lighten the load, she at first reacts with typical British upper-class indignation:

> Out? Get out? My dear man, your impertinence is only matched by your incompetence as a driver. It is my duty to ride in this coach from Toronto to Niagara. It is yours to get me there. Now I am doing my duty. Kindly do yours.

Eventually, of course, she is forced to accept the realities of the situation. She gets out and instructs her man, Johnson, to help push: "Johnson, push with a will — the eyes of England are upon you." Ironically, an Indian who happens to be passing stops to watch the procedure; Johnson, in terror, flees the coach and climbs a tree, only to be called back instantly by Lady Backwash, whose imperial instincts have been aroused by the sight of the native: "Johnson, come down from that tree . . . Johnson, it [referring to the Indian] speaks English. And if it speaks English, it can take orders." The "savage" is then put to work to help push the coach, and the journey continues.

"The Head" is nothing less than a mimed pun on the name of the then lieutenant-governor of Upper Canada, Sir Francis Bond Head: while a narrator describes his features, four actors assemble the face, two heads for eyes, two arms for arching eyebrows, two more arms for the nose, until the entire head, complete with dimple, stands before the audience. The "head" then proceeds to speak. Pronouncing the words of a speech made by the lieutenant-governor at the time, the actors use the various parts of their anatomy to provide such appropriate facial expressions as a frown or a smile. While this scene offers some light-hearted relief, "The Dummy"[19] represents a bitter indictment of colonial oppression. In the framework of a political rally, a ventriloquist show is announced. The performer is none other than "John Bull, your Imperial ventriloquist," with his companion, "Peter Stump, the Canadian axeman." Their dialogue is a brilliant illustration of the colonial spirit:

> Peter: "Hello."
> John: "Aren't you forgetting something, Peter?"

Peter: "God Save the Queen."
John: "Good, Peter. Very loyal. I say — what is that in your hand?"
Peter: "My axe."
John: "What do you do with your axe, Peter?"
Peter: "Chop down trees . . . Timber!"
John: "And what do you do with the wood you cut?"
Peter: "Send it to you in England, John."
John: "Very fine, Peter. What else do you have there?"
Peter: "My rifle."
John: "Aha — and who are you going to shoot?"
Peter: "Yankees."
John: "Good. And quickly, too."

Very clearly, this scene reflects not only the situation of 1837, but also the nationalism of the 1960's — even if the battle by that time had shifted from political to cultural colonialism. In the "Dummy" scene, Peter eventually demands to be released from the ventriloquist's hold. To the latter's utter surprise and indignation, he slowly finds a voice of his own, and his first independent words are "Thank God for the man who is giving me a voice — William Lyon Mackenzie!"

The two last scenes of the first act bring us up to the revolution itself. "The Speech," a highly inflammatory piece of rhetoric by Mackenzie, incites the farmers to open rebellion, using the metaphor of the "turkey hunt." In the last scene, "Lount's Forge," we find the blacksmith manufacturing spikes rather than horseshoes.

Act two takes us logically and chronologically through the events of the revolution itself: preparations; the march on Toronto; the disastrous defeat; and the tragic aftermath of exile, imprisonment, and execution. Because the second part deals more closely with the historical facts, it is somewhat less theatrically effective than the more imaginative first act. The focus shifts back and forth between the leaders of the revolution, Mackenzie and Van Egmond, and the ordinary people.

The first scene presents a strategic meeting called by Mackenzie; December 7 is set as the date for the revolution. Van Egmond marches on Toronto, with his rebel troops; however, the battle breaks out earlier than originally planned, and utter chaos ensues. Mackenzie escapes, but Van Egmond is captured. A number of gripping scenes illustrate the debacle. The first of these is entitled "Knocks On The Door," "an old Canadian tradition . . . break-ins by government forces at the homes of suspected rebels." The three final scenes depict the ultimate outcome of the revolution for the rebels: prison, emigration, and execution. The play ends with the announcement of Van Egmond's death in his cell and the hanging of two other rebel leaders: Matthews and Lount, the blacksmith. Lount makes an impassioned last speech, a plea to continue the freedom fight, come what may. With the rope already around his neck, he still insists on his hope for a better future:

> Matthews: "Sam, we lost-"
> Lount: "No! We haven't won yet."

The trap falls, and the two men dangle by the ropes as the lights go out.

Buffalo Jump, produced jointly by Carol Bolt and Theatre Passe-Muraille, follows the same technical and ideological principles as *1837*: a historical episode is given contemporary relevance and also used as a basis for the creation of national hero figures. As Carol Bolt states in her introduction to the play:

> Myth is more appealing than fact. It postulates that heroism is possible, that people can be noble and effective and change things. . . . I think that what we were doing in Buffalo Jump was making those characters tragic heroes.[20]

In order to produce such a tragic hero of mythological proportions, Bolt combined two historical figures into one: Red Walsh and Slim Evans are blended into "Red Evans," hero of the play.

Buffalo Jump is based on Carol Bolt's earlier show, "Next Year Country," which was produced at the Globe Theatre in Regina in 1971; the work was completely revised and a new version, with a new title, developed in collaboration with the Passe-Muraille company.

The subject of *Buffalo Jump* is the unemployed workers' protest march to Ottawa during the Depression; the title represents an attempt to find a truly "Canadian" metaphor for their desperate move: the workers' march is equated with the Indians' method of driving a herd of buffaloes over the edge of a cliff. Its loosely connected sequence of scenes is divided into two acts, and the tone grows increasingly more sombre and tragic as the play progresses. Fact and fiction are mixed freely to create the desired effect.

As with the revolution in *1837*, the first act provides the background for the workers' march; act two describes the march itself and its unfortunate conclusion.

The play opens with an election rally in Estevan, Saskatchewan, where R. B. Bennett's unfortunate tendency towards mixed metaphors is duly satirized:

> My friends in Estevan, in the warp and woof of the Canadian cloth which is our fine British heritage, our immigrants are the embroidery on our sleeves. We want to roll up those sleeves and get to work.

Unemployment statistics are counterpointed with the announcement of the Conservative victory. The play then moves on to a description of the misery, drought, and unemployment in the Canadian West. The unemployed are kept busy with such heavy and useless work as moving rocks in relief camps where living conditions are untenable. Red Evans arrives at one of the camps and attempts to organize the men into a union. Counterpointing the purposeful activity of Red Evans, the next scene shows a totally ineffectual Bennett at the Commonwealth Conference, ending his speech with an emotional rendering of Kipling's "If." Meanwhile, the men from the relief camps get organized, take strike action against the useless "work" expected from them, and organize protest marches. Mass scenes alternate with glimpses of individual lives. There is a particularly moving inner monologue by one of the men, Peter, who meditates out loud on the contrast between his own poverty and isolation and the luxury he sees around him. He feels unsure of himself, confused, and somewhat guilty: "We see . . . we think. We see red . . . and we think Red. Can you blame us? . . . Where do we go from here??"[21] His question is eventually answered: the workers decide on the long trek to Ottawa via freight cars.

The second act presents a sequence of scenes from that trek: the men suffer from cold and hunger, and they nearly choke to death as the train passes through tunnels; but they do not give up. In Golden, British Columbia, food is found at last. This scene provides some much-needed relief in the grim picture of the Ottawa trek; it is handled in the form of a mock opera, with the entire population of the town, involved in the preparation and serving of food to the hungry workers, singing lustily as they go about their chores. The workers happily join in the chorus, "A stew! A stew!"

Before the actual confrontation in Ottawa takes place, the "Stampede" scene presents another stage metaphor (as we have seen, a typical feature of Passe-Muraille style) for the impending meeting: Red Evans rides a bull named R. B. Bennett. Eventually, of course, the government succeeds in its efforts to stop the workers' march; only eight men are allowed to come to the Capital. When they do, it turns out an exercise in futility: all of their demands are rejected, and they are quickly turned away: "Good morning, gentlemen. We have been glad to listen to you." The play ends logically enough, with the Regina riot.

Although *Buffalo Jump* does not read as well as *1837*, because of the many abrupt transitions and place changes, it is a highly effective theatrical piece. Song and dance routines, as well as some clever satire, serve to lighten an otherwise oppressively pessimistic work. Its political message nevertheless comes across clearly. The relevance of its basic theme, the clash between a conservative government and the needs of the working people remains undiminished in the 1980's.

Them Donnellys (1974, unpublished) is probably Passe-Muraille's most ambitious historical play in terms of its sheer theatrical fireworks. A collective creation with Frank McEnaney, it takes up the gruesome story of the Irish-Canadian family who are eventually massacred in the small Western Ontario community where they attempt to make a home. The play has been described as a mixture of "folk drama, action comic, tragedy, and country and western ballads";[22] it is particularly successful in its alternation of realistic and stylized scenes. The prologue to the play gives a good introduction to the various techniques used in the production. As the audience comes into the theatre, the actors, in costume but not in character, are already present; some stroll among the audience, engage in conversation, others are on stage, building the set; a fiddler moves in and out. This is, essentially, the same technique as that used for *The Farm Show* to put the audience at ease and create the proper atmosphere for the performance. The prologue itself consists of three parts: the "Realistic Fight," in which Donnelly kills Farrell; the "Mythic Fight," where the fight itself is mimed while the grandfather (a tiny figure) tells the grandson (a huge figure) the story of the Donnellys; and finally, an introduction number, where the actors are introduced to the audience through a routine of song and traditional step dance.

The play itself follows the same pattern, a mixture of realism, stylization, and song and dance interludes, some in country and western style, others heavily Brechtian. An exceedingly long play, *Them Donnellys* is divided into three acts of seven scenes each; the action follows the Donnelly story from the time of Jim Donnelly's imprisonment for murder, through the years of violence after his return, to the final massacre of the entire family, except for Will Donnelly, the lone survivor. While the Passe-Muraille version of the Donnelly story is very different in style from James Reaney's well-known trilogy on the same theme, the mythopoeic intention of both works is quite apparent. Through the dramatic recreations of their fate, the Donnellys have become legendary folk heroes for the Ontario region.

In relation to the myth-making aspirations of Passe-Muraille, *Maggie and Pierre*, a minor, but extraordinarily successful show of 1979 deserves mention. "A fantasy of love, politics and the media," the play was developed and performed by company member Linda Griffiths and directed by Paul Thompson. In her introduction to the published text [23] Griffiths states:

> Margaret and Pierre Trudeau are heroes to me. . . . I find the struggle of any two people trying to stay together heroic. The struggle of a family trying to stay together is heroic, especially in 1980. I find avoiding the inevitability of corruption in politics heroic. I think there was a real vision in what Trudeau wanted to do . . . the play is a metaphor for the country's involvement in politics and love. . . . I like to think of Maggie and Pierre as "epic" characters. They are heroes in that they contain all the elements of humanity, magnified.

The two-act play features three characters, Pierre Trudeau, Margaret Trudeau, and a journalist named Henry who both provides the frame story and represents the Canadian public: "I'm the guy who just can't stop watching."[24] All three characters are portrayed by Linda Griffiths, with some quick costume changes and the use of representative props — an impressive tour de force. The script manages to avoid sensationalism; the story of the prime minister's marriage is told with sympathy, understanding, and a touch of humour. Maggie is shown as a victim, first of her parent's conservative home, then of the entrapment of being the prime minister's wife. There are some excellent lines in the play, especially for the character of Maggie, who reveals herself fully through these lines. For example, on her first meeting with Trudeau, at the Tahiti Club Med, she describes to him her goal in life: "I want to be world-renowned, to shape destiny, to be deliriously happy. You might say, I want it all."[25] Pierre feels exactly the same way. They fall in love, and Maggie describes her newfound ecstasy in terms which indicate her hippie past:

> It's like flowers in the springtime and every atom in my body feeling alive. No, exploding. It's like really good acid and being on mescaline for eight hours and sitting up in a tree, thinking you're a bird.

Under the pressure of marriage and Ottawa etiquette, depression soon replaces the high, and Maggie decides to "freak out":

> I got bored, just this moment. A frozen moment in time. Boredom came crashing through the ceiling and landed right there on the carpet like a piece of rotten meat. What am I doing with this man? We have nothing to say to each other.[26]

Although the author/performer's sympathies are clearly with Maggie, the prime minister is also treated with much admiration and respect. Griffiths's little play is definitely a contribution to the Trudeau legend and an attempt to elevate Margaret also to the level of a folk heroine.

While collective creation has always been the central concern of Theatre Passe-Muraille, the company has also made a contribution in producing the work of young, experimental playwrights. The most important name in this connection is probably Hrant Alianak, who saw eight of his plays premièred at Passe-Muraille between 1972 and 1976;[27] several of these were later taken up by Factory Theatre Lab. Alianak's technique represents an interesting antithesis to the concept of collective creation: while collective creation produces dialogue without script, Alianak often produces a script without dialogue. We have already seen *Mathematics*, his play without characters or words. When he does use characters they express themselves in the comic strip style; often the author simply indicates action to be mimed but supplies little or no dialogue. This is the case, for example, in his short [ten page] play *Western*, a spoof on Western movies and cartoons. *Western* was first produced at Theatre Passe-Muraille in 1972 and subsequently published by Playwrights Coop. Here are the author's initial stage directions:

Arizona, 1874. Three stage coach travellers ambushed by 500 hostile Indians have managed to hide behind some rocks up in the hills:
Bart, a yet untested gunfighter.
Lili, a pampered Eastern belle.
Jean, a tough farmer's daughter.
    Below, the 500 wait. Tense music heightens the immediacy of the moment.

There are ten scenes in all, using all the techniques of caricature, absurdism, and the theatre of the grotesque, complete with killings and return of the corpses. Alianak's style here comes close to that of George Walker's later plays. The first scene establishes the satirical tone with a litany-like calling out of Western themes by one character and the response with the appropriate movie star by another; "John Wayne" and "Shane" hold the record of six times each. Scenes are separated from each other by blackouts punctuated by "whirling music." Some of the scenes consist of mime only. Instructions for these are provided in telegram style by the author (obviously suggesting an equally telescopic style of acting), for example, scene seven:

Bart and Jean now. Alert Bart looking for Indians. Jean looking for love. Tactless Jean is ignored by preoccupied Bart. No-nonsense Jean offers some friendly persuasion. Helpless Bart feels the pointed gun and decides not to argue. Brazen Jean forcefully kisses Bart. . . . Revived Lili walks in with determined eyes. She kicks Jean out of position and fires her gun. Right in between Bart's eyes. Bart's death is quick.

In this scene, as throughout the play, exaggerated versions of all the clichés of the traditional Western are presented. In the same tradition, the three characters finally meet their end as three shots are fired at them from offstage in the penultimate scene; as they die, a voice offstage is heard proclaiming "high noon!" Scene ten brings the play to a conclusion with "Silence. No one. In the distance, the cavalry are heard as the columns rush to do their duty."
    Alianak's anti-theatre, so completely opposed to the essential naturalism of the Passe-Muraille style, is a testimony to the company's openness and genuine interest in experimentation in various directions. Of course, the Passe-Muraille style itself has left its mark on a considerable number of younger alternative theatre companies. But the group made a perhaps equally important contribution through its hospitality to other and different theatrical endeavours. .While only some of its productions have been recorded, and will thus remain a part of the body of Canadian dramatic literature, Passe-Muraille's influence on the development of that literature cannot be underestimated.

Les Maudits Anglais, a collecive work performed by
Theatre Passe-Muraille in November 1978. Directed by
Paul Thompson. Left to right: Diana Belshaw, Linda
Griffiths, Paul Kelman, David Fox.

2. *Under the Greywacke,* one of Passe-Muraille's sociological plays, where the actors and director, Paul Thompson,
moved into the community before beginning improvisation. Left to right: Jacquie Presley, Clare Coulter, Greg
Malone, Saul Rubinek, Ann Anglin, Miles Potter, and Ted Johns.

3. *Them Donnellys,* a collective work with Frank McEnaney, directed by Paul Thompson, is probably Passe-Muraille's most ambitious historical play, highly successful in terms of alternation of realistic and stylized scenes. Left to right: David Fox, Eric Paterson, Ted Johns, Dean Harves, Gary Reineke.

4.-5. Edward Astley, left, and Stephen E. Miller, right, in Tamahnous Theatre's 1975 collective creation. All eleven members of the cast contributed to this examination of contemporary society in a tribal context.

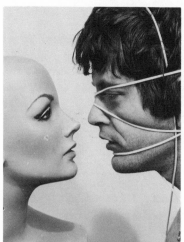

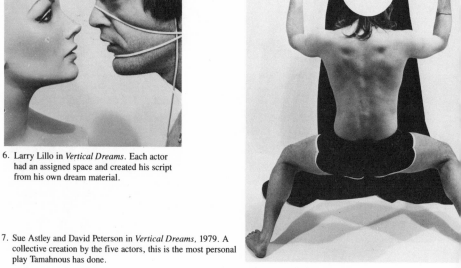

6. Larry Lillo in *Vertical Dreams*. Each actor had an assigned space and created his script from his own dream material.

7. Sue Astley and David Peterson in *Vertical Dreams*, 1979. A collective creation by the five actors, this is the most personal play Tamahnous has done.

8. Nicole Leblanc in one of Jean-Claude Germain's most ambitious plays, *Les hauts et les bas d'la vie d'une diva: Sarah Ménard par eux-mêmes.*

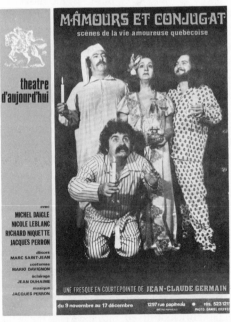

10. Germain's *A Canadian Play*, subtitled "un exorcisme ritual," in which Lord Durham is forced to confront the disastrous consequences of his report.

9. Germain's *Mamours et Conjugat* follows "bedroom history" from the seventeenth century to the present. Produced by Théâtre *d'Aujourd'hui*, it starred (left to right) Michel Daigle, Nicole Leblanc, Richard Niquette, and Jacques Perron.

4

Western Magic: Tamahnous Theatre and Savage God

In Western Canada, the major innovative thrust of the alternative theatre movement came from Vancouver. Of course, other large cities also developed alternates to the regional theatres: Theatre Network, Catalyst Theatre, and Theatre Three in Edmonton; Alberta Theatre Projects in Calgary, and 25th Street House in Saskatoon. Most of these followed the pattern of alternative companies as set in Toronto, and more specifically, by Passe-Muraille. In Vancouver, however, the movement developed independently of Ontario; rather, it shows the influence of the American West Coast, a powerful generator of counter-culture throughout the 1960's and into the 1970's. While alternative theatre in the rest of Canada belongs largely in the "committed" or socially concerned category, the most interesting work done in Vancouver was strictly introspective, reflecting the West Coast interest in the drug culture, Freudian psychology, Gestalt, and other psychotherapies as practised at the Esalen Institute. Theatre, then, is seen not so much as a tool for social action, nor as a comment and interpretation of life, but rather as an integral and potentially enriching part of living itself. If no-nonsense Brecht was the supreme deity of alternative theatre in the East, the West Coast stands under the more flamboyant aegis of Artaud and Grotowski.

Underground theatre started early in Vancouver and developed vigorously for a while. During the decade between 1965 and 1975, some forty small companies were active in the city. However, most of these were short-lived and exerted little or no permanent influence on the local theatre scene. As with the Toronto underground theatre, only one company survived to commercial viability: Tamahnous Theatre. Savage God, more of a cultural phenomenon around the personality of director John Juliani than a company in the strict sense of the word, also continued its work into the 1980's; its centre moved from Vancouver to Edmonton in 1976. These two groups not only proved remarkably long-lived; they have also made the most original contribution to the alternative theatre movement in this country: Tamahnous in the direction of self-exploration; Savage God in the attempt to fuse life and art into one creative whole. Because the work of Savage God has been considerably more diversified and far-reaching than that of Tamahnous it will be discussed at much greater length.

Tamahnous Theatre was founded in 1971 by John Gray,[1] who had just completed a Master's Degree at the University of British Columbia, and a group of younger University of British Columbia graduates. They protested against their university training, which they considered reactionary, and against the "rich" theatre represented by Vancouver Playhouse. Followers of Grotowski, they believed that only by setting themselves up as a "poor" theatre would they be able to achieve the kind of magic they dreamt of; and they chose as a name for the company, "Tamahnous," the Chilcotin Indian word for magic. Gray proclaimed his basic principle from the start: "What I wish to see is not a production machine, but a group of people who will create a reality for me with their voice and bodies."[2] Tamahnous, then, was to be an actor-oriented company in the spirit of Grotowski and Artaud.

The experiment proved highly successful. By 1981, Tamahnous had produced thirty-eight plays. Of these twenty-one were original and either collective creations or collectives in association with house writer Jeremy Long. Their first shows were done in the Vancouver Arts Club. After Larry Lillo took over from John Gray in 1974, the company acquired a home of their own on Maple Street in Vancouver; since 1977, they have been operating as the resident company at the Vancouver East Cultural Centre. Besides their regular productions, the company has done street theatre, workshops, and children's plays in parks and on playgrounds during the summer.

Members of Tamahnous attribute their success largely to the fact that they have managed to create a genuine ensemble — an unusual situation for an alternative theatre group, whose memberships are usually irregular because of financial exigencies. The number of actors in Tamahnous varies between six and thirteen at any given time; but there is a solid core who have been together from the beginning. Because the group has also experimented with communal living, they look upon themselves as a "family," rather than a group of people associated for purely professional reasons; the resulting sense of mutual trust and openness has made possible the kind of self-exploratory shows at which they are best.[3] The group obviously has its roots in the "flower children" ideology of the 1960's. Their early productions show a great deal of naive idealism, which later makes way for nostalgia and a somewhat more realistic approach. In their programme notes for the 1976 production of *Nijinski*, they included the following quotation from the Russian dancer's diary — obviously because Nijinski's statement mirrors so well the hippie-type of exaltation which lies at the origins of Tamahnous:

I love everybody. I do not want war or frontiers. The world exists. I have a home everywhere. I live everywhere. I do not want to have any property. I do not want to be rich. I want to love. I am love — not cruelty. I am not a bloodthirsty animal. I am a man. I am man. God is in me. I am in God. (1919)

Another reason for the success and commercial viability of Tamahnous is the company's dedication to the art of theatre *per se*; they have no specific political orientation. When they do perform works with a "message," it is more in response to audience demand than out of any special social or political concern. Their official statement of aims and objectives makes this quite clear:

The members of the group are working together because each individual in the company is searching for a means of expression through theatre that exists outside traditional forms. We are concerned with the breaking down of the roles that exist in production — i.e., writer, director, actor — and with developing a working situation in which everyone is concerned with the central concept of the project. We believe that we should work to develop our own form — one that will allow our productions to live and have significance for more than a few historians and an elitist audience. We are dedicated to developing new forms and plays, providing audiences with a wider choice of theatre, maintaining a high standard of production and making theatre an important element in the lives of a large number of people.[4]

To achieve these goals, Tamahnous developed its own collective creation technique. The process is fully democratic. Instead of allowing itself to be formally "directed," as do Passe-Muraille and The Mummers, the group simply chooses one of their members to act as an outside "eye" in each production. Where conflict arises, it is solved by majority decision rather than by directorial fiat. This type of approach obviously presupposes a long period of harmonious collaboration. Where the services of a writer are used, he too is drawn into the collective process. Because of this approach, and because of Tamahnous's special interest in exploring inner rather than outer reality, memories, dreams, and fantasies, their productions tend to be more effective in their visual images and sense impressions than in their verbal expression. It also means that any production script produces a poor record of the actual performance; videotapes (which the company could rarely afford) provide the only effective means of preserving their type of show.

In order to develop an original technique, Tamahnous actors went through an apprenticeship period when they experimented with productions modelled on those of other radical companies, and with adaptations of the classics. Like Passe-Muraille with its opening show, *Futz*, Tamahnous started its first season with shock tactics: 1971 productions included *Dracula II*, an original work by the

Stable Theatre of Manchester, and *The Bacchae*, modelled after The Performance Group's controversial *Dionysus in '69*. *Dracula II*, based on Bram Stoker's Gothic novel, mixed techniques of the theatre of cruelty (including stage directions such as "Rivers of blood. Freak out the audience") with a collage of poetry going from Blake and Coleridge to nursery rhymes, the whole presented by five actors on a bare floor, with a few suggestive props (Dracula's cape) and highly elaborate lighting effects covering both the stage and the audience. Critics found the production "mindblowing"[5] "a shattering theatrical experience"[6] — and Tamahnous had made its mark. *The Bacchae*, a political allegory which sought audience involvement and included scenes of total nudity, created an even more violent reaction. Christopher Dafoe accused the director, John Gray, of having turned Euripides' tragedy into a "ceremony of hysteria and blood"[7] — not quite fair when one considers the essentially gruesome nature of the Greek original!

Tamahnous's most ambitious classical adaptation was their production of *Medea* by Jeremy Long and the company (1973). Long's interpretation clearly reflects the strong hold of both the theatre of cruelty and the "happening" on the company at the time. While Euripides presents his characters at one particular moment of crisis and puts the emphasis of the tragedy on the presentation of arguments on both sides, Long chose to tell the story chronologically from beginning to end, heavily stressing the physical violence. A chorus with percussion instruments accompanies the sequence of gruesome events. All physical action is shown on stage; it includes ritual killing (the sacrificial victim being shown nude); murder, suicide, and sexual intercourse. The two most blood-curdling scenes deal with the murder of king Pelias by his three daughters — the horror of which is heightened by erotic overtones — and Medea's strangling of her children. The play ends with Jason crying over the bodies of the little boys while Medea towers ferociously over him. The effect of the play is of course diametrically opposed to the kind of catharsis that Greek tragedy aims for. It is a reworking of a classic in typical 1960's fashion and anti-intellectual in its straight emotional appeal.

Also in 1973, Tamahnous experimented with the potential of Shakespeare's *The Tempest*. A first version was done environmental-style, the text a "collective adaptation" of the original. When this proved unsatisfactory because the actors were insufficiently trained to do justice to Shakespearean language, they attempted a mimed version of the play, the only spoken words a sermon by John Donne. This interpretation through "mime-dance" set the entire action within the mind of Prospero, with the other characters acting out his basic conflict between flesh and spirit. To create an emotional bridge for the audience, the production was introduced by a blues-style "Ode to Bill Shakespeare." This second version of *The Tempest* proved more satisfactory. In the years which followed, the Tamahnous company created increasingly original works. The best of these are definitely their introspective, self-exploratory productions.

The first in the series was a light-hearted musical called *Salty Tears on a Hangnail Face*, with text by Jeremy Long and music by John Gray (1974). It was the company's nostalgic reaction to the slow fading away of the hippie culture. The play centred on a communal house, its decline witnessed by a sympathetic feline named Quixote Cat and shown to the audience from his point of view. In the process, the musical manages to probe into a number of serious issues of the period: the Protestant work ethic; the drug problem (should catnip be legalized?); rising crime in the alleyways; and the corruption of the establishment (here represented by the veterinary clinic). In the best musical tradition, the lines between Good and Evil are clearly drawn. The human characters are divided into two opposed groups: the hippie community, with their idealization of brotherhood and love, and "heavies," such as the landlord, the "man in uniform," and the veterinarian. On the animal level, the devoted and heroic Quixote Cat and his pretty girlfriend Blossom Pony are counterpointed by Mafia Monster, a feline version of the neighbourhood godfather, and a growling Dog. The lives of people and cats run parallel, and Quixote Cat provides a central pivot for both actions. When the community finds itself under heavy stress from outside pressures, the flower children have to go out to work to meet the landlord's ever-increasing demands. Not to be outdone, Quixote also joins the work force; he gets a job as mousecatcher in a factory. Soon, however, he becomes the victim of a horrible industrial accident. His tail is caught in a machine and badly mangled. The veterinarian, a heartless and callous representative of authority, suggests putting the now useless animal "out of his misery"; but Quixote's loving humans will not hear of such a thing and insist on an amputation, although they can ill afford such expense. Nevertheless, poor Quixote fails to recover: cancer develops, and eventually the young people have to choose between letting him die a slow and painful death or opting for euthanasia. They decide on the latter, and Quixote goes to his rest.

However, since this is a musical and not a tragedy, the play does not end here, but on a double note of hope: we meet our hero again in Kitty Heaven, where he is informed by the good Kitty Fairy that he has only used up three of the nine lives which, as a cat, he is entitled to; and he is given instructions on how to be reborn. Meanwhile, on earth, a blessed event takes place among the hippie community: one of the girls gives birth, and the child is named, symbolically, Lazarus (surely, he must be Quixote reincarnated!).

The play succeeded very well in presenting a realistic portrait of a waning counter-culture, and it was especially effective in its attempt to render the typical hippie way of expression. Production techniques also underlined the basic theme of communal spirit and co-operation: every actor, besides playing one or more roles, also took part in the production chores, either as a member of the technical crew or as one of the five-men band. In this way, the production itself provided a living illustration of the spirit of togetherness which it celebrated, and whose demise it mourned.

The Shaman's Cure, a collective creation of 1975, used techniques of ritual and incantation to explore in a more serious fashion the relationship between the individual and society. It examined contemporary society in a tribal context, again a link with hippie culture.

The theme of the play is simple: a member of the tribe, a young girl named Moth, is ill; for the good of all, she must be cured. All conventional methods having failed, a shaman is called in to perform a healing ritual. When this does not bring the desired result, it becomes clear that the group itself — society — is sick. Eventually, one of the group, a "man with a gun," kills Moth: a thoroughly pessimistic ending, reflecting the violent nature of contemporary society.

This production was the group's first fully co-operative venture, with input by all eleven members of the cast. It represented the result of a year and a half of earnest work, from discussion and research to improvisation and rehearsal. A great deal of improvisation was also used throughout the run of the show, so that the story line varied: some versions included more than one killing, others a suicide. The basic plot line, of course, remained constant. The shaman's curing ritual itself was based on careful research of the Kwakiutl Indians.

The show opened with an imaginatively choreographed scene showing the gradual emergence of the family circle, or tribe, from a primordial heap of bodies. One of the group is left writhing in pain away from the others: she is Moth, "sick" or "unhappy." The company then intones an anthem in which they give voice to their feeling of belonging:

> We are one
> We are one
> Face not the night with fear[8]

A speech by the sick girl's father echoes a similar hippie philosophy: "Happiness is fundamental to our lives. Unhappiness cannot be tolerated." Such naive idealism, of course, does not correspond to the facts of life: there is no cure for Moth, just as there is none for the evils of society.

When the shaman is brought in, accompanied by an assistant and a pair of live snakes, the healing ritual starts. Each member of the family is made to step forth and "witness" his or her attitude towards Moth by re-enacting a scene with her. It soon becomes clear that in spite of all their protestations of love and goodwill, they all secretly hope to get rid of the girl. Moth alone tells the truth, as her final, impassioned, and chaotic "speech from the tower" reveals. Although it could be argued that this play deals with a sociological theme, the emphasis is not on that theme, but rather, in typical Tamahnous style, on the "magic" evoked through ritual act and stage image.

Perhaps the most interesting of all the company's experiments along the line of introspective theatre was their 1979 production of *Vertical Dreams*, a collective creation by five actors and actresses. It is the most personal play Tamahnous has ever done, with all of its material taken from the dreams, fantasies, and memories of the participants themselves. It also illustrates the use of theatre as therapy: the company was undergoing an internal crisis at the time, and members felt that by baring their subconscious selves to each other and to an audience they would solve their problems. In fact *Vertical Dreams* turned out to be effective therapy for the actors, as well as exciting and stimulating theatre for the audience.

The entire creation process started with discussions based on June Singer's *Androgyny: Towards A New Theory of Sexuality*, a book which aroused the actors' interest about the way in which mythological images turn up in the collective unconscious. To help them in their search, they brought in two professional therapists and went into a series of workshop sessions. These sessions served to explore Jungian theories of animus, anima, and shadow, on the basis of which sex roles were then acted out. The production itself was constructed from the dreams which developed during the workshop, both during the sleeping and the waking state. Each actor created his own script out of his or her dream material.

Eventually a "play" consisting of twenty short scenes emerged. The set was designed as a maze, within which each actor had his own assigned space. Elaborate lighting effects in a broad spectrum of colours and intensities helped to create the dream-like atmosphere, as did props such as a profusion of Japanese lanterns and papier-mâché hearts suspended from the ceiling. The dreams, or stories, were not told consecutively, but meshed — bits and pieces from many different dreams following each other. To enact these scenes, the actors stepped out of their own dream space and into that of the character whose dream was being told at the time. All of the props carried symbolic significance, with each character assigned one particular identifying symbol, such as a baby carriage, a petfood dish, a fashion dummy, or a media gadget. The stories suggested by the characters all illustrated archetypal situations: a neglected young girl taking refuge in a fairy tale she tells to herself; a young boy stifled by his family environment; violence between two young men culminating in homosexual passion. The intent was to create a rich, theatrical dreamscape. Judging from the videotape of the performance, Tamahnous fully achieved this goal. Audiences were fascinated and intrigued: frequently, many stayed for long discussions with the cast following the performance.

In 1980, Tamahnous combined the techniques of *Shaman's Cure* and *Vertical Dreams* in a new production, *Foolproof*. This show attempted to explore the relationship between "normal" behaviour and "madness" and to show the blurring of the lines between the two. The star and motivating force of this show came from outside the company: it was Ronnie Gilbert, the actress and clinical psychologist who had worked with Peter Brook in England and Joseph Chaikin's Open

Theatre in New York. At the time of *Foolproof*, Ms. Gilbert was living in the Slocan Valley of British Columbia, where she had founded Theatre Energy, a *Gestalt* type theatre combining performance and therapy. Commenting on the Tamahnous production, she formulated one of the basic beliefs of that company, and, as we shall see, of *Savage God*:

> The theatre is one of the few places left where people can pose questions that aren't normally asked, and put them to both themselves and the audience at the same time . . . what we have been trying to do with this play is to find the fool — perhaps the Holy Fool — in all of us.[9]

The show was done revue-style, a sequence of short scenes related to each other only casually by the theme and the central character, "Norm." Many portions of the show were humorous or satirical, although they all conveyed a serious message. Stage images, as in *Vertical Dreams*, carried certain archetypal connotations: one scene, for example, showed an old bum, his rubber chicken named Toto on a leash, lecturing earnestly to an assembly of battered baby dolls, with occasional asides to Toto. The production also included a healing ritual. This time the shaman does succeed in curing the patient, Norm — with the result, however, that the latter, freed from inhibition and social control, vents all his violent existentialist desires — thus crossing the border to behaviour no longer considered "normal."

In the area of social and political, "committed" theatre, Tamahnous produced both classics of the genre, such as Brecht's *St. Joan of the Stockyards* or John Hare's *Fanshen*, and original productions. These definitely fall short of the introspective type of play. *Eighty-four Acres* (1976) by Jeremy Long, for example, a play about the land freeze, fails as political theatre because of the discrepancy between theme and treatment. A serious social problem is presented; the villain in the case is established (the land developer); and the call for revolution, sounded: "guns, blood, revolution!" However, one can hardly take the political message seriously in the setting of a light-hearted musical, with a pair of ducks, Jim and Jemimah, as the spokesmen of the author. *Liquid Gold* (1978), by Bruce Ruddell and Glen Thompson, deals with the formation of a fisherman's union on the West Coast, and it succeeded better in conveying its basic theme. Although *Liquid Gold*, too, is a musical, it presents strongly drawn characters and believable, sometimes gripping, situations. There is a central conflict, focused on Mort Wheel, capitalist, middleman, and exploiter, and the vigorous fisherman's widow Sophie McCafferty, a highly intelligent and resourceful rum runner. It is Sophie who organizes the fishermen and instills in them the courage to stand up to Mort and his henchman on the police force. Her outburst against Mort, an impassioned plea for fishermen's rights, is also an effective piece of Brechtian rhetoric:

But who has given you that right? Who, in his almighty wisdom, has decreed that you should own us? Is it the men who control the factories and the armies, or is it the people who till the soil and fish the sea? No, we are the wealth of the world; we own you, because we own these (holds up her hands).

Tamahnous was more successful when it used collective creation techniques to express its social concerns, rather than the somewhat ambiguous medium of the musical. *Deep Thought* (1977) is described in the programme notes as "an entertaining look at the ironies of life in the global village; images, melodies and lyrics from our own fears and dreams." Clearly it is closer to the introspective shows than to political theatre. *Deep Thought*, however, does carry a serious message: it is a revue-style satire of contemporary consumer society in the form of an allegory: a family of clowns (the people) is threatened with extermination by three vicious giants: the Multi-nationals, Mr. Progress, and The Media. The structure takes on the form of a series of news stories broadcast by a television station; the audience watches the trials and tribulations of the three clowns in their attempt at defection from the Circus of Dreams (consumer society), pursued by a hit man in the employ of Harold P. Progress. The news reports are interspersed with topical stories, such as skits about the coffee and sugar crisis and satirical songs on consumerism ("I'd like to teach the world to spend a dollar more each day"). There is also some bitter comment about the way the consumer society corrupts and abuses artists: the Mutant Poets, a rock group, are discovered by the media, catapulted to instant fame, and dropped just as soon as they show the slightest subversive tendency.

It is unlikely that any of the Tamahnous productions will become part of Canadian theatre literature; but the company has made an important contribution throughout the 1970's by its injection of unique and original approaches into the country's theatre scene. While Tamahnous has done this in an informal way, simply by pursuing its alternative goals, Savage God formally proclaimed its position as alternative and complement to traditional theatre.

Like Passe-Muraille, Savage God began under the auspices of an avant-garde educational institution. In 1966, John Juliani joined the theatre department of the newly founded Simon Fraser University on Burnaby Mountain outside Vancouver. In July of that year, the Simon Fraser University Theatre Company made its first appearance before the public under the name of Savage God, with a double bill of Ghelderode and Arrabal. The choice of name for his company attests to Juliani's fondness for literary allusion; it is based on Yeats's reaction to *Ubu Roi*, an awe-struck "After us, the Savage God." By way of further elucidation, Juliani later added a triple "e" exponent to the name, which made it Savage God[eee] — signifying "emergent, experimental ensemble."

Although Savage God began as a student company, it soon developed far beyond any such narrow confines. As has been mentioned before, it is a phenomenon centred on one person charged with cultural energy, rather than a group or movement in any conventional sense. Savage God defies definition; but it could perhaps be described as an ever-changing, ongoing experience of explosive multiple happenings on the counter-culture scene of Canada. Juliani himself has issued many statements in which he attempts to delineate the perimeters of Savage God; his flamboyant prose is convincing, but not necessary illuminating. Nevertheless, it is well worth looking at the pseudo-definition he provided with his programme notes to the first Savage God production:

> The modern theatre is still waiting for a form that will harmonize with the moral, intellectual and emotional viewpoint of our age — an age that has been accused of wearing its complacency like a laurel wreath. The history of the theatre arts in our century has been to shatter that complacency by means of a bombardment of the senses. . . . The apparently arbitrary and often violent juxtaposition of eccentricity, conventionality, the grotesque, the sublime, innocence and cruelty, has, paradoxically, become a cliché of contemporary art. It is through the reconciliation of these discordant qualities in an orchestration of shapes, sounds, colors and movement that the imagination reveals itself in a new language, the hieroglyphics of which are designed to lure our demons to the surface . . . for every new form, a glaring question mark. *The Savage God is an anthology of such question marks.* (Author's italics)

Juliani may have seen Savage God initially as an "anthology of question marks"; but he certainly proposed some answers, albeit always only tentatively. First of all, he defined his radius of operation. As he stated many times in programme notes, press releases, and interviews, he sees his task as revitalizing the theatre at its four "essential roots": acting, actor-audience relationship, text, and direction. To achieve this, he has developed a philosophy of theatre which borrows heavily from Artaud, Grotowski, and Schechner.

Later, he gave the following elaboration on the initial definition: "Savage God is simply the Imagination — insatiable, unrelenting, fiercely energetic, wary of categorization, fond of contradiction and inveterately iconoclastic."[10] This statement seems to describe the man as much as the organization.

Looking upon the work of Savage God in retrospect, one can isolate five major points of Juliani's philosophy.

1. *The fusion of life and art.* Juliani's attitude to the fusion of life and art here comes close to that of the French Symbolists, the Dadaists, and some representatives of Expressionism, who sought, through their flamboyant and often outrageous lifestyles to make the events of their daily lives into works of art, while at the same time making art a part of daily life. For Juliani, creating art is part of the total life experience. He has consistently demonstrated this belief by making the

rituals of his private life into public functions, with the audience invited to share in the creation of a "Work of Art." His wedding ceremony, for example, took place in the Vancouver Art Gallery, an integral part of a Savage God production, *Celebration*; the audience were handed out masks to wear for the occasion and invited to participate. A similar ritual celebration took place on the occasion of his son's baptism. The principle applies equally well beyond the Julianis' personal lives. Asked to choreograph a ballet on the Canadian ethnic scene and immigration, Juliani came up with *Mosaic*, an impressive performance by Ernst and Carol Eder — with the production built into the ceremony which conferred Canadian citizenship on the lead dancer. Juliani objects violently to the typically Western attitude which sees in art an escape from life, and points out instead the Oriental trend to create a harmonious whole out of the two — as exemplified in the Japanese garden.[11]

2. *Process as product.* Unceasing experimentation follows as a natural result of the first principle, and Savage God productions are therefore never "final products"; rather, they are stages along a dynamic process of trial and error. In fact, it is one of the central features of Savage God that no one performance is ever seen a second time in exactly the same way. The same script may be produced many times but each production will be distinctly different. Juliani may decide to change the location and thus force the actors into a totally new approach. Beckett's *Happy Days*, to give one example, was performed both in a small indoor space and outdoors in Stanley Park: they were two separate shows. Or the changes may be made in setting and costume; in acting technique; in production style. The director may decide to experiment with a change of sex roles within the same play. Strindberg's *The Stronger*, for example, was played by both male and female performers. Often it is necessary for the audience to be present at an entire series of experimental productions of one play in order to get the full impact of the work. Unwary members of the public are warned in the programme notes about the tentative quality of the performance they are about to witness. The formula is always basically the same:

> You will have noticed that many of the works are "incomplete" or "in progress." For instance, you may have been puzzled by the glaring absence of costumes on one night and their extravagant presence on another. You are sure to have noticed the absence in any conventional sense of decor. Hopefully, you will also have noticed a wide range of experimentation with seating arrangements and admired, perhaps, the work of what for lack of a better word, might be called an "ensemble."

In the programme notes to *Celebration*, 1970, Juliani expounded further on his basic philosophy of experimental theatre:

Life and Art must ultimately seek to be reconciled or else cease to remain organic. . . . Life cannot be institutionalized. It is, in one sense, a continuous public mistake, an unfinished work of cataclysmic proportions. It is pointless to seek the identity of the perpetrator of that mistake when we ourselves continue the perpetration. *Deliberate public mistake is the essence of experimental theatre. All theatre is experimental. Experimental means 'Process as Product.'* " (Juliani's italics)

3. *Free theatre.* In keeping with Juliani's philosophy on the fusion of life and art and the powers of art as a product, it is a basic principle of Savage God not to charge admission for any of their productions. Juliani follows Grotowski's belief in a "poor" theatre; he also feels that in return, this poor theatre must be absolutely free in its forms of expression. By charging admission, a company severely handicaps its freedom of action: the ticket buyer feels entitled to a "performance" according to his own, preconceived notions. In a free theatre situation, the conventional consumer/distributor relationship between the actors and the public no longer exists; instead, the members of the audience have become voluntary participants in a joint undertaking, free to leave if the event does not meet their approval. The actors, on the other hand, need have no fear of making the "deliberate public mistake" which Juliani sees as the essence of experimental theatre.

4. *Emphasis on the non-verbal aspects of theatre.* Juliani is a fervent disciple of Artaud in his belief that the essence of theatre does not lie in the scripted text, but in the sum total of sensory impressions created by the production. This results in an emphasis on the non-verbal aspect of theatre. With Artaud, Juliani also believes that only through an affective rather than a conceptual appeal can theatre make its mark on an audience. He openly attested his indebtedness to Artaud when he called his theatrical "laboratory research" for a number of years "Research Institute of the Plague" (1973 ff). A more recent influence is Richard Schechner's theory of environmental theatre; Savage God has implemented every one of the criteria for a "new theatre" proposed by Schechner.[12] Juliani's statements in this area could come directly from Schechner; they also echo Artaud's teachings of some forty years earlier: "Communication in the theatre is essentially non-literal and connotative. . . . I believe that the word, as sole arbiter and conveyor of meaning in the theatre, is dead."[13]

5. *Theatre as therapy.* Artaud's whole concept of "theatre of cruelty" already suggests its therapeutic value; he speaks in terms of "exorcism," of "draining abscesses," of the purging effect of theatre as "plague." Savage God, however, went far beyond such a metaphorical interpretation. Instead, Juliani turned to the more practical teachings of modern psychology, especially *Gestalt*. Because role-playing forms an essential part of Gestalt therapy, he felt that theatre is an area where the two separate endeavours of art and therapy come together: just as theatre

can be used as therapy, therapy should lend itself to use as theatre. To explore the thin line between the two was a major research goal of Savage God from the beginning; and formal Gestalt sessions were incorporated into its 1971 "PACET" ("pilot alternative complement to existing theatre") project. Even for his "straight" dramatic shows, Juliani emphasized the psychological value for the audience; he considers theatre in any form "a continuous Rorschach test" for the public.[14]

This summary of the philosophy of Savage God makes it clear that the entire operation hinges on the driving force of one man. The Juliani chronology *is* the history of Savage God. It is useful, therefore, to establish this chronology briefly, before examining the actual productions.

John Juliani was born in Montreal in 1942. As his work clearly shows, he obtained a thorough classical/humanistic education: Loyola University, the National Theatre School, apprenticeship at the Stratford Festival. After working for a brief period in Montreal, acting, directing, and translating (he produced the first Canadian versions of several Arrabal plays), he came to Simon Fraser University in 1966 and founded Savage God. Juliani's flamboyance, however, did not meet with the approval of even so modern a university as Simon Fraser, and Savage God was forced to move its headquarters from gown to town in 1969. Operating out of a variety of spaces, such as the Vancouver Art Gallery and the Public Library, Juliani, unperturbed, continued his experimental work in a number of areas: scripted texts, both classical and modern; improvisation; and readings of contemporary local playwrights and poets. In 1970, he demonstrated his fusion of life and art theory with the public *Celebration* ceremony of his wedding to actress and dancer Donna Wong. Donna has remained the second mainstay of Savage God, both as performer and administrator. A highlight of Juliani's Vancouver years was a three-week, high-powered series of experiments funded by the Canada Council ("PACET"), which led to his book, *The Free Theatre*, a report on the results of his work, together with recommendations for new and better cultural policies on the part of the government.

Following a year of world travel and theatre research, Juliani was again offered an academic post. In 1974 he was invited by the theatre department of York University to set up a programme of graduate theatre studies. The result was PEAK ("Performance, Example, Animation, Katharsis"), an experiment in theatre education which combined art and therapy. The PEAK ensemble of young actors proved extremely successful in Canada and abroad: they were invited to perform at the Wroclaw Festival of International Avant-Garde Theatre in Poland. Nevertheless, the director's association with academe again proved less than happy, and in 1976, the Julianis moved to Edmonton, which has served as headquarters for Savage God since.

To obtain a clear idea of the many-faceted aspect of Savage God, it is best to follow the four major stages of Juliani's progress chronologically:

1. Savage God at Simon Fraser University.
2. The Vancouver period, especially the PACET project.
3. The York period and PEAK.
4. The most recent Savage God events in Edmonton.

Of all these activities the PACET project of 1971 is the most far-ranging and will be given detailed treatment.

Juliani's first productions at Simon Fraser bear a distinct resemblance to the flamboyant, *épater-les-bourgeois* style of the beginnings of both Passe-Muraille and Tamahnous. Savage God began with a sample of international avant-garde drama, the Arrabal-Ghelderode double bill. It included two short plays by each author: Arrabal's *Orison* and *Fando and Lis*, Ghelderode's *The Blind Men* and *Escurial*. Since he had the resources of a well-funded and equipped theatre department at his disposal, Juliani could afford to mount spectacles considerably more lavish than anything produced at independent alternative theatres. He made full use of these resources with *The Devils*, (1967), a play by John Whiting based on Aldous Huxley's novel, *The Devils of Loudon*. The plot lent itself perfectly to theatre of cruelty techniques, as well as mass spectacle. Set in France at the time of Louis XII, the play deals with the fate of a priest wrongfully accused of witchcraft by a group of vengeful nuns and burned at the stake. Juliani turned this play into a marathon performance of four and a half hours, with a cast of fifty and eleborate technical effects. The production involved a great deal more than just the performance itself, however. Many features were added which later became hallmarks of Savage God: special environments both outside the theatre and in the lobby; seminars conducted alongside the performance; an appendix to the programme, featuring the *dies irae* in both Latin and English. All of this was calculated, of course, to create a "total experience" for the public. Environments included: a special arrangement of illuminated crates outside the theatre entrance, to illustrate the "we and they" theme; a "psychedelic garden of good and evil" in the lobby, and a "regression chamber" in the shape of an igloo, for the use of audience members. To complement the acting, Juliani designed a bombardment of sense impressions: sound effects, visual effects through film and projection, and even olfactory effects (the acrid smell of burning flesh to accompany the scene at the stake). In the programme notes, the audience found an elaboration of the ambitious goals of this production:

> *The Devils* . . . seeks to reach a synthesis of the technical innovations and psychological research of this century, and the traditional role of the spoken word in drama . . . through a mise-en-scène that is cinematic; the synthesis sought in Savage God is through an investigation of the principle of simultaneity.

Critics, of course, protested the length and noise of the production, as well as the showing on stage of sex and violence. For the first season of Savage God, *The Devils* represented a typically high-powered, no-holds barred plunge into all of their theatrical concerns at once, exciting "process," if not polished "product." Other interesting experiments at Simon Fraser included exploration of both Passe-Muraille documentary style and investigation of a dream-play technique later developed by Tamahnous. *The Centralia Incident*, an attempt at documentary theatre, failed. Arthur Kopits provided the texts for the dream-play productions with *The Conquest of Everest* and *Chamber Music*. In his programme notes to these short plays, Juliani stressed the importance of Freudian psychology for modern society, and its link with the thematology of the subconscious in contemporary theatre, which led to the "happening" type of events. His own production was based on a combination of montage and dream-play technique. It also included some social satire, an attempt to make fun of, and debunk, the "American dream."

From the beginning, Juliani never rejected the "classics," whether ancient or modern. Savage God projects usually include productions of plays found in the repertory of traditional theatres, as well as original works. But these plays were given radically new and original treatment — again in the spirit of Artaud, and, in this case, Brecht. At Simon Fraser, Juliani decided to do an up-dated version of the much-performed *Glass Menagerie* by Tennessee Williams. Like many of his productions, it aroused a great deal of controversy because of the profusion of multimedia effects added to the original script, which many saw as "stage gimmickry":[15] projections of films and photographs combined with recordings and even scent effects to subject the audience to a multiple bombardment of their senses. To create a more contemporary atmosphere, the actors were dressed in leotards and dominoes. This, of course, also meant a strong move away from the realistic aspects of the play, towards abstraction and stylization, further emphasized with a dance sequence. Finally, Juliani introduced a satirical local touch, when he decided that the vanished father of the family should be not a restless American, but a member of the respectable Royal Canadian Mounted Police.

Obviously, all of these early productions were flawed through sheer exuberance. For the students who took part in them, however, they represented an invaluable learning experience, totally new insights into the potential of the theatrical experience once it is taken out of the traditional framework.

Juliani began and ended his stay at Simon Fraser with Arrabal. His farewell performance, *Arrabalesques*, included *Orison, Solemn Communion* and *Impossible Loves*, staged as a multimedia production. He justified this approach as usual in a programme note: "Theatre is pure art form and not merely a vehicle for the illustration of dramatic literature . . . [it is] a metalanguage."

After leaving the campus, the work of Savage God continued in various locations in the city. An important new element was added to their already wide spectrum through the support of young, local writers and an organized series of readings; the texts included poetry and monologues as well as drama. Most of the readings were held at the Vancouver Public Library. To give the young writers maximum public exposure, Juliani also organized a seven-week television series as well as public forums for discussion of their work. In this way, a whole new wave of little-known dramatists found an opportunity to come before the public; some of them have since established solid reputations, such as Peter Hay, Anne Hungerford, and Sharon Pollock.

The most important contribution of this period, however, was the PACET project of 1971. PACET (a Pilot Alternative Complement to Existing Theatre), was Juliani's attempt to demonstrate to the government funding agencies and the boards of directors of the establishment theatres that an artistically and financially viable alternative to the existing situation on the Canadian theatre scene could be found. Like founders of alternative theatres everywhere, Juliani was outraged at the policies of the regional theatres, where, he felt, vast amounts of taxpayers' money were wasted on unimaginative productions which did nothing to foster the development of theatrical creativity in Canada. Unlike most other young directors, however, Juliani did not simply retire from the mainstream to cultivate an alternate garden of his own; instead, he decided to challenge the establishment.

In May 1970, Juliani met with the Theatre Arts Officer of the Canada Council to present his case. As a result, he was asked to formulate a proposal for a pilot project to investigate the possibilities of alternative forms of theatre for Canada. Eventually, funding was granted, and Juliani launched into the preparations for the project. Six months later, in April 1971, Juliani and his company swung into action for a three-week, non-stop marathon of theatre events in a wide variety of Vancouver locations.

Following the experiment, Juliani drafted a five-hundred-page report, entitled *The Free Theatre*, which he submitted to the Canada Council. It included a detailed step-by-step documentation of the PACET project, as well as a formulation of Juliani's theatrical philosophy. The report concludes with a set of recommendations for changing existing conditions on the Canadian theatre scene. This document is well worth examining in detail. It gives the best possible insights into the workings of Savage God, and beyond this, into the problems of alternative theatre generally, as well tentative solutions.[16]

In his Introduction to *The Free Theatre*, Juliani reviews the evolution of a theatre establishment in Canada between 1950 and 1970; although he admits that much of a positive nature was accomplished, he objects violently to the direction taken by the newly emerging regional theatres, which he sees as squelching all creativity: "The most startling feature of the theatrical landscape is the virtually faceless nature, at home and abroad, of Canadian drama and of the Canadian dramatist." Juliani admits this is not necessarily the result of ill-will or any conspiracy against the Canadian playwright on the part of regional theatres; rather, it is the logical outcome of an administration policy which expects the theatre to be a commercially viable enterprise. It is not possible under the present system for a regional theatre to work without compromise, because:

> [it] is chained in practically every aspect of its operation to predominantly financial concerns. Its mentality and that of its employees . . . is virtually undistinguishable from that of the average North American business corporation.

PACET, then, was to point the way to a truly "free" theatre. In order to underline its message, the alternative it presented was deliberately extreme. To the "exorbitance, elitism and museum theatre" of the establishment, it opposed "poverty, democratization, and contemporaneity." The key to its success would be application of three essential principles often overlooked by traditional theatres: "economy, flexibility, and mobility." The report then goes on to a detailed description of the preparations and implementation of the project. Preparation covered three basic areas: hiring of actors to create an ensemble; finding suitable performance spaces; and the setting up of a repertoire.

For the first time in the history of Savage God, actors could be paid — which meant that the PACET project was carried out by trained professionals. In assembling his company, Juliani had some difficulty in separating applicants who were eager for a summer's "experience" from serious actors. Eventually, he ended up with an ensemble of ten young actors fully committed to the project. In return for the actors' total commitment, Juliani proclaimed their development as "performer, therapist, priest and human being" his first priority.

In looking for possible spaces, the criteria were simple: they had to be free or very cheap, available for rehearsals, and easily accessible to the public. Many existing public facilities proved useful: The Public Library, the Vancouver Art Gallery, the Art Gallery's Satellite Studio. In addition, many environmental settings were also used: Christ Church Cathedral, various locations in Stanley Park, downtown cafés, shopping malls, even the airport lounge. For the duration of PACET, the people of Vancouver literally lived amidst a bustle of theatrical events wherever they went; many times, the lines between theatre and real life became blurred or lost altogether — when this happened, Juliani did nothing to clarify the situation, but enjoyed seeing his ideal of the fusion of life and art become reality.

The PACET repertoire was chosen on the basis of three principles which Juliani defines clearly in the report:

> 1. To provide a spectrum of theatrical experience drawn from a national and international repertoire of classical and contemporary products that, qualitatively and quantitatively, would be easily equated with the annual offering of the average Canadian regional theatre.

In other words, Juliani proposed nothing less than to telescope a full, "average" season into a three-week schedule which also had to accommodate a number of other events — certainly a provocatively ambitious project.

2. To incorporate in the presentation . . . the poles of product and process, art and therapy.
3. To provide opportunity for growth and development for actors and writers.

All of this could be accomplished only with an administrative set-up very different from that of the regional theatres. Juliani proposed to run his group in a democratic style with collective decision-making and no specialization; actors were to be active in administration as well as technical aspects of production. Another essential principle was that monetary considerations would be given low priority. Production cost was to be kept low, and no admission charged ever. In fact, when PACET ended, the company had not only managed to stay within its modest budget of $18,000, but even showed a small surplus. To Juliani's contention that he had set up a possible model for the regional theatres to follow, it has to be objected, of course, that his production costs were low because of Savage God's use of free public facilities, a saving not possible for the conventional theatre. He was also helped financially by the enthusiasm and dedication of his youthful company, who were willing to work for extremely low pay; again, a situation not tenable on a permanent basis.

Eventually, a schedule of some fifty events was drawn up, including scripted plays, happenings, Gestalt sessions, and readings. Rehearsals, of course, were hectic, since many activities had to be carried on simultaneously. A large proportion of the productions had to be self-directed by the actors involved, with only occasional advice from the director. This feature contributed greatly to the development of self-confidence and creativity in the actors; it also created much stress and some internal crises. However, on the scheduled production dates, everyone was miraculously ready to perform. Juliani provides a rationale for his choice of each one of the "classical" plays chosen for performance, as well as some production information. The list is impressive.

Fernando Arrabal: Juliani has always given prominence to the work of Arrabal, partly as a challenge to the staid taste of Anglo-Saxons, who tend to consider his plays "excessive." Arrabal plays serve as ideal Rorschach tests, since they invariably elicit new responses in an audience. PACET included excerpts from five Arrabal plays (*Striptease of Jealousy, Fando and Lis, Solemn Communion, Erotic Bestiality,* and *The Architect and The Emperor of Assyria*). Arrabal's work was also used as the basis for a happening type of event, in which Juliani, playing Arrabal himself, was "interviewed" by members of the company. The setting was quite informal, with wine being offered to the audience and the actors mingling with the public. While microphones, video equipment, and cameras reinforced the idea of the interview, other props were chosen to demonstrate and recreate the dream/fantasy world of Fernando Arrabal: a Bible, handcuffs, a whip, a chamber-pot, balloons, toys, female undergarments. Much of the evening was improvisational, although Juliani, in control throughout, did use actual texts by Arrabal. The evening ended quite wildly, with balloons and confetti thrown to the audience, much noisy fraternization between members of the audience as well as between actors and public; and finally the voice of Juliani-Arrabal proclaiming over the general din: "I think as a playwright, I am greatly overrated" — a typical Juliani touch.

Samuel Beckett was chosen, first of all, because of his stature in contemporary theatre; also, because his minimalist tendency meets the "poor theatre" concept of Savage God. Finally, the part of Winnie in *Happy Days* presented an ideal challenge to the actress. As mentioned earlier, *Happy Days* was produced twice, once in the Vancouver Art Gallery and a second time in Stanley Park. The outdoor performance used a huge hollowed-out tree-trunk, instead of the traditional mound of earth. The performance was timed to coincide with the sunset — a demonstration of perfect "found space" utilization.

Ugo Betti's *Crime on Goat Island* was included in order to acquaint Canadian audiences with a little-known modern playwright. The play was used as basis for multiple experimentation: it was first presented in the rehearsal stage, as "process"; then as a finished performance. Next, the two acts were separated, each one being performed on a different evening in an attempt to determine "ideal" performance length from an audience point of view.

Lodewyk de Boer: this dramatist, musician, and composer, heavily influenced by Oriental drama, provided a different type of challenge for the actors. His *Darts*, based on distortion of words, stylized and acrobatic movement, and hypnotic use of repetition, forced them to learn to "dance," rather than recite, their parts.

Anton Chekhov: Juliani chose two of Chekhov's much-beloved short plays *The Bear*, a farce, and the monologue on *The Evils of Tobacco*. The latter was given a contemporary, controversial turn with the substitution of marijuana for tobacco; the speaker himself was presented, not as a befuddled old professor, but a young prison parolee.

Henrik Ibsen: Ibsen's inclusion in the list was Juliani's tribute — somewhat tongue-in-cheek — to "classical respectability." Again, the play chosen for production, *Little Eyolf*, was used as material for a variety of theatrical experimentation. *Little Eyolf* was rehearsed in a perfectly orthodox fashion; the performance itself, however, did not adhere to the prepared costume and set models. Instead, these were displayed in the lobby, to show to the audience what they would *not* see. Two separate spaces were used for the production. From the conventional proscenium of act one, the audience moved to the space-staging of act two; for the third act, they returned to the first act space, only to find a totally changed seating arrangement.

William Shakespeare: for obvious reasons, Shakespearean scenes were included in the PACET schedule. These were presented in a variety of styles, both as process and product, with audience reactions solicited.

August Strindberg: as with Chekhov, Juliani chose two short plays by this author: *The Stronger*, a dialogue for two women, and *The Pariah*, a dialogue for men. *The Stronger* was once done, unannounced and unscheduled, in a Gastown café, to give the company an opportunity to observe the reaction of patrons as they slowly realized (some never did, of course) that "theatre" had invaded their real life scene. The same dialogue served to explore sex roles, since Juliani chose two male actors to perform the "female" roles.

Besides these classics, Juliani's schedule also called for the production of a number of works by new, local playwrights. The most interesting of these was probably a production of three short plays by Merv Compone, *Act of Love, The Song*, and *Heritage*, which combined environmental staging with audience participation. On entering, the members of the audience were handed a slip of paper which read:

In the course of this evening's experience, there will be a progression from room to room, from darkness to light, and from standing to sitting. We consider you a vital, integral part of this evening's soundscape and ask you to please sense and follow the players and the action.

The first play was performed in darkness, with stereophonic sound produced by the actors mingling with the audience. Following this, the actors lit tiny penlights of various colours, and with their help led the audience into the next room. Here, an arrangement of stools was provided, leaving a narrow strip of empty space in the middle for the performers who were now dimly visible. The third room featured chairs and candlelight. Following the performance, the audience was taken to a fully lit room and invited for coffee and a discussion of the experience.

Other new Canadian authors featured during PACET were Jackie Crossland, whose "black fairytale," *The Fairy Kiss*, was presented as an outdoor pageant; and Tom Grainger's *I'll Take One Breath*, the monologue of a hallucinating old man on his deathbed. Play readings and criticism were provided for both Grainger and Michael Mirolla.

Savage God itself contributed a number of happenings to the PACET project. All of these used non-theatrical spaces, mostly outdoors. Intended to explore the possibilities of street theatre, they naturally presented the actors with a whole new set of challenges. The intention was to achieve a deliberate fusion of life and art. Because these happenings had to appear totally spontaneous, their effectiveness depended on "surprise, unpredictability, and precision timing." Some of the events also carried a strong message, such as a group of three Savage God actors cycling through Stanley Park at peak traffic time, wearing gas masks — a demonstration against the high pollution level of the Park. Again, gas masks were used for shock effect and to test the reaction of people exposed to them: actors in gas masks appeared in a downtown coffee shop; others casually pushed a shopping cart through a supermarket. Not all of the Savage God happenings carried such gruesome overtones, however. Some proved quite idyllic, such as a group of actors joining the crowd in a shopping mall, licking ice cream cones, organizing games and sing-songs. With all of these, the city itself provided a laboratory for unlimited exploration of unconventional audience-actor relationships.

Alongside the more specifically theatrical events, PACET also featured two weeks of Gestalt sessions. These were justified both by Juliani's concept of the function of the actor as "priest" and "therapist" and by his belief that therapy constitutes one of the essential components of theatre. Under the direction of a professional therapist, members of the company and of the general public went into two weeks of Gestalt sessions, "Instant Drama" and "Dream Work." In the first instance, volunteers from the group were asked to act out a story, in the second, a dream. The significance of their role-playing would then be analysed by the group, led by the therapist. In both cases, the actors were to function as catalysts, providing volunteers to get the session underway. In practice, it turned out that the members of the public performed with greater conviction than the professional performers in these sessions.

At the end of the experiment, Juliani encouraged all possible comment and criticism from those who had participated. Three "post-mortem" sessions were held, one hundred questionnaires sent out, and interviews conducted with audience members and actors. It turned out that PACET had reached people from all social strata, including many who had never attended a theatrical performance before. Armed with all the experience gained from the experiment, Juliani proceeded to set up a list of fourteen points which were to be the trademark of Savage God from then on, and to suggest models for other theatre companies:

1. Free theatre — no admission charge.
2. One performance only in any one space.
3. Limited advertising, to preserve a sense of surprise, spontaneity for the audience.
4. Programmes delayed until after the performance, for the same reason.
5. Direct feedback encouraged.
6. Non-technical bias.
7. Integrated intervals — no arbitrary intermission.
8. Flexible seating and staging.
9. The audience as critic.
10. A sense of the whole.
11. Non-regular seasons.
12. Ensemble acting.

13. Non-corporate status.
14. Mobility.

Finally, *The Free Theatre* addresses the various levels and agencies of government with a list of recommendations. The two most important ones are addressed to the federal government and the Canada Council. To the federal government, Juliani suggests the establishment of a permanent centre for applied cultural research at the national level, as well as greatly increased input by creative artists in administration. The Canada Council is asked to "articulate a lucid and distinct cultural policy premised on democratization, decentralization, experimentation in, and demythification of, the artistic process." Other recommendations address themselves to the provincial governments, the regional theatres, and to a "potential" alternative. This portion of the document concludes with three dramatic statements in the typically flamboyant style of its author:

> The necessity of the changes suggested in the above recommendations can no longer be denied;
> The feasibility of such changes can no longer be questioned;
> The implementation of such changes can no longer be delayed.

Now, more than ten years after the conclusion of the PACET experiment, it has become clear that the project did not have the desired effect of changing Canadian cultural policy in a drastic manner. However, the enterprise itself will certainly be remembered as one of the more daring and exciting ventures in the history of Canadian theatre.

In 1974, John Juliani was put in charge of organizing a graduate programme in theatre at York University. His official title was that of "co-ordinator," but he preferred to refer to himself as "provocateur." And provoke he did, to the point where the university decided to abandon the programme two years later (financial considerations, of course, also entered into the decision). In the meantime, however, Juliani managed again to build up a strong ensemble and perform a number of virtuoso feats of avant-garde theatre.

The acronym chosen as a name for the new group, PEAK (Performance, Example, Animation, Katharsis) suggests the orientation of the director: there was to be heavy emphasis on actor development, with therapy playing a major role. Because he realized that the success of the new venture depended heavily on the student material he would have to work with, Juliani proceeded to pick these students in a most unorthodox fashion. He and Donna Juliani toured the entire country holding auditions for prospective applicants. Out of all the young people interviewed, they eventually chose twelve to enter the graduate programme, and with it, the PEAK experience. Juliani outlined the major features of his proposed programme in a paper he submitted to the university administration before the beginning of the academic year. This "Philosophical Blueprint for PEAK"[17] made three main points which proved highly controversial to the university: development of the actor as a person was to be the central goal, his professional training referred to as a "by-product"; the performing group was not to remain stationary at York University, but rather to move about the country giving the students first-hand experience of every part of Canada; graduates of the programme should become prime movers for change as they entered the professional theatre world. In Juliani's words:

> The graduate program in theatre at York University is primarily designed, within the matrix of the theatrical discipline, as a series of individual and collective learning experiences. . . . The principal *by-product* [author's italics] of those growth experiences will be the advanced training of young theatre artists in the spheres of performance, playwriting/dramaturgy, criticism, direction and design. . . . a unique feature will be the mobility of the performing ensemble . . . it is as catalysts for constructive, ongoing change that alumni from this program can make their most pertinent and lasting contribution to the Canadian theatre. . . . PEAK emphasis will be on creating a microcosm of the ideal professional producing unit.[18]

The group was exceedingly successful with their productions both at York University and on their Canadian tours; they were also invited to the Esalen Institute in California, and, as previously noted, the Wroclaw Festival. Their repertoire consisted of a blend of ancient and modern classics and contemporary Canadian plays. As in the PACET project earlier, the classical works served mainly as a basis for experimentation of various kinds. *Prometheus Bound*, for example, was performed in several versions, with Prometheus as male, female, and androgynous; *Peer Gynt* was given environmental staging. Canadian playwrights in the PEAK repertoire included Peter Hay and Ann Hungerford, whose *The Plague* was chosen for performance at Wroclaw. The company also performed *Cue to Cue*, a play by one of their own number, Raymond Cosgrove.

In spite of this positive record, Juliani was not able to convince university authorities of the value of his avant-garde approach, and PEAK ended in 1976.

Savage God was an unknown concept in Edmonton when Juliani arrived. As he had done before, he chose to introduce himself to his new public with an Arrabal production — *Fando and Lis*. However, staging plays turned out to be almost impossible in the absence of either funds or an ensemble. Juliani therefore turned to poetry readings and choreography as his major Savage God projects. Readings took place at the Edmonton Art Gallery. Juliani himself chose the theme for each reading, selected the appropriate texts, and performed the readings. His range of authors and themes was far-reaching and always exciting. "The Road of Excess Leads to the Palace of Wisdom: Poetry and Prose of Madness," for example, included excerpts from Nijinski, de Sade, Nietzsche, Lautréamont, Artaud and

Gogol; "Oh, For a Muse Of Fire" presented Aeschylus, Watts, Blake, Ginsberg, Yeats, St. John the Evangelist, Genesis, Milton, Brecht, Plato, Nijinski, Ferlinghetti, Wilhelm/Baynes, and Fared ud-din Attar. Seven such readings were held under the auspices of Savage God[eee], providing a new and stimulating cultural experience for the people of Edmonton. Other readings featured the work of new playwrights from the Western provinces.

In 1977, Juliani turned to choreography. He produced two original dance-dramas for Tournesol ("Canada's smallest dance company," made up of Ernst and Carol Ederer). *Mosaic* illustrated the ethnic composition of Canada and was performed as part of Ederer's citizenship awarding ceremony. *Separation*, which was also performed at the Théâtre des deux portes in Paris, dealt with the theme of separation from an individual and national point of view. The programme note describes it as "an exploration, in sound and movement, of the tensions emanating from the state of being united." Although the emphasis of the production was on the couple, it ended on a strong political note with the release of ten balloons, each one inscribed with the name of a province.

The most ambitious and artistically exciting project of the Edmonton period to date, however, was the 1979 production of *The Seven Ages of Picasso*. It was performed at Latitude 53, a tiny art gallery seating twenty-five at most. In spite of this small audience potential, the production was ambitious, with a team of thirty artists working together to reproduce the "spirit" of Picasso. The performers and audience were surounded by full-size copies of Picasso's art works, with a bronze goat sculpture as the main feature. Juliani's "original performance score" for the actors was built around Picasso's own short play *Four Little Girls*. It was complemented by a collage of Picasso texts, mime, music, and light and sound effects. As with *An Evening With Arrabal*, the artist himself, Picasso, was the central figure of the show. In the beautifully illustrated programme note for this performance, Juliani as usual gives the rationale for his production. His statement also gives a clear indication of the direction he intended Savage God to take in the future:

This work . . . is an extension of the ongoing research into the art of performance begun by Savage God in 1966 in Vancouver, B.C. From the outset, these investigations have focused on those threshold areas where the various art forms can be seen to coalesce and have been concerned with the exploration and articulation of the parameters for possible hybrid forms in the future.

5

A Voice From The East: The Militant Mummers

Of all the Atlantic provinces, Newfoundland has produced the most interesting and long-lived ventures in the area of alternative theatre. However, local playwrights, like Michael Cook, directors, and actors insist that the term "alternate" in the Toronto sense of that word does not apply here: there simply is no "mainstream" theatre in Newfoundland. This seems paradoxical indeed in view of the fact that the province boasts an extensive and flourishing system of Arts and Culture Centres. The first and largest of these opened in St. John's in 1967, a centennial project. Others followed: Cornerbrook, Gander, Grand Falls, and Stephenville. Clearly, there is no shortage of performing space; what is lacking is a clear-cut cultural policy.

The five elaborately appointed and equipped buildings which together form Newfoundland's concrete establishment function strictly as community centres: the facilities are made available to local groups for events of all kinds, from high school graduations to concerts and amateur theatricals. John Perlin, currently director of the Arts and Culture Centre in St. John's (which sets the policies for all five centres) sees his mandate as two-fold: he is administrator of the facilities and acts as impressario for a number of annual shows which appeal to the "general public." (The ratio of theatre to music in these shows is about one to one.) Newfoundland plays are notoriously absent from the programme of the Art Centres; nor is there a resident company. Indeed, with the rapid decline of the once-flourishing tradition of amateur theatricals, the alternative companies remain as the only groups to keep alive a creative theatrical tradition — as opposed to museum theatre. Of these groups, The Mummers' Troupe is the most long-lived and probably the most interesting because of their unusual combination of concerns: while trying to preserve the native heritage of the past, they are also militantly political. Their nationwide tours have made their work known from St. John's to Vancouver.

Like alternative theatre companies everywhere, The Mummers' Troupe grew out of a specific combination of social and cultural forces. As Chris Brookes, founder and director of the Troupe, has said: "We are what we are because of where we are. Newfoundland frames and motivates us."[1] The Newfoundland situation is unique in English Canada, although it bears many resemblances to Quebec. Like Quebec, Newfoundland suffers from the impact of a double colonialism: a sense of dependence on England which did not end when the province joined the Canadian Confederation in 1949; and a sense of inferiority towards the mainland after that date. Like Quebec, Newfoundland is a small, economically deprived, but culturally rich society whose members felt like second class citizens as they hit the North American mainstream. Joey Smallwood's policies for Newfoundland bore results similar to those of Duplessis in Quebec. By the late 1960's Newfoundlanders were suffering from a severe identity crisis: they felt they no longer knew "who they were, or who they wanted to be."[2] Just as the Quiet Revolution followed the Duplessis rule in Quebec, an outburst of cultural activity took place in Newfoundland after the end of the Smallwood era. The central problem there, as in Quebec, was that of establishing an identity. The various aspects of native culture had been looked down upon for so long that it was difficult to bring them back to respectable status. So strong was the colonial complex that even by the late 1960's, local music such as fiddling or playing the accordion was simply "not done" in "cultured" circles. In the field of drama, the problem of the vernacular presented a serious obstacle. Newfoundland dialect, like *joual* in Quebec, was a *lingua non grata* in polite society and its use as a stage idiom unthinkable. It remained for the alternative theatre groups of the 1970's to restore the local speech to respectability, and to demonstrate its inherent poetic quality.

In response to this situation, Chris Brookes formulated the two-fold goals of his company: to create a sense of identity through a restoration of the heritage of the past (renewal of the ancient tradition of mummery was one aspect of this programme) and to battle for social and economic justice through a theatre of political agitation, using collective creation techniques.

Like Garrard and Thompson at Passe-Muraille, Brookes came to the theatre with a solid academic background. He had studied at Dalhousie, Michigan State, and Yale. His theatrical apprenticeship included work with Neptune Theatre in Halifax, with Juliani's Savage God in Vancouver, and with Passe-Muraille in Toronto. In 1971, he returned to Newfoundland, determined to create the kind of theatre which would "link up immediately" with the people. While working as resident artist at Memorial University Extension Service, he began experimenting with workshops in small villages. So great was the response that Brookes and five other young enthusiasts decided to pool their resources to start a small professional theatre for regional and community development, somewhat on the model of the Teatro Campesino. The group originally called itself "Resource Theatre Company"; but after the popular success of the first season of mumming, 1972, the name was quickly changed to The Mummers' Troupe.

Brookes chose to revive the *Mummers' Play* as a part of his goal to restore pride in the local cultural tradition: "We wanted to do the Mummers' Play because it's the only traditional theatre we had in Newfoundland."[3] Of course, one might point out the irony that this, the only "traditional theatre of Newfoundland," really does not originate in Newfoundland at all, but is simply a continuation of a British custom which goes back to the Middle Ages and beyond;[4] however, within the North American context, Brookes's interpretation of local tradition is probably justifiable. Another reason for starting his theatrical endeavours with the *Mummers' Play* was to break the population's natural suspicion of theatre as "art": for "art" at that point meant a foreign, rather than an indigenous, endeavour. The *Mummers' Play*, on the other hand, was considered a local "custom" rather than an artistic event, and as such became instantly popular.

The *Mummers' Play* goes back to pagan customs preceding Christianity, but it reached its greatest popularity during the Middle Ages. The central feature is the battle between good and evil, or light and dark, represented by St. George (white) and The Turkish Knight (blackface); other characters were added with the influence of the *commedia* tradition which flourished during the Renaissance. The Newfoundland version of the play features a "doctor," who revives the slain knight — obviously a *commedia dell' arte* character. From British folklore comes the figure of old Father Christmas who acts as M.C. for the play. He is accompanied by a "hobby horse" (a huge, handcarved, horsehead puppet on a stick, manipulated by an actor under sackcloth), a burlesque figure and fertility symbol.

The *Mummers' Play* is traditionally performed between Christmas and Twelfth Night by members of the community who go from house to house with their show; the characters of the play may be accompanied by other masked and disguised figures, playing instruments, or just contributing to the general merriment. This "mummering" from house to house in disguise served another purpose as well: many persons disguised as mummers took the opportunity to play practical tricks on those against whom they bore a grudge. Because of the abuses this led to, mummering, which had been popular all over Newfoundland early in the 19th century, was forbidden by law in 1862. The tradition then slowly died out, first in town, then even in the outports. When the Mummers' Troupe attempted to revive the custom, it had not been done in St. John's in living memory; in small places, the tradition was kept alive into the 1920's. It had to be reconstructed largely on the basis of oral tradition, from bits and pieces remembered by older people.

When the Mummers' Troupe first announced its intention to perform a Mummers' Play in 1972, they were warned by the St. John's chief of police about the illegality of the undertaking; eventually, they were given permission to go ahead, on the understanding they would only visit the homes of friends. Needless to say, they gave a wide interpretation to that term, and the *Mummers' Play* received a great deal of exposure. It was an instant success, and the annual mummering has since become a regular feature of the St. John's Christmas scene, with the Mummers welcome guests at holiday gatherings. The *Mummers' Play* also regularly goes on a tour of Newfoundland schools, thus providing the young generation with a sense of their cultural past.

The Mummers' Troupe has also expressed its concern for the local heritage through several of their original productions such as *East End Story* (1976), an attempt to recreate the atmosphere of the "old downtown" at a time when the city of St. John's was undergoing rapid and drastic changes. It was made into a twenty-seven minute film by local filmmakers. *The Bard of Prescott Street* (1977) was dedicated to the memory of a colourful St. John's balladeer and street character, Johnny Burke. This show included most of Burke's original songs. It was enthusiastically received by a nostalgic audience. On CBC radio, Jeanne Beker reflected the audience's feelings with her lively review, written to fit the tune of one of Burke's songs, *Kelligrew Soirée*:

> The Mummers did a show last night
> About old Johnny Burke,
> And such a show I ne'er did see
> In Paris or New Yurk:
> They were swinging from the rafters
> They were dancing on their toes
> I tell ya b'ys in St. John's town
> This's the show of shows![5]

This concern with their own past reflects the Mummers' fierce local patriotism; many of them are avowed separatists — another parallel with the Quebec scene! Donna Butts, one of the members of the company, echoes the general feeling when she says "I was born after Confederation but still I wouldn't think of calling myself anything but a Newfoundlander — certainly not a Canadian!"[6] Nevertheless the Mummers' most important contribution, from a national point of view, has been in another area, that of socio-political theatre. Chris Brookes firmly believes that "artistic creation does not exist in some sort of artistic limbo — it is a social act."[7] While he obviously follows the pattern set by Theatre Passe-Muraille, his emphasis differs. More literally Brechtian than Thompson, Brookes is more concerned with the message than the form of his productions. Such an approach accounts for the often obvious weaknesses in the Mummers' shows: because actors are chosen more for their political conviction than their professional skill, the productions lack polish and sophistication, and tend to appear heavy-handed; as John Fraser of the Toronto *Globe and Mail* pointed out in connection with their tour of *The Price of Fish*, political theatre can indeed be "a monumental bore."[8] Referring to the same show, Audrey Ashley of the *Ottawa Citizen* suggested that

"perhaps it's time for The Mummers to make up their mind what they really are —
a political group or a theatre."[9] On the other hand, all critics agree that the
company has succeeded brilliantly in developing techniques which portray island
lifestyles, mores, and social concerns. Like Passe-Muraille, The Mummers zero
in on individual communities and present to them an accurate mirror-image of
themselves. In this way, again like Passe-Muraille, they have helped preserve
pieces of the mosaic which, put together, forms Canadian reality. Michael Cook,
whose dramas also concern themselves with the particularities of life in Newfoundland, saw the significance of the Mummers' work very early. In 1974, he
accurately described their role for the community:

> If we are to emerge, at the end of the century, with our identity and our culture
> intact, then art must be placed at the service of the people from which it draws
> its strength, and not ape the subculture of the media. When this responsibility
> has been recognized to the full, we will begin to know each other and our
> reason for being may become a little more clear to us.
>
> The *Mummers' Troupe* . . . use their resources and their skill to help us to
> share in our common heritage. Theirs is a living theatre, rich, functional and
> vitally necessary to us in Newfoundland."[10]

Although the Mummers' basic approach is so similar to that of Passe-Muraille,
Brookes's attitude to collective creation differs essentially from Paul Thompson's.
Whereas Thompson is entirely actor-oriented and uses collective creation as a
vehicle to display his actors' skill and versatility, Brookes feels that he must work
in that particular genre because he does not have professionally trained actors at his
disposal. It is his belief that the level of skill and training of his actors would not
allow them to attempt anything more demanding than collective creation, which
maximizes the assets they do have.[11] Unlike the situation at Passe-Muraille, then,
the choice of collective creation as the basic production technique is here not based
on artistic criteria (Brookes admits he would love to produce traditional/classical
plays as well), but simply dictated by the necessities of a literally poor theatre.
Funding is more difficult in Newfoundland, of course, than anywhere else in
Canada. The process of creation itself is somewhat less democratic with the
Mummers than with other collectives: the director usually suggests the theme,
does the research, decides on the style and format of the show before the actors
become involved. They are then programmed through an "information" process,
sometimes with the assistance of resource people, and go into improvisational
sessions from there; but the final "shaping" of the material again remains the task
of the director — unless a writer is involved, which has happened occasionally
(for example, Rick Salutin for *IWA*, the story of the loggers' strike). With this
system, the director clearly controls the particular slant of each production.
The technique used by the Mummers was not modelled directly after Passe-

Muraille. Rather, it was developed as a result of Brookes's work with the film unit of Memorial University Extension Services on Fogo Island. The unit prepared films of the community, did interviews, eventually played it back to the people as a mirror image of themselves, and thus actively influenced the decision by the community not to leave the island. Brookes was impressed with the possibilities of the technique for social action and decided he would try to use theatre in the same way. The result was the "documentary community drama" developed by the Mummers Troupe.

Just how theory and practice work together can best be illustrated if we follow in detail the genesis of one particular production. Brookes has published the diary he kept during the creation of *Gros Mourn*, in 1973.[12] It provides some excellent insights into the specific Mummers' approach and style.

The manner in which the Mummers literally hit upon the subject of *Gros Mourn* is typical of the spontaneous, action-oriented approach of the company. They were touring the province with their first production, *The Mummers' History of Newfoundland*, when they accidentally discovered that a difficult situation had arisen in the Gros Morne area: as they learned from the local people in the course of the discussion which followed the history play, the government was about to expropriate and resettle several communities in order to create a large National Park. The Mummers were impressed with the grim determination of the people to resist government pressure:

> If they goes ahead and ruins our lives, then we got the right to spoil their dream, too. If they drives me out they'll have to rename the Park Charcoal Park, 'cause I'll put the torch to every tree in 'er before I goes.

These and similar statements were enough to convince the company that here was a job to be done. They decided to interrupt their tour for three weeks and stay in the area to do a play about the National Park problem. For a title, they chose a pun on the name of the area: "Gros Mourn." The date was 2 August 1973; at the insistence of the local population, they agreed to have the show ready in time to precede the official opening of the Park, scheduled for 12 August. Ten hectic days followed. The Mummers took up quarters in an empty school bus in the village of Sally's Cove; the schoolhouse and grounds provided rehearsal space. Working day and night, they proceeded to research the situation and put together a play. The pressure caused by the impossible deadline they had set themselves was of course enormous and caused friction among members of the company, moments of panic, but also exaltation whenever things seemed to fall into place. The actors were greatly helped by the support of the community. The people of Sally's Cove provided them with food and unlimited quantities of much-needed coffee. More importantly, everyone seemed genuinely interested in what the actors were doing. Schoolchildren organized themselves into work gangs to help with props and sets;

in the evenings, villagers and actors would come together over drinks; the people would talk freely about their lives, the Mummers took note of every detail that might be incorporated into the production. These late night sessions generated a great deal of warmth and mutual respect. As Brookes notes,

> We are feeling very close to the people here. Their hopes and fears are becoming ours. . . . When I'm talking with someone here, I'm trying to get inside his skin, to see things with his eyes, because I may be portraying him on Sunday night, speaking his words, using his inflections, believing his beliefs.

The experience gave Brookes new insight into the poetry of ordinary language, and helped shape his populist philosophy of art:

> Working like this . . . one begins to notice the poetry in the speech of ordinary people. Not poets cloistered in attic rooms, but lobster fishermen over a kitchen table: how magic is their choice of phrase! This play will at least have some beautiful lines. The whole myth of Art is autocratic nonsense — everyone, not just the artist speaks with poetry, breathes with music. It is simply a matter of listening not just in the art galleries and concert halls, but out in the dust of the street.

As in *The Farm Show*, which also used words "given" to the actors by the people, *Gros Mourn* eventually contained many speeches and bits and pieces of dialogue recorded directly in the community — sometimes these were based on interview situations; other times on casual remarks made to the actors. Some of the lines were simply bits of daily life accidentally overheard by one of the company and recorded for the play, such as a child's somewhat unorthodox evening prayer: "God bless Mommy, God bless Daddy, and God damn the National Park." Another child provided the following bit of dialogue, which also became part of the script:

> Brookes: "Well, is your family moving out?"
> Boy: "Yup."
> Brookes: "Are you glad?"
> Boy: "Yup."
> Brookes: "Why?"
> Boy: "Because when we moves, I gets a bike. My father's getting me one."
> Brookes: "Wouldn't he buy you one anyway, if you were staying here?"
> Boy: "No. 'Cause, when we moves, see, the government gives us lots of money, and I gets a bike. We don't gets no money if we stays."

This theme of the "baiting" of simple people with the promise of a sum of ready cash later became one of the focal points of the script. The Mummers discovered a great deal of confusion among the people about what sort of a deal they were being offered; an enormous information gap between government officials and the people, partly owing to the lack of a local newspaper. Most of all, they felt a sense of frustration, resignation, and doom which they tried to mirror in the play.

Of course, their research had to go beyond the eventual victims. The Mummers tried to get the other side of the story by talking to the staff of the provincial government co-ordination office and to Park officials. They were somewhat taken aback to discover that the Park officials, far from being the villains they expected, all turned out to be "so nice"; a fact which made the Mummers' task more difficult, since they could not present a clear-cut black-and-white picture of the situation.

On the evening of Sunday, 12 August, the Mummers were exhausted, but ready with the show. They played to an enthusiastic audience of about two hundred people, who gave the actors a standing ovation and remained for a serious discussion of the situation afterwards. The members of the company felt elated. Like Passe-Muraille with *The Farm Show*, The Mummers' Troupe had found its true identity with *Gros Mourn*:

> Each of us in the company has come to feel a part of this place. . . . As artists we have done something directly useful. We have given birth to a work of art which is also a real and tangible tool. We have clearly put our hands to the wheel.

In fact, little of practical significance was achieved by the intervention of the Mummers. Following the play, the people decided to hold a community meeting the next morning to decide on a strategy. At the meeting, they agreed to attempt a formal protest against the Park policies of the government at the time of the official signing ceremony that afternoon. The Mummers were asked to repeat their show at that time, but Park officials refused to give permission.

The protesters then began by boycotting the government bus sent to take them to the Park site. Arriving in their own cars, they immediately confronted the Minister of Indian Affairs and Northern Development, Jean Chrétien. It became clear at that time that the Mummers' play had provided the people with a terminology for their battle; images and metaphors from the show kept cropping up as they presented their arguments. The minister, however, remained adamant and insisted that all the decisions had been made; nothing could be done to change them now. As the ceremony proceeded, government officials faced an angry crowd; most of the speeches were drowned out by choruses of shouts from demonstrators. But the Park project went ahead.

Although *Gros Mourn* had come too late to influence developments there, the play was used later as a tool in fighting similar situations; and this time it was more effective. In October 1973, the show toured three other Atlantic provinces communities threatened with eviction to make room for National Parks. As a result, the first People's Conference of National Parks was held in Halifax on 1 December, with three delegates from Sally's Cove present. As a result of pressure from this Conference, the much-disputed Ship Harbour, Nova Scotia, National Park project was cancelled in favour of a series of provincial recreation areas.

Looking back on the *Gros Mourn* experience, Brookes tries to de-emphasize its agit-prop aspect and stress instead the concern with indigenous theatre which is the second major interest of the Mummers' Troupe. Considering the history of the Mummers' involvement in the situation, his argument is not fully convincing; rather, it reflects a certain basic ambiguity in orientation, not uncommon in proponents of political theatre:

> this sort of theatre should not be interpreted simply as political "outside" agitation. It is *mirror*-oriented, along a certain axis, of course, but not *necessarily* designed to rouse a community to action. One of our main reasons for working this way is that in Newfoundland we have very little in the way of a *people's* expression in art or politics, and this is a way of creating indigenous theatre material which speaks to the people.

As a piece of theatre, the play itself,[13] hastily put together in ten days, obviously falls short of more elaborate productions in a similar vein, such as *The Farm Show*. Nevertheless, it contains some surprisingly good material: several music hall type dialogues between "Freddy Federal" and "Percy Provincial," which pack a lot of information together with some robust humour; a number of highly satirical scenes; and several felicitous stage metaphors. The final scene of the play achieves genuine pathos.

The Freddy Federal/Percy Provincial exchanges always follow the same pattern: "And today we have some good news and some bad news. First the good news." The juxtapositions of "good" and "bad" items testify to the Mummers' careful research into their subject and provide the audience with much useful documentation. Here are some of the ironic combinations:[14]

Good news:	Bad news:
"You are going to get a brand new National Park"	"Your houses will be destroyed"
"There will be one-hundred new jobs"	"Ninety-eight of them will go to mainlanders"
"You will get brand new houses"	"They will be on a bog, with ⅙ of an acre each"
"Some of you won't have to move at all"	"Your children will"

Equally ironic is a minstrel-show routine between a "Mr. Doody" and a "Mr. Maynard" in Ottawa, who have found a simple solution to the whole problem:

> Mr. Maynard: "How are we going to get the moved fishermen back to fish?"
> Mr. Doody: "Why, that's easy, Mr. Maynard, we simply put them on a bus and bus 'em up to Sally's Cove, and then we bus 'em back again in the evening. Simple."
> Mr. Maynard: "How we gonna let the fish know the bus schedule?"

Through their work with the Park officials, the Mummers came upon another interesting tidbit of information which they incorporated into the show: the arctic hare was chosen as the official Park symbol; but the hares' main habitat was not part of the Park because it was a large tract of woodland owned by the powerful Bowater Pulp and Paper Company. In the play, a Park information officer brings in a slide show to explain the project to the people:

> We've chosen to make the arctic hare our Park symbol, because he's one of the animals we're doing the most for . . . now this virgin forest is essential to the survival of the hare. . . . You'll notice it's not in the Park. Well, that's because it was too valuable for Bowaters and they wouldn't let us have it. But in our Park we have created a brand new home for the little fellow. . . . Here he is now, frisking and gambling right around the ruins where Philip Decker's house used to be. Closely watched by Joe Tourist.

While these scenes make their point through bitter verbal satire, others rely on metaphors for their message. These metaphors are all taken from the ordinary everyday experience of the people. The "Lobster Trap" scene, for example, compares the way a fisherman catches lobster with a bait of herring to the way in which the government baited the people with a promise of cash; it ends with the lobster's warning song to the people: "If they try to take away your freedom, tell them to go to hell." In another scene, an "old professor" delivers a lecture in which he tries to explain to the people the difference between the "old times" when life was simple and responsibilities clear-cut, and the present, when events seem to take over without anyone being able to stop them or even to find out who is to blame. He demonstrates his point with two types of toilet paper — the old type has individual sheets; the new type is one long roll with each section connected to the others. The following scene, however, suggests that there is a way to stop the infernal machinery of modern bureaucracy after all. Here, specific protest actions are suggested to the audience, such as collecting funds to hire a lawyer to fight the project; blocking off the roads to the campsites; informing the tourists of the situation and collecting their reactions, and so forth. All of these are intended to embarrass the government, on the assumption that, if the government is embarrassed, it will "go away." This is the most overtly political, agit-prop kind of scene in the play. The finale, by contrast, is highly theatrical. A row of model houses is brought out, each one inscribed with the name of one of the Gros Morne houses which were phased out. Jean Chrétien appears for the christening cere-mony of the National Park; with a bottle of champagne, he demolishes each house in turn, following which a hand slowly strikes a match and sets fire to the demolished houses. In the background are heard the sounds of the official signing ceremony, along with "O Canada." The residents slowly begin to sing the hymn "O God our faith in ages past" as onstage the actors are silhouetted in the flames from the model houses. This finale obviously aroused the feelings of the audience to a high pitch; it also provided an effective counterbalance to the documentary character of some of the earlier portions of the play.

The Mummers Troupe's first production, *The Mummers' History of Newfound-land*, which brought them to the Gros Morne situation in the first place, deserves brief mention as an example of the company's attitude towards historical subjects. The Mummers' approach to history is strictly sociological. Unlike Passe-Muraille, which is concerned with the creation of national hero figures and legends from the material of history, the Mummers' historical plays are intent on demythification. Their orientation in this area comes a good deal closer to that of the alternative theatre in Quebec, which is also much more concerned with destroying prevailing myths than creating new ones. The Mummers present the facts of history from the point of view of ordinary people. Their history of Newfoundland is simply a history of the exploitation suffered by Newfoundlan-ders from the beginning; its relevance for the contemporary situation is obvious. To bring home even more the fact that the play deals not with history alone, but also with an ongoing social and economic problem, anachronisms are frequently built into the fabric of the play. For example, in the scene where John Cabot provides himself with cheap labour for his crew, he uses the "manpower training on the job program."[15]

The History of Newfoundland is not one of the Mummers better productions; too long, uneven, and often irritatingly obvious in its propaganda, the script taxes the reader's patience. The production was successful in Newfoundland, however, because many theatrical qualities added to the impact of immediate relevance. The play condemns the conspiracy of capitalism, Church, and State against the workingman. Some of the "historical" scenes obviously create instant identifica-tion on the part of the members of the audience. There is, for example, a scene where a fisherman named Henry returns from a successful fishing expedition to Newfoundland, only to find that the pay for his labours will not buy enough fish to feed his family:

> How is it, how is it, I catch 20,000 fish, I can clean them, I can split them, I can salt them, I can dry them, I can load them on the ship in Newfoundland

and unload them in England, and I buy three fish and I have nothing left. How is that?

Clearly, history is used here strictly as a device for the demonstration of social ills. The bitterness of the tone is reinforced by the addition to the script of a document which is calculated to prove beyond doubt the capitalist conspiracy against the workers' fight for justice: it is an address by Bishop Howley, pronounced in 1912, in which he urges the faithful to remain obedient to the Church and follow the wishes of His Holiness the Pope, who only wants to "calm the passions of the workmen."

Such heavy-handed and direct political propaganda is bound to interfere with the effectiveness of a show as a work of theatre; the result can hardly be art. On the other hand, the Mummers achieved a high level of professionalism with their more restrained productions, shows which presented a mirror image of a community while underplaying the message. Their most successful production belongs to this genre. It is a study of life in a Newfoundland mining town.

Buchans — A Mining Town drew standing ovations from audiences at home and impressed critics and public alike when it went on tour. Michael Cook has called it "the most meaningful statement ever made theatrically about the Newfoundland way of life."[16] Sandra Heindsmann of Vancouver termed it "an inspired and accomplished product of Documentary Drama."[17]

Like *Gros Mourn, Buchans — A Mining Town* developed out of direct contact between the Mummers and the people of the community. The company happened to stop in Buchans to perform their *History of Newfoundland* play during one of the many strikes by the local miners. Impressed with the *History* play, the people of Buchans asked the Mummers to come back and do a show about their own town. They returned a year later and set about exploring the community. This was accomplished, Passe-Muraille style, by sharing experiences as much as possible. All seven members of the company lived with the people of Buchans, the men in the company bunkhouse, the women with the kitchen staff. As the programme note later stated:

> The Newfoundland Mummers Troupe lived and worked in Buchans alongside miners and their families to create this documentary play out of the actual words and memories of the Buchans people. The words of this play are theirs.

While the words and characters of the play which developed were taken from life, many of the situations were in fact invented to make a certain point. As conceived by the director, the play was to present an accurate portrait of the community, as well as give an idea of its labour problems. The emphasis of the play was on the workers, with management treated in a much more abstract fashion, either heavily caricatured or portrayed through puppets rather than live actors. This removal of management to another level of reality was intended to reflect the alienating effect on the miners of being "owned" by a foreign company (American Smelting and Refining). Again because of his wish to stress the problems of the miners themselves, Brookes intended to underplay the role of the women in the production, a decision which met with protest from the actors and was greatly modified. Eventually, the play achieved a good balance between vignettes of daily living and the progress of trade unionism and strike politics. After playing Buchans itself, the show went on a tour of the Atlantic provinces and from there to Toronto, where the name was changed to *Company Town*.

The play is made up of a sequence of loosely related scenes, structured into two acts. The scenes alternate between first person narration — "stories" culled directly from the people of Buchans — and documentary information; this basically naturalistic approach is relieved through the use of song and dance routines, and the substitution of puppets for live actors to represent the undesirable characters (police, management). The audience is first given a glimpse into the history of the town with reminiscences by some of the oldtimers who recall life in the 1920's and 1930's. In spite of many hardships, the families who settled there developed a fierce loyalty to the place. Donna, one of the women, is quoted: "You know, that's the way it is with Buchans. Once you comes in here, you never wants to get out of it no more." Some grim statistics follow, which give ample foundation to the growing unrest among the miners. Frustration on the part of the union leaders and oppression by company officials eventually led to a series of strikes, the last of which culminated in violence.

But while these developments along the labour front are sympathetically and convincingly portrayed, the play's real strength lies in the small vignettes of daily life; it is through these everyday scenes that the town becomes a living reality for the audience. The focus here is mostly on the women, their hardships, the loneliness of their lives, and the total inadequacy of the housing provided by the company. There are also occasional touches of humour, such as the monologue in which Donna looks back on a lifetime of feeding her man — and comes up with some astounding statistics:[18] every year she has produced 66,000 cookies, 257 cakes, 1,600 slices of homemade bread, 342 sandwiches . . . "and . . . and . . . and . . . I'll tell you something . . . I'm never getting married again." Thinking back to the starvation among miners described by Zola and other 19th-century writers, one might fail to respond to this episode with the intended sympathy; Donna's plight appears as welcome comic relief. Another humorous episode concerns one of the miners who is inordinately fond of strong drink. He regularly repairs to a quiet spot in the woods with a good supply of 2 per cent beer and 80-proof hair tonic, there to feast on this unusual and powerful mixture.

The most pathetic scenes of the play deal with the problem of silicone disease among the miners. To underline the severity of the situation, it is shown in three different versions — from three different points of view.[19] The first scene shows Donna reminiscing about how she watched her father slowly dying from the disease while she was a child. The next episode presents Bembo, a sick miner, who is told by the doctors to have an operation; when he confronts them with his opinion that nothing can save him, they confirm his belief, and he goes home silently, to wait for death. The third story concerns Howie, a sick old miner who refuses to stop working because he feels he must go on until he reaches the pension age of sixty-five.

Of the three stories, Donna's is the most moving. It is told in the first person:

> My father died of silicosis. I used to lie awake in bed nighttime and I'd listen to him coughing up his guts sick. Every night before he went to bed and before he would get up every morning, I'd haul a pillow over my head to try to bar the sound of it. I was twelve, thirteen years old then maybe.

At the end of the second act, the play returns to the central theme of labour unrest. The story of Buchans is brought up to the date of the 1973 strike partly witnessed by the Mummers. This unusually long strike eventually leads to violence, and the RCMP is called in to restore order. The miners are further subdued by rumours circulated by management that there is little ore left and the future of the town is uncertain. The play ends with one of the characters addressing the audience directly: "Well, now we have told you a story. We could have told you a very dangerous story. You know that."[20] The implications are obvious.

The success of *Company Town* was due, in a large part, to the Mummers' effective staging devices. The set made no attempt at naturalism. The main feature was a huge backdrop, stencilled with company rules and regulations; against this background, some scaffolding served to suggest the various locations. These were indicated verbally during the play: "This is now a mine shaft." Sound effects and light switches were operated in full view of the audience. In the same way, only minimal costuming was used — suggestive props such as an apron or a hat, rather than full costume.

In spite of its enormous success in Newfoundland, the production was not invited to the St. John's Arts and Culture Centre. When it went on tour, it proved strong enough to appeal to audiences outside of Newfoundland. The Toronto *Globe and Mail's* review of the show explained the essence of the Mummers' appeal:

> the Mummers' Troupe offers a kind of theatre that is startlingly right. Because of its roots in actual experience, the evening lacks the stale, cut-and-dried impression so many scripted plays give. *Company Town* is about real events on the way to being folklore; that accounts for its strengths and for the players' commitment.[21]

Another successful Mummers production in the same genre — the political portrayal of a community — was their exploration of life in the far North, *Weather Permitting*, subtitled "Glimpses of the North Labrador Coast" (1977). To collect material for this show, five members of the Mummers' Troupe moved into an Inuit community. They stayed in the Eskimo section of town, again trying to share as closely as possible, the life of the people they were portraying. They eventually came up with a show which combined photographic recordings of real-life scenes with a highly imaginative approach: the staging involved the use of slide projections and impressionistic suggestion of locale (huge bolts of white cloth, for example, served to indicate blizzards and frozen rivers). The play deals with three aspects of Northern life: traditional lifestyle, now largely a thing of the past (hunting expeditions, feats of men and dogs, glorification of hand-made products); social problems created by the transition to a more modern way of life; and the political implications of rule by a white government. The sympathies of the Mummers are clearly with the native people, and the entire play is one long plea for preservation of the native cultural heritage and lifestyle. Problems with the assimilation process enforced by the Department of Labrador Services go all the way from the inadequacy of food ("store food don't fill you up like de wild food do"), to the deterioration of the huskies through cross-breeding, to a total loss of pride in being Inuit. The play also demonstrates how Eskimos are fully unable to cope with a system of justice which is to them incomprehensible; when taken to court, they automatically plead guilty. This section ends on a song which sums up the frustration of native peoples:

> And you ask him why he kept drinking
> He replied: What else is there for me to do
> It hurts so much to keep thinking
> Of days when living was good.[22]

The grim picture is relieved with some satirical scenes. Tourists and especially "university people" come in for some biting satire; the "professor," for example, conducts a research experiment which involves measuring Eskimo noses and recording these measurements. In another humorous scene, "What If," the tables are turned: two Labradorians come to St. John's to take over the place. The entire downtown area is expropriated and buildings are torn down in order to create a herding ground for caribou.

From the lighter tone of this scene, the play then moves into the serious propaganda which provides a finale of strong rhetoric:

> Our claim is a moral and political claim to the right to continue to live lives which have sustained us in the past and which we believe will be meaningful and coherent for our children. We do not want decisions about our country to

be made for us. We do not want to be owned. . . . we want the ultimate authority over what happens in our own country.

Although all of the Mummers' plays are controversial in some way, none aroused as much heated argument as their 1978 production of *They Club Seals, Don't They?*, which dealt with the annual seal hunt off the Newfoundland/Labrador coast. The Mummers researched the topic at length, but the production eventually turned out to be heavily slanted in favour of the hunt. For the first and only time, the usually subversive Mummers found themselves on the same side as their provincial government. Not only that; the government also provided money to help defray the cost of taking the show on tour across Canada. On their return, the Mummers received an official message of thanks and congratulations from the premier of the province, Frank D. Moores.

Jubilation on the part of local government authorities notwithstanding, it remains dubious whether *They Club Seals, Don't They?* made any converts for the seal hunt, simply because the Mummers were not able to make their show appear like an objective presentation of the facts of the hunt, in spite of programme notes to the contrary. In fact, the programmes for this show provided an elaborately devised introduction to the topic, emphasizing detachment and fair play. Each programme consisted of an envelope containing a number of cards, each stating main arguments, for and against such major issues surrounding the seal hunt as "Economic," "Extinction," "Tactics," and "Inhumane." The envelope also contained a prefatory note with the following information:

"They Club Seals, Don't They?" was created collectively by the cast and is based upon extensive research. The views expressed in the play are our own and arise from a careful study of the facts. Other groups or individuals may hold differing views on the seal hunt, and we will be glad to make the theatre available for discussion after the performance, if desired.

The play itself, however, belied the objectivity implied in the programme. The general setting was that of the circus — an imaginative way of indicating how the hunt has been handled by the media. In setting up the two opposed parties, however, the Mummers were unfair. The seal hunters were represented as honest, hard-working men, struggling to keep their families alive under difficult circumstances. The positive emotional impact was further reinforced by zeroing in on one particular family, with whom the audience could fully identify. The anti-sealhunt forces, however, were represented as a group of buffoons, dressed in clown costumes and equipped with red rubber noses. To create a particularly dramatic finale for their show, the Mummers ended it with a film sequence showing the horrors of a pig being killed in a slaughterhouse. Most critics considered this as a shock tactic in dubious taste. The implied argument ("all those who eat meat accept the slaughterhouse, so why object to the seal hunt'') certainly carries little conviction.

Reaction to the play was mixed and depended on the attitude towards the seal hunt of individual reviewers; but most critics, even those who favoured the project in principle, condemned the Mummers for their heavy-handedness in trying to preach their pro-sealhunt gospel. Their main argument, that seals "remain a renewable, thriving and unendangered marine resource," making the annual hunt "a humane, and ecologically sound, harvest" certainly aroused the ire of Green-peacers everywhere, especially in Vancouver, the heart of Greenpeace country, and in the presence of Paul Watson, one of the characters lampooned in the show. On the other hand, the Montreal *Gazette* praised the Mummers' effort as a long overdue "antidote for the poisonous mass hysteria being mounted against the annual Newfoundland seal hunt."[23]

Pro or con, *They Club Seals, Don't They?* certainly put the Mummers' Troupe on the theatrical map of Canada. The following year, they branched out into a new genre with *Some Slick*, a cabaret-style rock musical, at the time of composition "a musical fantasy of off-shore oil development in Newfoundland." History quickly caught up with the Mummers, and they found themselves in a race with reality. The show opened in April 1979; by October, its prediction had come true, and oil had indeed been discovered off the Newfoundland Coast. In spite of the fact that their fantasy had become reality, they found that little had to be changed in the show. The events and situations they predicted were based on careful research of what had actually happened in Scotland after the discovery of North Sea oil. The Newfoundland situation turned out to be predictably similar.

Some Slick was a totally new venture for the Mummers' Troupe, a highly polished production consisting of twenty original songs alternating with comic skits. Chris Brookes directed the show, which was performed, not by his usual ensemble, but by the members of Iceberg Alley, St. John's top four-man rock band. It was a virtuoso performance, as the four men had to perform as band, actors, and singers all at the same time. This tour de force came across suc-cessfully with the help of a highly sophisticated set and lighting design which included huge rotating pillars from which the actors emerged for various scenes. Television monitors recorded the production from different angles with a port-a-pack camera. Although totally different in performance style from usual Mum-mers' productions, *Some Slick* did retain the traditional Mummers' concern with social problems. The skits deal with such serious problems caused by the oil discovery as the struggle for control between the government and the oil company; the effect of sudden affluence on the community; and the difficulties faced by other industries because of the sudden exodus of the entire labour force to the oil rig. In spite of this sociological component, the show never loses its fast-paced tempo nor its light, sparkling tone. If the Mummers' Troupe can rightfully be described as the angry young men (and women) of Newfoundland, *Some Slick* proves that they, too, are capable of a more light-hearted approach. With the prediction of *Some Slick* come true, and the traditional Newfoundland lifestyle rapidly making way for the new affluence came the dissolution of the Mummers' Troupe in 1982. Their work remains an important and integral part of Canadian theatre history.

6

In the Wake of The Quiet Revolution: The Alternative Theatre Movement in Quebec

In Québec, as in English Canada, the rise of an alternative theatre movement signifies the end of the first, and the beginning of the second, evolutionary stage in a dialectic pattern: the once revolutionary "nouveau théâtre québécois" of Dubé, Tremblay, and their contemporaries has thus become "mainstream," while a new wave of theatrical counter-culture, the "jeune théâtre," sets itself up in antithesis. The two groups are diametrically opposed in both their form of expression and their general approach: the nouveau théâtre québécois is a *théâtre d'auteurs*, a literary theatre, while the jeune théâtre consists of groups whose work is based on collective creation. The nouveau théâtre québécois concerns itself first and foremost with demythification, a clearing away of the colonial past, and the creation of a truly *québécois* identity; the jeune théâtre groups the concerns of alternative companies internationally, no longer so self-conscious about being québécois. Although their work is rooted in the realities of life in their province (or country, as they prefer to say), they no longer see flaunting their *québecité* as a first priority. Instead, they carry on the search for new theatrical forms, and the battle for social justice in much the same way as similar groups in both Europe and America. While there is some doubt about the "quality" of much of the work of the jeune théâtre, there can be none about the impact of the movement on the future development of the Québec theatre scene. As Claude Des Landes wrote in 1978:

> Libérée de ses emprunts littéraires et de ses prétensions purement "esthéti-santes," l'expression théâtrale refère maintenant à des données pragmati-ques. . . . Si des auteurs tels que Robert Gurik, Michel Tremblay ou Jean Barbeau . . . ont eu comme principale préoccupation de nous sortir des ornières passéistes et colonisantes de notre histoire, la présente generation,

celle des collectifs de création, nous laisse présager une utilisation de la scène dont on ne pourrait se contenter de scruter les resultats immediats selon une mesure-étalon. La dramaturgie toute entière vient de franchir un premier cycle.[1] (Liberated from its dependence on literature and its purely aesthetic pretensions, theatrical expression now relates to pragmatic given facts. . . . If authors like Robert Gurik, Michel Tremblay or Jean Barbeau . . . had as their major preoccupation to extricate us from the ruts of passivity and colonialism of our history, the present generation, that of collective creation, lets us foresee a utilization of the stage whose immediate results one cannot be satisfied to evaluate according to a certain scale. Our entire dramaturgy has just gone through a first cycle.)

Like alternative theatre in English Canada then, the movement in Québec represents a second thrust in the development of an indigenous dramaturgy; as in English Canada, it originates in a protest against established forms of theatrical expression and traditional training methods. There is, however, an essential difference between the two movements. In English Canada, the encouragement and support of young Canadian dramatists constituted one of the essential components in the ideology of all alternative theatre groups; some, such as Factory Theatre Lab, devoted themselves entirely to providing workshopping experience and public exposure for new playwrights. In Québec, this function was taken over entirely by the Centre d'essai des auteurs dramatiques, leaving the jeune théâtre groups free to exercise their own creativity. The Centre d'essai, founded in 1965, served as a meeting place for young authors; it also provided round table discussions, public readings, and, eventually, publication and/or help towards the production of new plays. In the first six years of its operation, the Centre d'essai received 150 scripts, of which 82 were retained and 17 published. Practically all the important authors of the nouveau théâtre québécois group came through the Centre d'essai — Robert Gurik, Jean Barbeau, and especially Michel Tremblay.

The jeune théâtre, then, set itself up as a deliberate alternative both to traditional theatre and to the more literary nouveau théâtre québécois, whose authors, it was felt, sought success only in order to defect immediately to the well-funded mainstream establishment. The Québec movement tends to be more radical than most of the English-Canadian groups, both in its aesthetic creed (reliance on collective creation almost exclusively) and its political orientation (committed groups align themselves fully with a marxist philosophy). Again, the ideological foundations for the use of collective creation differ in Québec from those of the English-Canadian groups. George Luscombe at Toronto Workshop Productions and Paul Thompson at Theatre Passe-Muraille emphasize the importance of collective creation for the development of the full potential of the actor, who, they feel, is reduced to the status of a reciting puppet in traditional scripted theatre. However, this essentially artistic aspect is not seen as the most important one in

Québec; what is, is that collective creation represents a political act. The results of the Quiet Revolution of the early 1960's did not satisfy the radical young people in Québec, who felt it had done nothing to eliminate the state of oppression and exploitation in which the majority of the people was forced to live. Young theatre artists went along wholeheartedly with these radical views. Jacques Vézina wrote in *Jeune Théâtre*, the official organ of the movement:

> Notre société québécoise est basée sur l'exploitation: celle de la classe bourgeoise sur la classe des travailleurs, celle d'une classe bourgeoise améri-caine et canadienne sur le peuple québécois, et celle de l'homme sur la femme.[2] (Our Québec society is based on exploitation; exploitation of the working class by the bourgeoisie, of the people of Québec by an American and Canadian middle class ["Canadian" meaning English Canadian, of course], and exploitation of women by men.)

In the view of the radicals, such a system makes the development of a national culture difficult, if not impossible: "Au Québec, la culture nationale véritable naîtra avec la nécessité d'en finir avec l'oppression et l'exploitation"[3] ("In Québec, a true national culture will arise with the need to put an end to oppression and exploitation.") From a historical point of view, one may well question the validity of this assumption: oppressed people have indeed produced cultures of their own, and often very impressive ones at that (the example of the Jews comes to mind immediately). However, for the members of jeune théâtre groups, social and economic change is a *sine qua non* of cultural development, and, as theatre artists, they feel called upon to help bring about such a change. Political disenchantment then carries over into the area of theatre: rejection of authority, of the "leader" figure in whom the young generation has lost all faith, and substitution instead of group action, "collective" — in the theatre as well as in social and political life. Although the theatre lacks the clear-cut orientation of political groups, it sees itself as an instrument for action through democratic, collective effort:

> La culture n'est plus posée comme une valeur manichéiste . . . mais comme le reflet d'une réalité individuelle et collective et comme un moyen d'action. C'est . . . la naissance d'un esprit collectiviste, comme solution de change-ment (Plutôt que la venue d'un sauveur, d'un chef, d'une vedette): coopera-tives, comités de citoyens, comités d'action politique . . . dans le domaine du théâtre. . . la création collective.[4] ("Culture is no longer posited as a Man-ichean value . . . but as the reflection of an individual and collective reality and as a means to action. It is . . . the birth of a collectivist spirit as a solution to change (rather than the advent of a saviour, a leader, a star): co-operatives, citizens' committees, committees for political action. In the sphere of theatre . . . collective creation.)

It is also felt that a single author is no longer capable of giving voice adequately to the general concerns, whereas this can still be achieved by a group working together earnestly and sincerely. Again, the validity of this argument is highly questionable, and it has been challenged frequently by practising writers. But it certainly reflects the general rejection of authority typical of alternative theatre groups. To them, the traditional author-director-script triad represents the hold of the establishment over the "oppressed" levels of theatrical creativity, actors and technicians who wish to gain full equality through a democratization of the creative process. Ironically, the collective creation movement, in spite of its violently anti-literary bent, also served as a springboard for a number of acknowledged playwrights who belonged to its ranks for a while: Jean Barbeau, André Simard, and, most importantly, Jean-Claude Germain. Germain eventually founded an alternative theatre of his own, the Théâtre d'Aujourd'hui, in which he functions as house writer, director, and chief actor rolled into one — an unusual answer to the problem of solving the tensions between the various levels of production. The next chapter examines the work of the Théâtre d'Aujourd'hui.

Interestingly enough, the technique of collective creation in Québec predates the formal beginnings of the jeune théâtre movement. It was first used in the early 1960's by students in several of the *collèges classiques*, who started with experimentation around collages of existing texts and from there proceeded further to improvisation and collective creation. From the educational institutions, the method then found its way to the growing number of semi-professional and professional groups across the province. (There is an interesting parallel here to the development of theatre in Québec generally, since it also goes back to the *collèges classiques* with their centuries-old tradition of performance.) As in English Canada, the methods of collective creation varied from pure collective creation to the use of an outside eye ("observateur") who helps shape the material and to the occasional addition of a playwright in the function of "special observer" ("observateur privilégié"); dramatists André Simard, Jean Barbeau and Jean-Claude Germain have all worked with collectives in this way. Simard insists that the writing process itself must emanate from the practical creative effort of a group, rather than taking place in isolation. Other Québec writers who have worked with collective creation groups take a more reserved view.[5] Robert Claing reports from his own experience:

> Curieusement, lorsque nous sommes rendus à l'étape des dernières répétitions . . . c'est la panique . . . le comédien cherche un "auteur" capable de finaliser le scénario ou de synthétiser théâtralement les resultats des improvisations.[6]
>
> (Strangely enough, when we have reached the stage of the final rehearsals . . . panic breaks out. The actor looks for an "author" capable of finalizing the

scenario or of creating a theatrical synthesis out of the results of the improvisations.)

By the end of the decade a gradual decline set in, and theatrical renewal was no longer sought along the lines of collective creation. As in English Canada, it is now looked upon as a transitional phenomenon which served a useful and necessary function within the evolutionary process. Marc Doré, currently director of the Québec Conservatory of Dramatic Art and formerly one of the leaders of the alternative theatre movement, expresses the views of most thoughtful critics of the Québec theatre scene in a 1979 article entitled "Quitter l'improvisation pour l'écriture" ("Leaving improvisation in favour of writing"):

> Moi, j'attends le poète! Je regarde aller le théâtre à Québec depuis trois ans, et je trouve qu'il est devenu très "secure," très "pantoufle." . . . C'est le temps que la poésie vienne au théâtre tant par l'écriture que par le jeu de l'acteur. . . . Il fut un temps ou je fis la guerre à l'écriture théâtrale. C'était dans les années soixante, au moment où l'on prenait la parole au Québec et que tant de belles choses sortaient de l'improvisation. J'ai mis l'improvisation à l'avant parce que les élèves n'arrivaient pas à jouer juste. Ca passait par la langue française! . . . Alors, il fallait qu'on nie l'écriture théâtrale. Ca nous a servi à ne pas attendre après la France. A prendre notre place.[7] ("As for me, I am waiting for a poet! I have been watching the theatre in Quebec for the last three years, and I think it has become very "secure," very "comfortable". . . . It is time for poetry to come to the theatre by way of the written text as well as through the acting. . . . There was a time when I was at war with written texts for the theatre. It was in the sixties, at a time when we in Québec began to express ourselves, and so many fine things came out of improvisation. I stressed improvisation because the students were unable to act properly. They had to go via the French language! . . . It was necessary, therefore, to do away with the written text. This helped us not to take our cues from France. To take up our own position.

Improvisation and collective creation, then, are seen as an essential stage, both in the development of a genuinely québécois theatre training, free of colonial fetters, and in the evolution of a native dramaturgy. From the vantage point of the 1980's, it becomes clear that it was no more than a stage. Looking at the history of the jeune théâtre movement, however, it becomes equally clear that this stage was an extraordinarily influential one which was bound to leave its mark on all future developments.

The self-definition of the jeune théâtre could apply equally well to alternative groups in English Canada. Jeune théâtre companies define themselves as belonging to the movement "dans la mesure où elles refusent, à cause d'un idéal de vie, d'être embrigadées dans un système où les structures prennent le pas sur la partie créatrice" ("insofar as they refuse, because of a life ideal, to be caught up in a system where bureaucratic structures are emphasized over creativity").[8] Decentralization, regionalism, research, and original creation are listed as basic goals. But while there is no formal link between the various groups operating in English Canada, Québec alternative companies actually form an organization, complete with a central office and an official journal. "Jeune théâtre," then, means both "alternative theatre" in the general sense, as in English Canada, and the association of most of the alternative companies in the narrower sense (AQJT, Association Québécoise du Jeune Théâtre); it is also the name of the journal of the association.

A brief survey of the history of the AQJT provides interesting insights into the growing radicalism of avant-garde theatre in Québec between the late fifties and the end of the 1970's. The association grew out of an earlier amateur organization, ACTA (Association Canadienne du Théâtre d'Amateurs), founded by Guy Beaulne in 1958. From the beginning, it emphasized regionalism with groups working in Montréal, Chicoutimi, Ottawa, Québec, Moncton, and Saint-Boniface. The most interesting work was done by the Apprentis-Sorciers company of Montréal, who represented ACTA at the International Amateur Theatre Festival in Monaco. They were also the first to introduce Brecht to French Canada. Although ACTA contributed enormously to the development of professionalism and a general awareness of theatre in Québec, representatives of the jeune théâtre later condemned the association and with it their own past with a fanaticism that can only be termed excessive. They saw the activities of ACTA as a continuation of the much despised Duplessisism — authoritarianism, centralization, and the supremacy of a foreign, that is, French, culture: "On fait du théâtre à ce moment-là pour propager des idées universelles, un esthétisme universel, des valeurs universelles qui permettent d'échapper à la réalité"[9] ("At the time, the purpose of theatre was to propagate universal ideas, a universal aestheticism, universal values which permit an escape from reality"). Throughout the 1960's, this radical and nationalistic spirit increased on the Québec theatre scene. With the founding of the Centre d'essai, the literary side of Québec theatre was given an enormous boost, and the theatre exploded with a multitude of works, all violently nationalistic. At the same time, a movement started within ACTA to change the staid organization to a more aggressive association called "Jeune Théâtre." The political and theatrical events of 1968 gave further ammunition to the young radicals within the association: in Québec, the year saw the formation of the separatist Parti Québécois; the first production of Tremblay's *Les Belles-Soeurs*, with its revolutionary use of the *joual* on stage; and "Place à l'Orgasme," a counter-cultural demonstration proposing alternatives to the existing value system. Place à l'orgasme is especially important in the context of the jeune théâtre, as it can be seen as a dramatized ideological foundation for the developing alternative theatre movement. It is a manifesto which groups a long list of values, litany-like, into two categories, "mort à" ("death to") and "place à" ("make way for"). This "litany" was chanted by a group of young demonstrators during a ceremony at Notre Dame church in old Montréal. It reflects the contemporary hippie spirit and echoes the spirit of Artaud, both essential components of alternative theatre. Here is an abbreviated version of the manifesto:[10]

Death to!	**Make way for!**
Baptism	Colour
Extreme Unction	Light
The Commandments of God	Spontaneity
The Commandments of the Church	Play
Imperialisms	Joy
Dogmatisms	Rhythm
Clerical Capitalism	Lucidity
The Pigs of the Spirit	Folly
Communism	Poetry
Capitalism	Hope
Fascisms	Deliriousness
Totalitarianism	Magic
Bureaucratism	Love
Infallibility	Adventure
Servility	Blasphemy
Prestige	Anarchy
	Anger
	Integrity
	Instinct
	Sexuality
	Erection

(all together) Place à l'Orgasme!

This manifesto, which evokes echoes of the *Refus Global* of the automatists in 1948, illustrates very well the spirit of passionate re-evaluation of all values which was characteristic of the young artists of the Quebec theatre scene in the late 1960's. Within ACTA, this increasing radicalism became apparent when the organization decided against sending a representative to the Monaco Festival in 1971 because of the offensively "bourgeois" quality of the event. In 1972, under increasing pressure, ACTA finally became the "Association Québécoise du Jeune Théâtre," and the *de facto* change in orientation was formalized. AQJT defined its goals as follows:[11]

Qu'au niveau de son orientation politique, l'AQJT appuie les forces qui luttent pour se libérer de l'oppression économique, politique, idéologique que subit le peuple québécois;

Qu'au niveau de son orientation culturelle dépendant de son orientation politique, l'AQJT favorise le développement d'un théâtre qui serait le reflet de ces luttes (écoles, quartiers, milieux ruraux, usines, etc.) ou qui cherCherait à le devenir.

(That on the level of its political orientation, the AQJT support the forces which are struggling to free themselves from the economic, political, ideological oppression which the people of Québec are subjected to;

That on the level of its cultural orientation depending on its political orientation, the AQJT favor the development of a type of theatre which would reflect these struggles (schools, neighbourhoods, rural areas, factories, etc.) or which would try to provide such a reflection.

In spite of this overtly political statement of principles at the inception of the organization, many of the member companies did not, in fact, adhere to such a strictly agitprop approach. Instead, they emphasized the element of creativity and experimentation in production and in audience/actor relationships. Besides the Living Theatre, the concept of environmental theatre was a major influence. Schechner's "sociology" of the theatre reached Québec through the efforts of the sculptor and stage designer Maurice Demers, who published a series of articles on the subject in 1971.[12] The first of these, "Théâtre d'environnement I: le nouveau théâtre" provides an excellent illustration of a counterpoint to marxist aesthetics. It is worth quoting in some detail, since it reflects both the jeune théâtre's involvement with the concerns of alternative theatre generally, and their specifically québécois point of view. Demers writes:

Le nouveau théâtre est vécu. Il invoque non pas des situations factices, mais la vie de celui qui s'y exprime. Comme le pré-théâtre, il implique un cérémonial, une fête, une liesse. Il incarne une situation dans le vécu et la fait exploser. Les personnages deviennent des créateurs. . . . L'art s'en trouve relié à la vie. Le témoin de ce théâtre devient un participant, chaque spectateur devient un acteur, chaque module ou accessoire acquiert une nouvelle signification. Il s'agit, non plus de subir, mais d'agir. . . .

Le théâtre traditionnel . . . est un spectacle inauthentique où le comédien hypocrite feint des sentiments qu'il n'a pas, incarne un personnage autre que le sien et vit sur scène une vie empruntée. . . . Le nouveau théâtre élimine le comédien en tant que comédien. Le nouveau théâtre veut de vrais hommes et de vraies femmes et non des marionettes. L'avenir appartient aux êtres authentiques et créateurs.

Le théâtre d'environnement est un théâtre collectif qui exprime une activité de synthèse et non la pensée d'un seul auteur neurasthénique et bigot. . . . Le rôle du nouveau théâtre est de faire surgir le potentiel où il se trouve en invitant chaque personne à créer son dialogue, ses décors, ses environnements. Le théâtre d'environnement est un théâtre de participation où le but visé est d'apprendre à chaque personne à être créatrice. Nous ne visons plus le chef d'oeuvre. L'important est le processus, non le produit.

[Le nouveau théâtre] . . . doit inciter chaque individu, en son individualité propre, à se compromettre par sa libération totale.

Un peuple est en quête de son identité.

Nous sommes à l'heure de la prise de conscience.

Plus le théâtre d'environnement sera québécois plus il sera mondial.[13]

(The new theatre must be lived. It no longer shows an imitation of a situation, but the life of the one who expresses himself through it. Like pre-theatre, it implies celebration, feast, rejoicing. It incarnates a real-life situation and causes it to explode. The characters become creators. . . . In this way, art becomes linked to life. The one who witnesses this theatre becomes a participant, each spectator becomes an actor, each module or accessory gains new meaning. It is no longer a question of passivity, but of action. . . .

Traditional theatre is . . . a false spectacle where a hypocritical actor feigns emotions he does not feel, incarnates a character other than himself and lives on stage a borrowed life. . . . The new theatre eliminates the actor qua actor. The new theatre requires real men and real women, not marionettes. The future belongs to those who can be genuine and creative.

Environmental theatre is a collective theatre which expresses an activity of synthesis and not the thinking of a single, neurotic and bigoted author. . . . It is the function of the new theatre to activate a potential, wherever it may be, by asking each individual to create his own dialogue, his own sets, his environment . . . the environmental theatre is a theatre of participation with the goal of teaching each individual to become creative. We no longer aim for the masterpiece. Process, not product, is what counts.

[The new theatre] must incite each individual, within the limits of his own individuality, to compromise himself by total liberation.

A nation is in search of its identity.

We have reached the hour of awareness.

The more québécois the environmental theatre is, the more universal it will be.)

In spite of its occasionally naive extremism (why, for example, should an individual writer be *ipso facto* "neurotic" and "bigoted"?), Demers's statement can be seen as a theoretical basis for many of the jeune théâtre's practical experiments throughout the 1970's. However, the excessive emphasis on creativity and development of the individual through self-expression antagonized the more leftist-oriented groups. Eventually, tension developed within the AQJT between those companies who saw art exclusively as a tool for social action and the majority, whose interest lay along the lines of environmental theatre. As a result, ten of the more radical groups left the association, among them the Théâtre Euh! and the Théâtre des Cuisines, both of which will be discussed in detail later. They explained their position in a highly emotional manifesto which did little, however, except reiterate the marxist philosophy of art:

> L'art au service du peuple subordonne le culturel au politique. Il propage le socialisme . . . tous les arts qui se disent neutres sont des arts hypocrites. . . . Nous quittons l'AQJT parce que nous voulons subordonner le culturel au politique, ce que le Ministère se permet et nous refuse"[14] (Art in the service of the people subordinates the cultural to the political. It propagates socialism . . . all art which declares itself neutral is a hypocritical art. . . . We wish to subordinate the cultural to the political, which the Ministry [of Cultural Affairs] permits itself but will not allow us.)

After this schism, the term "jeune théâtre" continues to apply to Quebec alternative groups, even when they do not formally belong to the organization.

The jeune théâtre covered a wide spectrum of theatrical activity. Following a brief survey, the work of three particularly representative companies, Le Grand Cirque Ordinaire, an experimental group, Le Théâtre Euh!, a marxist company, and the Théâtre des Cuisines, a theatre by and for women will be examined in detail.

While most alternative theatre emphasizes its "popular" aspect, a small number of companies carry on highly sophisticated and elitist theatre research. L'Eskabel, for example, founded in 1971, considers itself a research laboratory. Members of the group explore new methods of creation, both improvisational and based on texts; they have used as a starting point for their experiments such classics as *The Trojan Women* and Thomas Mann's *Death in Venice*. Les Pichous, directed by Gilbert Lepage of the National Theatre School, attempt to create highly sophisticated and polished productions as an alternative to the establishment repertoire. La Grande Réplique, founded in 1976, a professional company linked to the Université du Québec, defines itself as a "théâtre d'art et d'essai." Rejecting introspective theatre, this group specializes in text collages presenting collective and historical problems.

The largest number of companies work along the general lines expounded by Demers; the Grand Cirque Ordinaire, to be discussed later, belongs in this category. Another interesting group in this context is Les Enfants du Paradis, established in 1975. Typically, the company takes its mottoes from Artaud and Meyerhold. Pierre Larocque, the founder, had studied mime and *commedia* techniques in Europe. His theatre, intended to create a "naive" theatrical idiom, addressed itself to children and adults equally. Using mime, acrobatics, juggling, techniques of the circus and the music hall, Les Enfants du Paradis performed on city squares, in parks, cafeterias, and shopping centres.

Some of the young companies went into highly specialized fields. The Groupe de la Veillée, for example, founded in 1973, performed for such marginal groups as delinquents, handicapped groups, and the old; La Gang des autobus, 1976, attempted (unsuccessfully) to establish a tradition of theatre in moving city buses.

A number of groups exhibit a high degree of social awareness and responsibility, without definite commitment to a socialist ideology. The most interesting of these is probably the Théâtre de Quartier, founded in 1975. This group of young people made it their mandate to fight against the anonymity and isolation of the big city by creating a sense of "neighbourhood" (*"quartier"*) in a specific area. They settled in the Hochelaga-Maisonneuve and Saint-Louis sections of Montréal, and started to perform carefully researched productions based on specific problems of the people in the area. Their main goal was audience involvement: once a theme was explored by the actors, they encouraged the audience to join in and give their own version. A similar attempt to bring theatre to the people of a small community was made by the Théâtre de Carton (1972), which established itself in Longeuil and also made it a point to tour its productions to the smaller communities in the province.

Finally, a number of jeune théâtre companies belong to a radically marxist aesthetic. The Théâtre Euh! will be discussed later. Another example would be the Théâtre d'la Shop, an agitprop group which has a history of moving in on strike situations in order to support the cause of the workers, or the Théâtre Parminou, which hires itself out on commission to various groups.

Women's theatre represents another significant and highly vocal portion of the Québec alternative theatre scene. It will be dealt with at the end of this chapter.

Of all the jeune théâtre companies, the Grand Cirque Ordinaire is probably the most representative, although it was a relatively short-lived undertaking (1969–78). In its history, philosophy, and spectrum of activities, the Grand Cirque Ordinaire illustrates all the essential elements of alternative theatre in Quebec.

The company started as an act of rebellion against the National Theatre School. Under the influence of the general ferment of counter-culture on the North American continent in the late 1960's and the rising nationalistic spirit in Canada around the time of Expo, students at the School became increasingly dissatisfied with the traditional methods used in their training, as well as with the exclusive orientation towards the French classics to which they were subjected. Nineteen sixty-eight was a year of violent protests and counter-cultural breakthroughs in Québec. Students at the School, aware of the discrepancy between the kind of training they were receiving and the "real world" of the avant-garde theatre scene,[15] confronted their administration with a manifesto demanding radical changes in the programme. When their request was refused, the entire graduating class (a group of seven students) withdrew from the School in protest and set up a collective creation group of their own. They were led by Raymond Cloutier, a graduate of the National Theatre School, who had spent several years working with avant-garde and itinerant companies in Europe. They first appeared before the public with a production of ten short skits entitled *POT T.V.* (a pun on "Pas de T.V." — "No T.V." and "pot" T.V.), which was performed at the Université de Montréal for a student audience.

The name chosen for the group reflects their basic philosophy: "Circus" indicates a popular, light-hearted, non-verbal approach to theatre; "grand" modifies this and indicates a seriousness of intent which transcends the usual context of circus performance; and "ordinaire" refers to the ordinary, everyday life which is a base of reference for the productions. The group called its productions "spectacles socio-poétiques," clearly indicating a desire to combine Brechtian fable and Artaudian communion. The actors within the company describe themselves as "comédiens-créateurs" ("actors-creators"), since their productions are largely based on improvisation. Raymond Cloutier often provided a basic outline ("canevas") to serve as a starting point for improvisation; he also helped to shape the final version. However, the company made no attempts to "finalize" their productions through a printed text, although a number of records, especially of the song numbers, are available.

Cloutier has since expounded on the company's philosophy of improvisation, which goes beyond the rationale usually given for the technique. Le Grand Cirque Ordinaire members see improvisation not only as an essential tool for the development of the actor, but also as an indispensable means of freeing themselves from the hold of a foreign language and culture and of rediscovering their *québécois* roots. Beyond these more practical points, the company also developed an almost mystical approach to improvisation. Cloutier summed up all these views in a retrospective interview given after the dissolution of the company:

> L'improvisation pour moi, c'est vraiment la clé de l'acting. La clé pour trouver et définir l'acteur québécois en lui remettant son droit de jeu fondamental. . . . Nous vivons à 400 milles de New York, et nous sommes pourtant restés branchés sur le jeu français. . . . Dans le *Grand Cirque*, nous avons misé sur l'improvisation non seulement pour créer un nouvel acteur, mais surtout pour créer une nouvelle dramaturgie. Toutes les pièces que nous lisions n'arrivaient jamais à la hauteur de cet acte parfait de l'improvisateur entraîné qui arrive à exposer le tableau de l'inconscient collectif qu'il partage avec la salle un soir donné. . . . Il y avait quelque chose de magique que je ne peux pas expliquer, quelque chose qui n'est donné qu'à ceux qui font de l'improvisation ou du jazz.[16] (Improvisation, for me, really is the key to acting. The key to find and define the québécois actor by turning over to him his basic right to act. . . . We live 400 miles from New York, but we have remained tied to the French way of acting. . . . In the *Grand Cirque*, we have

based our work on improvisation not only to create a new type of actor, but especially to create a new kind of dramaturgy. All the plays which we read never reached the height of that perfect act performed by a trained improvisor who succeeds in rendering the image of the collective unconscious which he shares with the audience on a given evening. . . . There was something magic about it which I cannot explain, something which is given only to those who practice improvisation or jazz.)

The productions of the Grand Cirque Ordinaire reflect the dual orientation of the group: introspection as well as consciousness-raising. Some of their performances came close to the social concern approach of the Newfoundland Mummers, while others parallel the soul-searching experiments of Tamahnous Theatre in Vancouver. The ultimate failure of the group is only partly attributable to the personality problems which developed; it is also probably a result, to a large extent, of the difficulty of achieving a workable synthesis between two opposed elements: a "socio-poetic" approach is not easy to achieve through collective creation techniques.

The first official production of Le Grand Cirque Ordinaire was an adaptation of the Brechtian version of *Joan of Arc* to contemporary Quebec circumstances, and it was eminently successful." *T' es pas tannée, Jeanne D'Arc? (Aren't You Fed Up, Jeanne d'Arc)* (1969) ran for some 180 performances and received much critical acclaim. In Cloutier's version, Joan of Arc represented an archetypal nationalist and idealist figure. The "voices" she hears are the same voices heard by the people of Québec from the time of Maria Chapdelaine to the present: "Pourquoi avons-nous duré en Amérique, pourquoi avons-nous envie de continuer? Parce que 'Jeanne' est là, au fond de chacun de nous:"[17] ("Why have we lasted in America, why do we feel like going on? Because 'Jeanne' is there, deep down within each one of us"). Brecht's radio play was used by the company as a point of departure, yet *T' es pas tannée Jeanne D'Arc?* remained a genuine collective creation, with 80 per cent of the text based on improvisation. The purpose was to link the story of Joan of Arc with individual and collective experiences of life in Québec. Scenes alternated, therefore, between historical and contemporary realities. The production included monologues, skits, mimed scenes, and Brechtian songs. To represent the forces of oppression — The Church, The Invader, and Justice — grotesque giant cardboard puppets in the style of the Bread and Puppet theatre were used.

In their next production, *La Famille transparente* (1970) (*The See-Through Family*), the Grand Cirque Ordinaire took on the two major values of contemporary bourgeois society, the family and consumerism, in an attempt at demythification through imagery and satire. Demythification of the family, of course, was one of the central themes running through all aspects of Quebec culture at the time — an obvious rebellion against a society which, under the impact of an all-powerful clergy, had been family-oriented for too long. Practically all of the nouveau théâtre québécois is violently anti-family: we have only to think of Dubé or Tremblay. However alternative companies tended to go a step further than the playwrights. Where plays like *Les Beaux Dimanches* or *A toi, pour toujours, ta Marie Lou* simply expose the reality behind the pious façade of family life as held up by society, with condemnation implied only, collective creations on the same theme tend to be more militant. Their purpose is not simply to expose a state of affairs, but to bring about a radical change. As Paule Baillargeon, an actress with the Grand Cirque Ordinaire, has stated: "Quelle que soit la forme, c'est 'non' à la famille. . . . C'est la famille qui est le fondement du système. Si la famille s'écroule, c'est foutu."[18] ("Whatever the form, it is 'no' to the family. . . . It is the family which is the foundation of the system. If the family is destroyed, that's the end of it.")

The production attempted to investigate relationships of power within the family (male/female; parent/child); and within the four "basic" social classes of "worker," "bourgeois," "artist," and "woman." These relationships were illustrated at the hand of six characters, all members of the "Famille Transparent":

Honoré Transparent, the father, an autocratic, domineering figure;

Desirée Transparent, the mother, totally subdued; the character hardly ever speaks;

Dommage Transparent, the first son, a drunk, who suffers from a mother complex;

Pacifique Transparent, the other son, a slightly crazed artist. He, too, "trips" on his mother;

Prospère Transparent, deceased, shown in capitalist heaven, surrounded by consumer goods and waited upon by St. Peter as maitre d';

Bébé Buick, youngest member of the family, a nightmare figure. Young, pretty, and exploited, Bébé Buick eventually drowns in a basin filled with her own tears.

La Famille transparente is a good example of socio-poetic play in its combination of social satire with lyricism and prose with poetry. Bébé Buick's song, written by Paule Baillargeon, gives an idea of the general tone of the work:

Complainte de Bébé Buick

J'ai marché, marché longtemps
pour arriver ici
J'ai ramassé plein de faux-cils
pis plein de perruques blondes
pis plein de larmes
des rigoles de larmes
des rivières de larmes
des fleuves de larmes

Je me suis mise toute nue

j'ai montré mon beau corps brun
mon beau corps Tropic Tan
mes seins Wonder-Bra
mon ventre plat
mes jambes Philishave
mon sourire Colgate
mes cheveux Miss Clairol
ma face de poupée

J'ai fait marcher mon coeur électrique
pour faire rire les vieux messieurs
y'a plein de bébés qui braillent
en-dessous de ma robe
les plus beaux des enfants des femmes
qui viendront jamais au monde

Comme la vie est triste
comme la vie est triste
comme la vie est triste
pour Bébé-Buick

J'ai les cheveux bruns
j'ai les yeux bruns
pis j'casse rien
J'M'APPELLE BEBE-BUICK[19]

Baby Buick's Lament

I have walked
walked for a long time
to make it here
I picked up plenty of false eyelashes
and plenty of blond wigs
and plenty of tears
rivulets of tears
rivers of tears
streams of tears

I took off all my clothes
I showed my beautiful tanned body
my beautiful Tropic Tan body
my Wonder-Bra breasts
my flat stomach
my Philishave legs
my Colgate smile

my Miss Clairol hair
my doll face

I turned on my electric heart
to make the old gentlemen laugh
it's full of crying babies
under my dress
the most beautiful children of women
who will never be born

How sad is life
how sad is life
how sad is life
for Baby Buick

I have brown hair
I have brown eyes
I don't do any harm

MY NAME IS BABY BUICK

This production depended for its success on the closest possible co-operation between the members of the company. Each actor had drawn up his own outline and wrote his own songs for the character he was to represent; yet these were eventually meshed together successfully. Cloutier attributes the effectiveness of the company with this production to their close sense of belonging. As in the case of Tamahnous, members of the Grand Cirque Ordinaire considered themselves a "family," perfectly tuned in to each other. As this sense of closeness and total mutual trust eventually began to wane, the company found it more and more difficult to overcome the inherent difficulties of their socio-poetic technique.

The next major production of the Grand Cirque Ordinaire was an excursion into full-fledged political theatre, and it was not successful. Their approach was very similar to that used by the Mummers' Troupe; members of the company moved into a community to research an existing social problem and followed it up with a production aimed at leading the way towards reform. The village in question was Pibrac, a small community which had been suffering from unemployment for ten years. When the Grand Cirque Ordinaire arrived, they found 150 families on welfare, while American workers had been hired by the one company capable of providing work. Unrest had at last set in, and plans were underway for the development of a lumber co-operative by the people of Pibrac. At this point, the Grand Cirque Ordinaire moved in. *T'en rappelles-tu, Pibrac, ou le Québecoi?* (*"Do You Remember, Pibrac*, or *The Quebec — What?*) attempted to encourage the co-op movement by presenting to the community a picture of themselves and their relationship with the government.

The production consisted of two parts. Part I mirrored the situation at Pibrac as it appeared to the company. As in real life, the co-op movement was shown originating with community meetings in a potato cellar. Three major lines of thought were represented: the Radical, who demands total reform, if necessary by using violence; the Moderate, who believes in using existing structures and dialogue; and the Moderate's Wife, who acts as a go-between. The Radical frightens the group because of his excessive romanticism and flamboyance. They look for direction to the past, but can find no acceptable model in history: the Patriotes of 1837 certainly will not do. Eventually, a decision is made to invite the Minister of Lands and Forests to attend a meeting. When he appears, the community enact for him their troubled situation; this play within the play also contains some biting satire of the traditional French-Canadian hero figures, such as Dollard des Ormeaux and Madeleine des Verchères. But the Minister is not moved, and refuses help.

In Part II of the play, the Wife is delegated by the group to try to enlist help from three major political figures: Jean Drapeau, Robert Bourassa, and Prime Minister Pierre Trudeau. Again, she is unsuccessful. In this section of the production, the Grand Cirque Ordinaire lost its usual sense of balance and good taste. The three key figures were not only shown as political "heavies," lacking all sense of responsibility or compassion for the people, but strong hints of homosexuality were also made in their direction. This slant eventually caused a scandal which forced the production to close down.

The play ends on a call to action: the villagers, unable to obtain help and unwilling to endure the situation any longer, use their own bodies to block the road for the American trucks — a powerful image of frustration and non-violent resistance.

Nevertheless, *Pibrac* represented a triple failure for the Grand Cirque Ordinaire: it had been closed down by the authorities; it had not achieved any practical result in improving the lot of the people of Pibrac; and it was less than successful from a formal and technical point of view. The experience provoked a crisis within the company. Deeply hurt by their experience with political theatre, the members of the group now withdrew into a stage of soul-searching and introspection, probing their private unconscious with the next production, *L'Opéra des pauvres* (*The Poor People's Opera*) (1973), and the collective unconscious with *La Tragédie Américaine de l'Enfant Prodigue* (1975) (*The American Tragedy of the Prodigal Child*). Both of these combine music with improvisation for their descent into the underground of the subconscious.

The *Opéra des Pauvres* appears as a rather naive and clichéd attempt to present on stage the inner crisis of a group of people who find themselves suddenly cast out from the make believe paradise of a hippie-type adolescence into an uncertain adulthood. As in several Tamahnous productions, this collective creation is essentially a nostalgia trip, with bitter comment on the realities of the present. Part I, performed in the dimly lit area in the back of the stage, presents scenes of adolescence: the "gang," happy and innocent, in the corner store, at the skating rink, at a party. Part II switches to an adult setting. The characters, now in their thirties, have achieved affluence, but also existential ennui, and their life becomes an unceasing battle against emptiness, solitude, boredom, and impotence. Eventually, the entire family drowns in their own swimming pool, only to reappear as old people, sick, poor, and miserable, in an acting area close to the audience. This naturalistic ending is transcended by the appearance of a white knight, who represents hope and the ultimate triumph of the imagination over crude realism.

While *L'Opéra des Pauvres* dealt with the private concerns of the actors, *La Tragédie Américaine de L'Enfant Prodigue* used biblical fable as the basis for a self-analysis of the collective and its history. A rock opera obviously patterned on *Hair*, *L'Enfant Prodigue* reflects the inner crisis of the company as they ponder the past and wonder about the future:

> Une tragédie rock/Sur un air biblique/Un mouvement acide/Quelques allegros pour l'Expo/Puis une descente en mineur/Vers un silence qui nous fait peur/Et demain, qu'arrivera-t-il/Aux enfants de la terre promise?[20] (A rock tragedy/On a biblical tune/An acid movement/Some allegroes for Expo/Then a descent in minor/Towards a silence which we fear/And tomorrow, what will happen/To the children of the promised land?)

In the Grand Cirque's interpretation, the Prodigal Son becomes an archetype of the eternal child (both male and female) and a symbol of the group itself. The child's travels from his father's house are seen as a quest: he goes out to find a "coffre," the treasure chest, archetypal image of happiness and solution to all problems. At the beginning, the Child is filled with hope, reflecting the enthusiasm and faith of the young actors at the start of their career. The strong religious overtones emphasize the seriousness of their dedication in the past: "Nous serons des pèlerins égarés qui cherchent le nouveau dieu"[21] ("We shall be lost pilgrims looking for the new god"). As the play progresses, however, the discrepancy between the ideal of peace and love and the realities of the "grey empire" (North American civilization) becomes more and more oppressive. The production ends on a tone of despair and total resignation: "Je croyais comme toi avoir changé la vie. Nous sommes des oiseaux de cabaret. Voilà que le spectacle nous ennuie."[22] ("I thought, like you, I had changed life. We are birds of the cabaret. And now we are tired of the show.")

Such a defeatist attitude clearly spelled the end of the group; it also indicated a slackening of creative energy, a lassitude, together with inner dissensions. In fact, there had been difficulties with male/female relationships in the company for a while, with the result that the women left the group to produce a show of their own. It will be examined later in the context of women's theatre. Definitely, the Grand Cirque Ordinaire had lost its momentum on all levels by 1975. Its last major production, *La Steppette Impossible* (*Impossible Highstepping*), no longer made any effort to reach out at all; rather, it was a further act of withdrawal, with the actors inviting the audience to observe "improvisation-in-the-making": *La Steppette Impossible* simply exposed the mechanics of collective creation.

Although Cloutier has blamed the cultural establishment which will "not give a chance to young experimental companies" for the eventual demise of the Grand Cirque Ordinaire, it seems obvious that the company simply exhausted its own energies and eventually lost its sense of direction. Cloutier's oft-expressed bitterness and sense of futility at the entire undertaking seems unjustified. During the period of greatest fermentation on the Québec theatre scene, the Grand Cirque Ordinaire provided a good portion of the general excitement and stimulation.

The Théâtre Euh!, Québec's most militant political group, started out on premises very similar to those of the Grand Cirque Ordinaire; in fact, its founder, Clément Cazelais, had been in France together with Cloutier during the agitated period of the late 1960's, and it was there that they decided to take active steps to reform the theatre of Québec. On their return, Cloutier joined the Grand Cirque Ordinaire in Montréal; Cazelais formed his own company in Québec City. A small group of six, the Théâtre Euh! started out as a working commune: each actor had a part-time job on the side, and each member of the group contributed to every aspect of the production. From the start, the Théâtre Euh! based its work exclusively on improvisation and collective creation. The group made heavy use of clown masks, mime, and *commedia* techniques in their emphasis on non-verbal theatre. They used only non-traditional theatre spaces and made conscious attempts to bring their productions to the people, rather than have the people come to them. The tone of their work was generally adjusted to the audience of each performance — workers, students — with the exception of intellectuals, for whom the group refused to compromise.[23]

Like the Grand Cirque Ordinaire and most of the other alternative groups, Théâtre Euh! began as a protest movement against the theatre establishment as well as against the National Theatre School. In fact, the founding of the company coincides with the beginnings of the Grand Théâtre, the official, subsidized theatre of Québec. Thus, Le Théâtre Euh!, from its very start, provided the people of Québec with an "alternative" to establishment theatre. In an early manifesto of the group, members of Théâtre Euh! accuse the theatre establishment of Québec of having removed itself from the realities of life around it, only to immerse itself in French culture; as for the Theatre School, it is accused of consciously "de-quebecking" its students.[24] A revealing list of opposites sums up the young generation's complaints against the School:

Pas l'adolescent . . . mais l'élève
Pas la vie . . . mais le théâtre
Pas le dedans . . . mais le dehors

Pas l'homme . . . mais le professeur
Pas le corps . . . mais le texte
Pas le théâtre d'ici . . . mais le Théâtre
Pas notre langue . . . mais le Français
Pas Les Belles-soeurs . . . Mais les Trois Soeurs[25]

Instead of the adolescent . . . the pupil
Instead of life . . . the theatre
Instead of inner experience . . . outer experience
Instead of the human being . . . the professor
Instead of the body . . . the script
Instead of a native theatre . . . Theatre
Instead of our language . . . French
Instead of Les Belles Soeurs . . . The Three Sisters

Although the point of departure for the Théâtre Euh! is the same as that of the Grand Cirque Ordinaire, its orientation quickly became aggressively political under the aegis of Mao Tse-tung and Brecht. The company's later manifestoes state its position unequivocally: theatre must be seen as a tool in the fight for proletarian revolution; this is its only justification. It was only natural, then, that the Théâtre Euh! should be among the leading groups which brought about the schism within the AQJT in 1976.

The Théâtre Euh! has engaged in a wide variety of activities since its inception: street theatre, commissioned plays, support of strike action, theatre for children, and public demonstrations, along with a number of more elaborate major productions. We shall examine three of these here: *Quand le matriarcat fait des petits (When the Matriarcate Has A Litter)* (1970), a vitriolic analysis of the woman and mother in Québec society; *Cré Antigone!* (1971) *(That Damn Antigone!)*, which examines the relationships between economic and political power; and *L'Histoire du Québec* (1973), a retelling of Québec history from the specific viewpoint of the Théâtre Euh!.

Quand le Matriarcat fait des petits is an example of the common contemporary attempt at a demythification of the family and motherhood. Loosely structured along the lines of epic theatre, it consists of eighteen short sketches treating the theme; however, not every sketch was actually included in each performance. As is usual with better productions in the revue style, it builds up from the more innocuous scenes at the beginning to a dramatic finale. The first series of sketches deals with such family problems as the mother who is too busy to answer her child when he asks "do you love me" and the husband who thinks his wife crazy when she asks him the same question. This is followed by a number of scenes which centre on the problems of sexuality and sexual frustration: the television set which takes the place of sexual activity; the generation contrast, with the young daughter bringing sexual information home to her mother; the woman as merchandise. Two sketches in the second half of the production are especially effective. "Le cordon ombilical," "The umbilical cord," is a violent parody on the indoctrination of mothers by the Church. In a wildly accelerated presentation, a child is born, grows up, decides to become a priest and missionary, and finally dies at the hands of hostile heathens. When the news of his death reaches home, the mother is exultant: she knows her son has won her immediate access to Heaven. The most vitriolic attack on the myth of the French-Canadian family, however, occurs in a sketch entitled "L'Histoire d'Oezipe," a québécois variation on the Oedipus theme. It presents "the terrifying story" of Oezipe, who killed his father Leo, violated his two sisters Cocogne and Philomène in the cradle, and killed his two brothers Théo and Paul-Emile in order to make love to his mother Jojo. The sketch concludes with the laconic comment: "encore une de nos belles familles canadiennes-françaises" ("another one of our beautiful French-Canadian families"). The final sketch, never omitted, concludes the production with a political message. Entitled "l'organisation ou comment s'organiser" ("organization or how to organize"), it demonstrates the benefits of solidarity with the image of a huge rock, which can be moved only if all work together.

Le Matriarcat remained a fairly simple production, both in theme and form. *Cré Antigone* represents a much more complex effort, with a universal, rather than specifically québécois, political theme, although it also obviously alludes to the political repression which followed in the wake of the October crisis.

Cré Antigone is an undisguisedly Brechtian play in its techniques and theme. Based on Brecht's radio play, it takes greater liberties with the Greek original than the Brechtian version. In the Théâtre Euh! interpretation, Creon is the oppressive leader of a police state who deceives, exploits and manipulates the people. Tiresias, the wise man and thinker, attempts to provide enlightenment; but it is Antigone who calls for open rebellion. In this version, she is not a princess, but a representative of the people, an ordinary working girl — ironically, a pacifist forced to work in a gun factory. The story line itself adheres to the original: the confrontation of Creon and Antigone, Antigone's refusal to back down (in fact, in the Théâtre Euh! version, she even hits Creon), her trial, and death sentence. However, instead of the lament found in Sophocles, this Antigone dies with a fiery last call to revolution, a speech entitled "éloge de l'organisation" ("praise of organization"), clearly modelled on Brecht, even in its rhythms:

> Celui qui vit encore ne doit pas dire jamais,
> Celui qui est assuré n'est pas sûr.
> Les choses ne restent pas comme elles sont.
> Quand ceux qui règnent en maîtres auront parlé
> Ceux sur qui ils règnent, parleront.
> De qui dépend que l'oppression demeure? DE NOUS!
> De qui dépend qu'elle soit brisée? DE NOUS!

Celui qui est abattu, qu'il se dresse
Celui qui est perdu, qui'il lutte![26]

He who is still living must not say never,
He who is assured cannot be sure.
Things do not remain as they are.
When those who rule as masters have spoken
Those over whom they rule will speak.
Who decides whether oppression remains? WE DO!
Who decides whether it shall be broken? WE DO!
He who is down, let him rise,
He who is lost, let him fight!

To bring the situation back home to the oppression of Quebec, Antigone concludes with a rendition of *O Canada* — sung to the tune of the American anthem.

L'Histoire du Québec proved the most successful of all their productions. It played in Paris, toured the French provinces, and was performed at the international theatre festival of Nancy. Subsequently, the company was invited to bring the play to Algeria — a newly liberated and socialist country where the parallels with the Québec situation became obvious. The journal *Jeune Théâtre* gave an enthusiastic review of the production which also reveals its own particular slant:[27] "(L'histoire du Québec) jouée par les clowns du Théâtre Euh! Pas celle des livres des Frères de l'Instruction Chrétienne, non, la vraie." *Jeune Théâtre* particularly praises the company for its correct evaluation of the present situation:

> pénétration de l'impérialisme américain que facilitent les marionettes politiques d'Ottawa et de Québec et les mythes soigneusement entretenus par l'Eglise: la revanche des berceaux, le retour à la terre, l'au-delà glorieux, la paix sociale.
> (The history of Quebec performed by the clowns of the *Théâtre Euh!* Not the one we find in the books of the Christian Brothers, no, the real one . . . penetration by American imperialism which is facilitated by the political puppets of Ottawa and Quebec and by the myths which the Church carefully keeps alive: the revenge of the cradle, the return to the land, glorious afterlife, social peace.)

Although this review implies an overly simplistic approach, *L'Histoire du Québec* was in fact a sophisticated production which successfully carried off its double theme of nationalism and class struggle. The history itself is set in a framing story about clowns. The production begins with a parade (a common feature of Théâtre Euh!). After some fooling around, the clowns announce that they are bored and decide to found a new colony on a desert island — and the history of Québec begins. As told by Théâtre Euh!, it is a history of unending exploitation: of the natives by whites, of the habitants by King and Church (under the slogans of "Dieu vous aime" and "La France vous aime"); of French Canadians by the English conquerors; and of the eventual triumph of American imperialism. The entire tragic process is summarized cynically at the end with the singing of "Alouette, je te plumerai." This history play comes very close in tone to the Mummers' Troupe's *History of Newfoundland*. Like the Mummers, Théâtre Euh! continues to put its productions to the service of specific social and political causes.

To complete this survey of major trends in Quebec alternative theatre, women's theatre, an active group within the movement, must be examined. Women's groups fall into two categories: dissidents who leave a mixed company in order to assert their feminist position free of the usual difficulties with male/female relationships and independent companies formed specifically by and for women. As previously mentioned, a disillusioned group of actresses left the Grand Cirque Ordinaire to produce a feminist play on their own. The result, *Un Prince, Mon Jour Viendra* (1974) (*A Prince, My Day Will Come*), was an interesting de-mythification and reinterpretation of well-known fairy tales along the lines of militant feminism (not unlike Tremblay's use of fairy tale motifs in his satirical musical *Les Héros de mon enfance*). The stories are set in a contemporary Canadian milieu: the fairy godmother is an aunt from Toronto; Snow White goes, not to a forest, but to a boarding school; and Red Riding Hood is a tough little girl from East Montréal. Traditional sex roles are explored: both Cinderella and Snow White see sex as a means to achieve wealth and security. When the Prince appears on the scene, complete with a golden penis, he brings "money, money, money" in exchange for the girls' unending love, faith, and tenderness. Only Red Riding Hood refuses to follow such a well-established pattern. A liberated young woman, she strikes out on her own, to use her body as she pleases — or so she thinks until the male of the species appears, no prince this time, but a Wolf — and she is raped ignominiously. At this point, the play switches to a documentary format, with newspaper clippings read out about rape and murder of women. The moral at the end points to the obvious: woman would like to look upon man as a brother, but he is an aggressor; as a prince, but he is only a murderous wolf.

The Théâtre experimental des femmes, set up in protest by the women members of the Théâtre Experimental of Montreal, follows a similar, hard feminist line. In recent interviews, members of the company have insisted on the continued fight for liberation, for still today, "la femme libérée n'existe pas"[28] ("liberated woman does not exist").

The Théâtre des Cuisines is the best known independent women's theatre group. A number of the company's collective creations have even been given finalized versions as scripts and are now available in book form.[29] The company grew out of several militant women's groups whose members decided to use theatrical performance as a means of propaganda for their causes. Their first venture was a show about the problem of abortion, which they considered most crucial at the time, *Nous aurons les enfants que nous voudrons* (1973) (*We will have the children we want*). It proved an immediate success and was seen by over 3,000 people, mostly women. Ironically enough, the performances took place in an anti-abortionist stronghold: a parish hall.

Following this success, five of the women regrouped for further action. They issued a manifesto stating the objectives, principles, and methods of the group.[30] Their reason for the existence of the Théâtre des Cuisines is the persisting exploitation of women on all levels: at home; on the job market; and in relation to their own body. Theatre is seen as a valuable propaganda tool. However, in their attitude towards production methods, the women of the Théâtre des Cuisines display a naive, if idealistic, lack of professionalism: they do not feel the need for any particular training in order to produce theatre. With almost religious faith, the manifesto asserts "Quand on a quelque chose à dire, on trouve les moyens pour le dire."[31] ("When you have something to say, you find a way to say it.") An equally unrealistic idealism inspires their group dynamics. The company operates on the principle of absolute democracy, and they feel that learning to work together in a small group represents a valuable beginning to an eventual world-wide co-operation between all human beings. Working methods are the usual ones of collective creation: research, round table discussion, improvisation, development of scenario, and preparation of the production. Topics chosen reflect the major interests of women; the major goal of the company is to provide a forum where women can discuss their problems with each other.

Moman travaille pas, a trop d'ouvrage (1975) (*Mummy Doesn't Work, She's Too Busy*) provides a good example of the approach of the Théâtre des Cuisines. The theme of the play is housework. Part one gives the facts, and part two suggests possible solutions. In the true Brechtian manner, no definite answer is given; instead, the audience is made to realize that options are indeed available.

A Prologue sets the tone of the play, pointing out the discrepancy of myth and reality: while three young brides sing at having achieved the blissful state of housewife, two messengers recite a list of chilling statistics (no salary, no vacation, a seventy-nine–hour week, no sick leave). In part one, we are shown the three young women at a later stage in their lives: Nicole, seven years later, married with two children, has kept her job as a school teacher. She lives in a state of unrelieved exhaustion. Yvette, fifteen years later, has become a deserted wife and mother of three. Living on welfare, she finds it hard to make ends meet. Rita, twenty-two years later, housewife and mother of four children, has quietly re-signed herself to her enslavement.

Part two displays two separate scenarios for possible change. The first option shown is revolt: a strike of all the housewives. This creates havoc in industry and government, as all the helpless fathers are left in charge of their offspring. Eventually, the women are brought to trial. They produce witnesses and proofs of their exploitation and demand, not just canteens and day-care centres, but a "total change." The second hypothetical scenario suggested is that of complete reform of sex roles within the family. Each of the three women is shown again as she responds to the new system. Nicole now has some time to herself, as she insists on her husband's co-operation with chores. Yvette improves her position by joining a co-operative. Rita goes back to school to make a life for herself.

The play concludes with a rousing song, "Debout les femmes" ("Women, arise"):

> Debout les femmes, prenons nos vies dans nos mains
> Soyons fortes pour demain
> Nous aussi il faut lutter
> Avec tous les exploités,[32]

> Women, arise, let us take our lives in our hands
> Let us be strong for tomorrow
> We also must fight
> Alongside all those who are exploited.

This militant song reflects the spirit of the entire alternative theatre movement of Quebec and its collective creation movement. We shall find a similar attitude in the scripted productions of the Théâtre d'Aujourd'hui.

7

From Folklore to Culture: Jean-Claude Germain and the Théâtre d'Aujourd'hui

"Le folklore, c'est l'âme, je sais! Et au fond d'elle-même, chaque nation se résume à quatre ou cinq chansons incompréhensibles et intraduisibles! Mais c'est la culture . . . qui donne une voix! Et sans voix, ce sont les autres qui parlent pour vous!"[1] ("Folklore is the soul, I know! And deep down, each nation reduces itself to four or five incomprehensible and untranslatable songs! But it is culture . . . which gives a voice! And if you are without a voice, others will speak for you!") This statement, put into the mouth of Lord Durham, sums up Jean-Claude Germain's theatrical creed and cultural mission. He believes that the people of Quebec have been forced, through political and economic oppression and cultural colonialism, to remain on a static level of purely "folkloric" self-expression, a precultural level which lacks a proper sense of history. Germain has set himself the task of effecting what he considers is a much-needed transition from this folkloric state to one of genuine culture and history. In political terms, this translates into the transition from province or region to nationhood.

Basically, his methods are the usual ones of "culture-building" among writers of colonial nations: demythification and mythopoesis. But Germain's approach differs radically from the pessimism of most contemporary drama: a Falstaffian character himself, he shares his indomitable high spirits with his audiences, producing lively, popular plays in the tradition of the late medieval farce, or *sotie*, plays to make an audience laugh, and through laughter, to become conscious of their own follies and those of the world around them. Germain's plays are one unceasing illustration of his most basic belief, that laughter is man's essential and inborn right: "le droit d'rire, ça s'acquiert pas. . . . ON VIENT AU MONDE AVEC!"[2] ("the right to laugh, — you don't acquire it. . . . YOU'RE BORN WITH IT!"). This attitude he shares with Rabelais — and there are a great many similarities between Germain and the creator of Gargantua and Pantagruel. In fact, if one were to attempt classification, one might describe Germain as a combination of Rabelais and Ionesco, his dramatic opus, a Quebec-style "Ship of Fools."

His multiple activities reflect the energy of the Renaissance man; they also appear fraught with contradiction. A fierce enemy of the classics, but also a highly erudite scholar; an anti-literary theatre man, but also the most prolific playwright in Canada today; a constant fighter against the establishment, but well on the way to becoming an institution himself, Germain represents the single most intriguing phenomenon on the contemporary Québec theatre scene. He offers a typically tongue-in-cheek solution to the paradox by declaring himself a "pataphysician"[3] — a member of that logic- and reason-defying clan which goes from Alfred Jarry to Eugene Ionesco and Boris Vian.[4] Critics have called him the "Louis Cyr" of dramatic writing,[5] and visitors to Germain's study will find a statue of the legendary strong man prominently displayed on the desk, a muscular latter-day patron saint.

A brief look at Germain's background may shed some light on the complexities of his career. Born in East Montréal (interestingly enough, on the same street as his fellow playwright Michel Tremblay), Germain attended a *collège classique*, which provided him with a thorough humanistic background. He then went on to study history at the Université de Montréal. This experience became a determining factor in his subsequent approach to theatre. He found the university a foreign territory, a land "ailleurs," "beyond" the realities of life in Québec,[6] without a bridge between the subjects he studied and their possible local or contemporary applicability. History, in the Québec of the late 1950's, meant the study of the Middle Ages; and Germain discovered to his consternation that Québec history was not being taught at all, a fact which seemed to imply that, academically speaking, it did not exist. It was this experience of his student days which created in him the desire to remedy the situation and to create, for the people of Québec, the awareness of their past which the educational institutions failed to provide.

Disillusioned with university, Germain left academic life and earned a living for three years as a grocer, an occupation which provided him with good opportunities for close contact with people and a chance to immerse himself in the popular language which he was to make into a dramatic idiom later. He then became a journalist, writing theatre criticism for a number of magazines such as *Le Maclean* and *Digeste-Eclair*. From the beginning, he revealed his fiercely nationalistic outlook. In his drama criticism, he freely gave voice to his disapproval of québécois reverence for the French classics, boldly flying in the face of the most hallowed traditions by declaring himself a "racinophobe";[7] not content with dismissing the great tragic writer, he went so far as to suggest that Molière, too, might have become irrelevant in the present age. This was the beginning of a career of "liquidation" which has continued from criticism through playwriting and production.

Soon he was given an opportunity to make use of his cultural nationalism in a more positive manner: in 1968, he became executive director of the Centre d'essai des auteurs dramatiques, a position which he held until 1971. Here he made his first major contribution to québécois theatre: the launching of Tremblay's *Les Belles Soeurs*. It was also during this period that he decided to establish a theatre of his own: in 1969, he founded the Théâtre du Même Nom, or TMN, its name a sly allusion to the "respectable" TNM, (Théâtre du Nouveau Monde). The company established itself at the tiny, fifty-seat Centre du Théâtre d'Aujourd'hui on rue Papineau in East Montreal, which has served as Germain's headquarters ever since, and is now known simply as Théâtre d'Aujourd'hui, in spite of some earlier name changes. His first group of actors called themselves "Les Enfants de Chénier," in deference to the French-Canadian freedom fighter; this was followed by "Les P'tis Enfants Laliberté," another name suggestive of the company's militant spirit. The first production of the Théâtre du Même Nom set the scene for all the theatre of "liquidation" which was to follow: *Les Enfants de Chénier dans un grand spectacle d'adieu*, a collective creation, attempted to systematically demolish the classical French repertoire and traditional performance styles. Germain was now launched in his career as director, housewriter, and chief actor; the next ten years saw fifty-three productions of québécois plays, of which twenty-two were written by Germain. (He was quite capable of producing as many as three or four plays in one year.) His Théâtre d'Aujourd'hui quickly developed a very specific character of its own. It was not only a small theatre exclusively dedicated to the production of québécois work, but it was also strongly marked by the personality of its "man at the centre." Germain himself, always aware of the practical aspects of theatrical production, attributes the specific "style" of his theatre more to the physical set-up at his disposal than to any conscious effort on his own part:

> les contraintes physiques nous permettent de travailler dans la proximité avec le spectateur, ce qui a influencé énormément le jeu et l'écriture, mis l'accent éventuellement sur les costumes plutôt que sur le décor et fait de la lumière l'agent principal de ce qui est devenu aujourd'hui un style de théâtre qui nous caractérise.[8] (the physical constraints allow us to work in close proximity to the public, which has enormously influenced both acting and writing, put the accent eventually on the costumes rather than the sets, and made lighting the main agent of what has become today the theatrical style which characterizes us.)

Germain's activities as a playwright, then, have always been closely linked to the specific theatre and company at his disposal; he calls himself an "écrivain scénique," a "stage writer." At the National Theatre School, where he teaches what he calls "gymnastique intellectuelle" as well as dramatic writing, he has insisted on the same approach: aspiring playwrights must be fully immersed in all aspects of production before embarking on a literary project for the stage.

It is not easy to evaluate the phenomenon of Jean-Claude Germain: moving freely between establishment and counter-culture, between the anti-literary alternative theatre and the literary élite of the nouveau théâtre québécois, he covers the full spectrum of theatrical activity. What, in fact, will be the ultimate mark left on the Québec theatre scene by this outburst of vital energies? To answer the question even tentatively, we must take a look at his plays, as well, of course, as at the theatrical philosophy underlying his dramatic opus. We shall then perhaps be able to answer Goethe's basic critical questions: What did he set out to do? How well has he done it? And — most important — was it worth the doing?

As was pointed out at the beginning of this chapter, Germain's avowed purpose is to effect the transition from a "folkloric" stage to the mature stage of "culture." Folklore, as he sees it, is a pre-historic or a-historic phenomenon; its manifestations remain static, fully divorced from historical evolution (for example, folk dances, folk songs). Germain sees Québec theatre as part of such a folkloric tradition; it concentrates on certain recurring themes of importance to the group (the family, the role of the mother), but lacks any historical perspective. Germain explains the fact through his own, rather unconventional interpretation of Québec theatre history. He rejects the traditional view, which sees the contemporary theatre of Québec as the product of a line of development which goes from the work of amateur companies and the classical performances in the *collèges classiques* to the impact of professional theatre that came with Father Legault's *Compagnons de Saint Laurent* and the subsequent rise of a number of high quality, professional theatres. Germain has repeatedly, and violently, attacked this view in which the theatre of Quebec is defined as a legacy of the "fils du Père Legault," the "sons of Father Legault." Because of the heavily classical, traditional, and especially French orientation of this entire movement, Germain refuses to accept it as the starting point of a genuine, native art form; in fact, he has referred to the establishment theatre artists working in that tradition disdainfully as "fils à papa," "daddy's boys," implying their colonial ties and lack of independence. According to Germain, the theatre of Québec did not depend on such ties with a foreign tradition; it had been alive and well, all along — albeit relegated to the level of "folklore" and unable to develop beyond the minor genres possible in an oral tradition: monologue, sketch, satirical revue. Germain insists that Québec has had an independent, dynamic theatrical life of its own since the beginning of the nineteenth century. But its manifestations were not considered "respectable," and thus they were never allowed to enter the mainstream of culture.

In the area of dramatic writing, Germain believes that the theatre of Quebec as such begins with Tremblay and Sauvageau (1968); he will admit, however, the importance of the first dramatist of French Canada, Gratien Gélinas, (*Ti-Coq*, 1948), and the subsequent contribution of Marcel Dubé. Even so, Germain insists that the direct line that leads from Gélinas to the nouveau théâtre québécois of the late 1960's connects, not to Gélinas's major plays, but to his satirical revue, *Fridolinades*, a bridge between the older, oral and popular tradition of minor genres and the later, mature and literary drama of Quebec.[9]

Germain's own plays deliberately take up the link with the oral tradition and revue style which he considers his theatrical roots. He describes them variously as "monologueire," "jonglerie," "gigue" — all titles chosen to emphasize their popular, non-literary quality; and he has evolved a special dramatic idiom to capture the exact sound and rhythms of popular language. At the same time, the purpose of his plays is to transcend this obviously anachronistic stage. He achieves this through distancing, telescoping of time elements, satire, and, most importantly, by superimposing a sense of historical perspective on his folkloric situations. His aim is clear:

> le théâtre que je veux faire, c'est celui du passage à l'Histoire [sic]. . . . Je crois que la problématique politique et culturelle du Québec depuis le début du 20ième siècle, c'est qu'il marque le pas, sur place, devant les portes de l'Histoire moderne . . . au théâtre, l'entrée ou l'accession de l'individu, la famille ou la collectivité à l'histoire devient le moteur dramatique le plus puissant[10] (the theatre I would like to create is a theatre which links up with History. . . . I believe that the political and cultural problem of Québec since the beginning of the 20th century lies in the fact that it keeps running on the spot, in front of the doors of modern History . . . in the theatre, entrance or access to history, for the individual, the family, or the community, becomes the most powerful dynamic force).

The most obvious way to achieve "access to history" for a character is through the historical play; Germain feels it is important that the many key figures of Québec history who have been known until now only through legend and oral tradition should be given cultural "status" and made part of a national heritage through dramatic treatment.[11] The historical play, then, forms an essential part of the Germain opus; his two other major themes are, not unexpectedly, the Family and Art.

Germain's dramatic techniques are carefully calculated to serve his particular goals. Although he started out working with collective creation, he did not remain long with this particular technique. Like many other directors, he considered improvisation and collective creation an essential stage in the formation of young Québec actors who had to shake off the "foreign" influences instilled in them at the National Theatre School. In fact, Germain claims credit for having been the first to introduce verbal improvisation into the work of his company, the Enfants de Chénier; previous improvisations had been based on mime only. Germain felt that verbal improvisation was essential in order to restore to the actors the "naturel

du parler" which they had lost through contact with too many French classics.[12]
His first production, *Les Enfants de Chénier dans un grand spectacle d'adieu*, was
entirely based on improvisation; no attempt was made to produce a script at all,
and performances varied greatly from one evening to the next. The second show
already switched to a different system: for *Diguidi, Diguidi, ha, ha, ha!*, improvisation provided a starting point, but Germain soon took over and eventually
produced a complete script. From then on, his productions were all based on
scripted texts — although he always remained very much aware of the potential of
his actors while producing these plays. Germain now rejects collective creation as
a valid long-term technique because he feels that it restricts the scope of productions to the actors' own, often limited experience.[13] It would probably be more
correct to say that Germain himself had very definite ideas of what he wanted to
achieve with his theatre and that he obviously could do so only through concen-
trated, individual creative effort; his personality does not lend itself to the
abnegation of self without which collective creation cannot work successfully. No
doubt he is quite aware of that fact, since he emphatically points out that he never
did share the "mystique de la création collective" of other alternative groups[14] (we
have seen earlier the mystical exaltation expressed, for example, by Raymond
Cloutier of the Grand Cirque Ordinaire). The dramaturgy which he eventually
developed has so far eluded critical analysis (in spite of many learned attempts)
because of its frankly "pataphysical" quality. A disciple of Brecht, Artaud, and
Genet, Germain has produced plays which combine the loose structure and
surface realism of epic theatre, with uninhibited excursions through time and
space. He also puzzles his audience through his use of multiple levels of reality,
while actors assume many different characters and often step out of their roles to
comment on their characters and situations. The spectator is also subjected to a
dizzying array of stage imagery and verbal metaphor. Watching a Germain play is
a total experience, but most of all, it is total entertainment. "Les rois passent, mais
les fous demeurent"[15] is one of the author's favourite mottoes. He fills his stage
with fool figures — most of whom, it turns out, are really remarkably sane viewed
against the background of the truly insane world in which they move. Perhaps the
most useful key to the works of Germain can be found in a statement made by one
of his characters in *A Canadian Play/Une plaie canadienne*: "Le ridicule tue le
respect! C'est ce qui en fait une arme efficace!"[16] ("Ridicule kills reverence! That
is what makes it into such an efficient weapon"). Like Rabelais before him, and
with a similar verve and abundance of expression, Germain uses ridicule to expose
the much-hated myths of a society incapable of reaching nationhood, which he
feels he must propel in that direction by sheer force of wit. Each of his productions
is an attempt at reviving these myths, only to dispose of them once and for all. As
he has said, "Le Théâtre du Même Nom ne ressuscite que mieux enterrer."[17]
("The Theatre du Même Nom resuscitates only the better to bury.")

There can be no question about the immediate impact and historical significance of Germain's contribution to the theatre. As to the inherent merit of the plays as dramatic works, it can be safely said that they will never be considered "great" additions to Canadian theatre literature. But in the context of alternative theatre, such a question has limited relevance: process counts more than product, and the creation of masterpieces is no longer an artistic goal. Germain himself concedes this point, and at the same time sets his work in to a realistic context. His statement in this connection is typical of his overall approach, always a mixture of cynicism, buffoonery, and disarming honesty:

> Ma meilleure pièce est un chef d'oeuvre qu'on a d'abord intitulé MacBeth de Shakespeare, puis, beaucoup plus tard, Ubu Roi de Jarry . . . ayant déjà tout écrit, je passe donc ma vie a créer des oeuvres mineures en joual et à solutionner divers problèmes de théâtre qui ont le grand avantage d' occupper utilement mon temps. . . . Certains verront là une thérapie plutôt qu'un art et ils n'auront pas tout-à-fait tort puisque, après une longue convalescence, je me guéris maintenant des chefs d'oeuvre en écrivant des oeuvres mineures.[18]
> (My best play is a masterpiece which was first called MacBeth, by Shake-speare, and then, much later, Ubu Roi, by Jarry . . . having already written everything, I therefore now spend my life producing minor works in joual and trying to solve certain problems of the theatre, which has the great advantage of giving me something useful to do. . . . Some people may consider this more a therapy than art, and they will not be quite wrong, since, after a long convalescence, I am now curing myself of masterpieces by writing minor works.)

An examination of the plays themselves through a few representative examples should prove that, in spite of certain inherent weaknesses,[19] writing these minor works was certainly worth doing!

It is not easy to select, from among the enormous wealth of Germain's production,[20] a small number of plays to illustrate his themes and techniques. I shall base my choices here on the plays' special relevance to Germain's avowed theatrical mission of "moving from folklore to culture." From within the three major thematic areas of the Germain opus, I shall briefly discuss the early family plays; examine several of the history plays in greater detail; and finally focus on *Les hauts et les bas de la vie d'une diva: Sarah Ménard par eux-mêmes*, on the theme of art and artists in Québec, which, I believe, provides an excellent synthesis of the Germain ideology and of Germain theatrical techniques.

FAMILY PLAYS

With his first independent play, *Diguidi, diguidi, ha, ha, ha!* (1969), Germain followed the contemporary québécois preoccupation with the family, a theme which runs as a major leitmotif through all of the nouveau théâtre québécois and also figures prominently in the alternative theatre of the period. Unlike the partially naturalistic family plays of Dubé or Tremblay, however, Germain's *Diguidi* is fully theatrical, his Mother, Father, and Son archetypal figures involved in the grotesque farce of a family life which has become a caricature of itself. The play ends on a plea for a freer way of life, thus making the transition from a mythical past to a militant present.

The stage set for *Diguidi* consists of three theatre-type arm chairs, marked respectively "Maman," "Papa," and "Gilles"; each one is equipped with a safety belt. The play consists of three parts. In part one, each character introduces himself through a long monologue. It becomes clear that each of the parents is trying to cope with the frustrations of life by escaping into a dream world: the Father waits for Santa Claus, the mother for the day when she will become the lovely Star Fairy. As for Gilles, the son, he has spent most of his childhood outwitting his parents' efforts to get rid of him (the Hansel and Gretel story); but he bears them no grudge and has become a model son. In his second long speech, Gilles reiterates all the home-and-church imposed formulas whose observance defines a dutiful child:

> Bonjour, papa . . . bonjour, maman . . . bonsoir, papa . . . bonsoir, maman . . . bonne nuit, papa . . . bonne nuit, maman . . . si vous plait, papa . . . si vous plait, maman — . . . marci, papa . . . marci, maman . . . J'vous demande pardon, papa . . . J'vous demande pardon, maman. . . . Ch'promets d'ete sage et obéissant avec papa et de ne plus ete impoli avec maman. . . . J'honorerai mon père et ma mère comme moi-même . . . Je confesse à Dieu Tout-Puissant . . . etc. (the entire *confiteor* now follows).[21]
> (Hello, daddy . . . hello, mummy . . . good evening, daddy . . . good evening, mummy . . . good night, daddy . . . good night, mummy . . . please, daddy . . . please, mummy . . . thank you, daddy . . . thank you, mummy. . . . Please forgive me, daddy . . . Please forgive me, mummy. . . . I promise to be good and obedient with daddy and not to be impolite with mummy again. . . . I will honour my father and mother like myself . . . I confess to God . . . etc.)

Having thus humiliated himself before God and his parents, as a good child should, Gilles turns into a dog — an eloquent metaphor for his abject condition. In part two, while scrubbing the floor, the Mother reveals a great deal about her unhappy marriage. The Father returns from the tavern. It is now his turn to change into a dog. As he goes about, barking on all fours, we also hear his side of the marriage story, a typically québécois tale of sexual frustration similar to Léopold's in *Forever Yours, Marie Lou.*

Part three completes the series of confessions, with the Mother now in the role of the dog, telling the story of her unhappy past and revealing the disastrous influence of a domineering parish priest. As she ends her monologue with dog-like howling, Gilles adds to the noise, imitating the sound of bombs exploding and machine-gun fire. This wakes up the Father, who dies from shock — the revenge of the younger generation?

This in itself would be nothing more than a fairly imaginative attempt to translate a social situation into grotesque stage metaphors. Germain adds considerably to the complexity of the play, however, by two devices: one is the Mother's finale, a speech in which she steps out of character and addresses the audience directly, obviously drawing the conclusions from the story enacted earlier. The second device is a framework of theatre-within-the-theatre, which gives the play a more interesting, multi-level structure and also adds the dimension of a satire on actors and acting to what would otherwise be a modest family play. With the addition of these two devices, *Diguidi* becomes genuine theatre of liberation. The Mother's closing speech sums up well the author's intention:

CHUS TANNEE D'PASSER MA VIE A M'EXCUSER. . . . D'accord, on a jamais rien eu. . . . MAIS C'ETAIT-TU UNE RAISON POUR SE TRAIN-ER A QUATE PATTES CA? D'accord, on a jamais rien eu. MAIS C'ETAIT-TU UNE RAISON POUR SE LAISSER MOURIR CA? . . . Moué, j'veux pus mourir . . . j'veux pus, j'veux pus. . . . J'VEUX PUS ATTENDE . . . J'AI PUS L'TEMPS D'ATTENDE . . . J'VEUX ETE LIBBEE . . . J'VEUX ETE LIIIIIIII-BBBBEEEE. . . . (Elle fait un long temps et retire lentement sa bouée de sauvetage) C'est pas facile . . . c'est dur . . . mais je m'en vas essayer . . . m'en vas essayer de l'dire au présent . . . Chus libbe . . . chus libbe . . . chus libbe . . . chus libbe.[22]

As this excerpt shows, Germain's "joual" is really a voice score which suggests to the actor exact sounds and rhythms; it is difficult to read and translations are obviously inadequate, although the basic meaning can be rendered without difficulty:

I'M FED UP WITH SPENDING MY WHOLE LIFE ASKING FOR FOR-GIVENESS. . . . Right, we never had anything. . . . BUT WAS THAT A GOOD ENOUGH REASON TO DRAG OURSELVES AROUND ON ALL FOURS LIKE THAT? . . . all right, we've never had anything. . . . BUT WAS THAT A GOOD ENOUGH REASON TO ALLOW OURSELVES TO DIE? Me, I don't want to die any longer . . . I don't want to, I don't want to. . . . I DON'T WANT TO WAIT ANY LONGER . . . I DON'T HAVE TIME TO WAIT ANY LONGER . . . I WANT TO BE FREE . . . I WANT TO BE FRRRRREEEEE (She makes a long pause, then slowly takes off her safety belt). It isn't easy . . . it's hard . . . but I'm going to try . . . going to try to say it in the present . . . I'm free . . . I'm free . . . I'm free.

In his next two plays, Germain expands his vision from the family unit to the social class — still retaining the metaphor of the family or clan for the larger unit to indicate the tribal level of development. Both *Si les Sanssoucis s'en soucient, ces Sanssoucis-ci s'en soucieront-ils? Bien parler, c'est se respecter!* a typical Germain title, virtually untranslateable except for the second part (*"To speak well is to respect yourself!"*), and *Le Roi des mises à bas prix (The King of the Discount Sales)* centre on the problems of the Sanssouci family, especially Farnand. This son finds himself encumbered with a multitude of possessions he does not need but cannot get rid of. The objects Farnand has inherited represent the cultural heritage of Québec, forced upon the family by outside forces with often disastrous results: there is a kitchen table in particular which inhibits virility, a problem passed down in the clan from father to son. Again, after much satire and clowning (a mock trial in *Les Sanssoucis*, much discussion between Farnand and the "television man" who inhabits his giant t.v. set in *Le Roi des mises à bas prix*), the cycle concludes on a serious note, another clarion call for freedom and an end to colonialism. Farnand:

CH'PEUX PUS SORTIR! Aussitôt que ch'sors, tout'l monde que j'rencontre, me courrent après pour me donner leu tabbe de cuisine. . . . On dirait que chus un aimant . . . j'hérite de toute . . . pis ch'peux pas m'en débarrasser. . . . Si ça continue d'même, y va m'falloir un entrepôt pour toute mette ça. . . . Pis, si ça s'arrête pas . . . y va m'falloir un pays UN PAYS . . . UN PAYS POUR ENTREPOSER LES MEUBBES A FARNAND! (I CAN'T GO OUT ANY LONGER! The minute I go out, everybody I meet runs after me to give me their kitchen table. . . . Looks like I'm some sort of a magnet. . . . I inherit everything . . . then I can't get rid of it any more. . . . If things go on like this, I'll be needing a warehouse to put all that stuff. . . . Then, if it doesn't stop . . . I'll be needing a country A COUNTRY . . . A COUNTRY TO STORE FARNAND'S FURNITURE!)

Farnand concludes his speech with a great outburst of laughter which is intended to transmit itself to the audience whom Germain would like to laugh first — and think later.

THE HISTORY PLAYS

As we have seen, Germain has been obsessed with Québec history since his early student days. He finds it an exasperating subject: "Au Québec, l'histoire et l'humour noir se confondent jusqu'à provoquer chez le chercheur soit la dépression catatonique soit l'émerveillement total."[23] ("In Québec, history and black humour become one to the point of inducing in a scholar either catatonic depression or complete wonder"). Never given to catatonic depression, Germain has obviously chosen the happier path of *émerveillement total*; and in his plays dealing with Québec history, he attempts to convey to the audience this same feeling.

I shall discuss three plays in this context: *Un Pays dont la devise est 'je m'oublie,'* 1976 (*A Country Whose Motto is 'I Forget'*); *A Canadian Play/Une plaie canadienne*, 1978; and, in a lighter vein, *Mamours et Conjugat* (another untranslateable title which contains multiple puns around "amour," "conjugal," and "conjugation").

The title of *Un Pays dont la devise est 'je m'oublie'* is an obvious pun on the official motto of the province of Québec, "Je me souviens," "I remember." The play attempts a demythification of the past, while at the same time impressing on the audience the fact that history does indeed exist for Québec. The episodes of the play are framed by two speeches which together define the theme. At the beginning, one of the two characters, in a long monologue, defines the meaning of identity and independence:

> L'indépendance . . . cé pas jusse là diusque on s'en va . . . cé là diousque'on vient! St'une vieille souvenance! . . . Cé l'futur du passé . . . on héritait toute du même BLANC D'MEMOUERE . . . qui, veux, veux pas, nous donnait un air de famille. . . . ON AVAIT TOUTE OUBLIE LA MEME CHOSE![24] (Independence . . . is not just where you're going . . . it's where you're coming from! It's an old souvenir! . . . It's the future of the past! we've all inherited the same memory blank . . . which, like it or not, made us look like a family. . . . WE HAD ALL FORGOTTEN THE SAME THING!)

And at the end of the play, Louis Cyr points out what had been forgotten: that the people of Québec indeed had a history, a culture, national heroes — all that was necessary to create a country. He ends on a note of hope that someday they will make this great discovery and "become what they already are."[25] Within this thematic framework, Germain develops a loose sequence of episodes in which the major events of the past, and some of the problems of the present, are acted out. Again, he uses the device of a play-within-a-play. The setting is an empty stage, featuring only a huge trunk, marked in large letters "Surprenant et Petitboire, comédiens ambulants." These two wandering actors, "specialists in local history," then act out the various episodes of the play against a background which shows black and white pictures of Canadian history as it is traditionally presented in the school manuals. The purpose, of course, is to make the audience aware of the discrepancy between the interpretation they have always known and the actual facts.

Part one deals with the beginnings of Québec. The first tableau shows a legendary figure, the "Canadien errant" of the folk song, discoursing on the theme of independence. He then changes his costume to become a *coureur de bois*, who comes upon a French explorer, Jacques Cartier, just as the latter is on the point of planting his famous cross. This Cartier, however, is not the idealist usually portrayed by the history books; as he talks to the coureur de bois, he reveals only disappointment and frustration with the land he has discovered: "Au nord, c'est le vide . . . bordé à l'est par l'inconnu . . . à l'ouest, par l'incertain . . . et au sud par une absence! Vacuité des vacuités! Ici tout n'est que vacuité!"[26] ("In the North, it is emptiness . . . bordered in the East by the unknown . . . in the West, by the uncertain . . . and in the South by an absence! Emptiness of emptinesses! Here all is but emptiness!") Surely, Cartier had imagined the Indies differently! The next tableau shifts to the French Intendant, who, in a magnificent trick of chronological telescoping, is shown trying to get Versailles on his long distance phone. He manages to get a connection after a year's efforts, only to be told that the colony is of little interest to the mother country at this point. He is left penniless and unable to pay his soldiers. Versailles even refuses to accept charges for the call. In the third scene, Germain gives his own irreverent version of the French defeat on the Plains of Abraham. He shows Montcalm quite resigned about losing the war; all he is interested in is gaining a place in history by engineering a dramatic death for himself. He is confronted by an outraged habitant who tries to call him back to a sense of responsibility, but he remains unmoved. Solemnly, he asks to be remembered to "the great Charles" who will appear in the fullness of time, and steps out in front of the British muskets. Following the war, the habitants are called to order by their bishops and impressed with the need to submit to British rule. This portion of the play concludes with a "First Epilogue" which demonstrates the logical consequence of the historical events: the habitant has been relegated as a tourist attraction to the elegant Hotel Québec, along with a plastic beaver and similar Canadiana; he has resigned himself to the fact that he has become "du folklore."

Part two brings the play up to the present. It deals with the corruption of the political scene in Québec, a "family affair"; the problems of the Church in the contemporary society; satire of the theatre. Clearly, the implication of Part two is that the difficulties of the present are mainly the result of an unquestioning acceptance of the oppression imposed upon Québec after the Conquest.

The play concludes with the second epilogue, and the more hopeful speech of Louis Cyr quoted earlier: again, the theme of the "pays," or nation, is underlined at the conclusion of the work.

A Canadian Play/Une Plaie canadienne is subtitled "un exorcisme rituel"; it attempts to exorcise the image of French Canada created by the famous statement of Lord Durham that French Canadians are a people "without history and without culture." Germain sets his ritual into the framework of a Masonic meeting. Lord Durham, brought back from the dead for the purpose, is confronted by the Grand Master with the consequence of his report, tried, and executed. The people are represented by the "Veuve (Widow) Saint Jean," a symbol of Quebec. As the play proceeds, Durham first tries to defend his attitudes, but is told by Caron, his accuser that he will have to "expiate" his sins vis-à-vis Canada. To do so, he is made to take on, one after another, the identities of the three political figures who are his spiritual descendants: first Sir Wilfrid Laurier, then Louis Saint Laurent, and finally Pierre Trudeau. In every case, it is clear that his initial misrepresentation has led to disastrous consequences for the people. Eventually Durham himself asks for his execution, a ceremony which concludes the exorcism ritual. As a "decapitated" Durham makes his exit, a red hood over his head, the Veuve Saint Jean entones a triumphant Song of Independence, in which she glorifies "indépendance," "équité" and the revolutionary triad of "liberté, égalité, fraternité." With the ultimate eradication of the image created by the Durham report, the folkloric stage can now make way for a new era of mature nationhood.

Mamours et Conjugat provides a look at the lighter side of Quebec history. Subtitled "Scènes de la vie amoureuse québécoise," it follows the path of bedroom history from the seventeenth century to the present. Although it is a highly entertaining, farcical play, it is perhaps more pessimistic than any of Germain's other works. Its conclusion seems to be "frustration, frustration — there is nothing here but frustration." The first scene, between a *coureur des bois* and a *fille du roi* starts an endless line of confusion and bedroom misery. Ovila, the man, is disappointed that the girl sent to him by the king is not a whore. He cannot remember her name and is quite incapable of "civilized" bedroom behaviour because he had previously lived with an Indian woman who was used to taking initiatives. Héloise puts up with him as best she can, and they resign to a life of quiet desperation.

The next couple belongs to the early nineteenth century. Hector, a patriotic but fearful French Canadian, spends all his time and energy searching for possible British soldiers. He has no idea how to explain his wife's frequent exasperation and attacks of insomnia. Cupid, who pops in and out of all of the scenes, meanwhile explains to the audience that female insomnia is a common malady in British colonies. For the following scene, Germain moves on the priest-ridden Québec countryside of the 1930's. Ephrème, a farmer, joins his wife Dalila in bed. He is hot and excited after having killed a horse. He eventually gets around to demanding some sexual action, only to be told that is impossible, since it happens to be "first Friday." Ephrème, unwilling to restrain himself, suggests Dalila make up for the sin by reciting a prayer during the act. This she agrees to, muttering the words of the *Ave* while he proceeds to a quick penetration. As soon as it is over, she expresses her hope that "after eighteen girls," it will be a boy this time.

The next tableau is set in 1953, and designed to illustrate the double standard of the period. Hérode, a notorious ladies' man, divides women ruthlessly into two classes: "Ouben sont mariabbes. Ouben sont fourabbes." ("Either you can marry them. Or you can make love to them.") When he finally decides to get married, and chooses a virgin, as he must, he finds himself unable to perform with her.

The final scene brings the erotic history up to the late 1960's. The characters, outfits, and language are modelled after Montréal's hippie headquarters, the rue St. Denis, "ca. 1968." The young couple of this scene illustrates the clichés of the period: the boy, named Elvis, is a drug addict and given to Oriental mysticism. His girl friend Chloé does all she can on her side to create a happy relationship: she dyes her hair blonde, dresses in sex shop lingerie, and studies all the best sex manuals. But nothing seems to work. When she tries taking an aphrodisiac, it only puts her to sleep. Eventually, they decide that something is needed — but they cannot imagine what. The scene ends on this question.

In spite of its frivolous theme, this little play represents as serious an indictment of Québec history and the effects of multiple oppression as any of the "straight" history plays Germain has written. It is also a thematic breakthrough. By shifting the emphasis from the couple seen as parents to the couple seen as sexual partners — a new approach in Quebec drama — *Mamours et Conjugat* served to break the persistent taboo against bedroom scenes on the Quebec stage.

DEMYTHIFICATION OF ART AND CULTURE

Demythification of art and "Culture" is one of Germain's central concerns and it is manifest in many of his plays. With the character of Sarah Ménard, he has created an intriguing double parody, partly modelled on Sarah Bernardt, partly on the Québec singer Emma Albani. His play, *Les hauts et les bas d'la vie d'une diva: Sarah Ménard par eux-mêmes* (1976) (*The Ups and Downs Of a Diva's Life: Sarah Ménard by Themselves*) uses the compound character of the diva as a basis for demythification and the investigation of a wide spectrum of issues, from grand opera to women's lib. It is one of Germain's most ambitious plays and possibly his most successful. Because it is essentially a one-character play, its effectiveness on stage depends to a very large extent on the performance of the actress who portrays Sarah.

The theme of Sarah Ménard is set in the Prologue, which takes the audience to the broadcasting room of an FM radio station, "là où, comme on le sait, la culture est si classique que même l'air qu'on y respire est antique" ("where, as everyone knows, culture is so classical that even the air you breathe is antique"). It is fully developed in the second part of the play. While Part one deals with lighter issues such as feminism, Part two concentrates on the problems of foreign vs. national culture and national identity. Grand opera, the most artificial of all genres, here serves as an effective symbol for cultural alienation.

The play is structured in the revue-style with a loosely connected series of episodes. Into this simple structure, however, Germain has built a highly sophisticated multiplicity of levels of reality: the theatre itself with its stage; the stage, set for a show; and Sarah's many different acts within the show. In addition, the actress playing Sarah cuts across all the levels to address the audience directly and to bring them back to the reality of the Théâtre d'Aujourd'hui, where they are seated. There are thus constant reminders of the connection between what is happening on the various levels of the stage performance, and the "real life" experiences of the audience.

Sarah carries the entire show, assisted only by occasional feedback from her accompanist, Tony Panneton, who appears as a caricature of the classical composer; dressed in "a white wig à la Mozart, round glasses à la Schubert, and eighteenth-century costume complete with jabot." His activities, however, situate him very much in the present, as he repeatedly interrupts the proceedings to put through phone calls to his bookmaker. Sarah's first appearance is in the guise of a "diva new look," a satire on the egomania of opera stars. As she sweeps on stage, she rhapsodizes over the near-orgasmic delights of fame and the thrills of being recognized instantly in a crowd. The next scenes, where she appears in an outfit of the 1920's — long, pink silk dress, and feather hat — focus on various aspects of man-woman relationships. The first episode, entitled "le grand blond," tells the story of her discovery of a handsome young man on a beach, her "adoption" of this beautiful specimen as a lover, and his eventual degeneration into overweight sloppiness. She now must get rid of him, since, as she informs the audience, being seen with such a partner has a most undesirable aging effect on a woman. The scene ends musically, with a spoof on the romantic farewell duo of grand opera. This is followed by a solemn discourse on the theme of the *femme fatale* in the rhythms of classical tragedy which culminates in a parody of the "to be or not to be" scene from Hamlet satirically adapted to the quandaries of modern women: "Mata Hari ou Jéhane Bénoit? Voilà la question!"[28] ("Mata Hari or Jéhane Bénoit, that is the question!") This part of the monologue leads up to a vexing paradox: men love to eat, but they insist that their partner be thin. In "L'étiquette des relations sexuelles" ("The etiquette of sexual relationships") Sarah exposes the double standard still applied by men. She tells the audience how it took her three years to lose her virginity because when she admitted her eagerness, men retreated in horror. As soon as she learned that demure behaviour is what is required, being deflowered was no longer a problem. In the next scene Sarah enacts the sexual fantasies of a housewife who takes her notions of *volupté* from television ads.

Part two introduces Sarah in the role of Marlene Dietrich, in a black pantsuit and top hat. Her seductive scene — demanding "fireworks" from Tony — is counterpointed by childhood memories. She sees herself as a Girl Guide who experiences the recurrent nightmare of having to get up early and as her shy teenage alter ego. Following this introduction, the play moves on to its central theme: the indictment of foreign culture which is here represented by grand opera. Sarah now slowly withers into the figure of an old woman. It is in this guise that she comments on the hardships of her past career as an opera singer. In particular, she points out the irrationality of the endless death scenes common to opera. A long series of operatic deaths follows, culminating in a parody of the "great dying aria," sung over and over to the names of famous composers, with ever-increasing speed: "Prestissimo: Rossini, Bellini, Puccini, Mascagni," until she finally collapses. But Germain goes beyond a parody of operatic scenes, and of the famous death scenes performed by Sarah Bernhardt. His Sarah is especially bitter about the fact that she must always perform her dying scenes in a "foreign language" — adding insult to injury. His intentions are unmistakeable when he has her cry out, in undisguised joual, "Pis y-a-tu queque chose de plus trisse que d'agoniser pis d'mouris dans-z-une aute langue?"[29] ("Is there anything sadder than to be in agony and then to die in a foreign language?") As she recovers from her death scene, Sarah makes another acid comment on the foreign culture that is forever imposed upon her: "La culture, moué, ça m'donne le shaque dans e gnoux pis ca mrend asthmatique. Chus pus capabbe de vive avec des morts qui sont plus vivants qu'nou-z-autes!"[30] ("As for me, culture just makes my knees shake, and what's more it gives me asthma. I can't stand living any longer with the dead who are more alive than we ourselves!") Her final accusation sums up the entire anti-establishment argument of the alternative theatre.

The problem of foreign culture brings her on to the subject of identity. For the final scene, the play shifts to an oneiric setting, with Sarah reliving childhood memories of village life, with fiddling, and the dancing of jigs. As she joins in the dance, happy to have found her real roots at last, the stage lights slowly dim. For the printed version, the author has added the following telling stage direction: "Sarah jigue maintenant pour elle-même: dans le noir, la jigue et le piano s'éloignent jusqu'à se perdre dans le silence du pays secret de tous: LA TRADI-TION."[31] ("Sarah now jigs for herself. In the darkness, the jig and the piano grow fainter until they fade into the silence of everyone's secret homeland: the land of Tradition.")

Sarah Ménard, monlogue in the form of grand opera, grand opera in the form of monologue, embodies all of the paradoxes of the Germain opus. The work is also the best illustration of his basic goal: Sarah has overcome folklore to enter the realm of culture; she is now able to return to her roots, and from them she takes strength for a new beginning. She thus becomes symbolic of a whole generation of Quebec artists — the generation for whom Jean-Claude Germain had made it his life's task to speak.

8

Summing Up

In the preceding chapters, I have tried to give a reasonably accurate and balanced overview of alternative theatre in Canada, its evolution and most representative manifestations; a critical evaluation of the phenomenon is now in order. Such an evaluation, however, presents enormous difficulties, not only because of the immediacy and historical closeness of the movement, but also because of the ephemeral nature of many of its productions. The essence of any theatrical performance is ephemeral, of course; but in the case of a movement in the theatre which defines its ultimate goal as process, rather than product, and often relies for its basis of operation on collective creation and improvisation, rather than a scripted text, the traditional difficulties of theatre criticism are increased to a formidable scope.

Nevertheless, it is possible to draw certain conclusions from the preceding study and to make some basic value judgments, which must, of course, remain tentative, rather than apodictic. Unconventional material is best approached in a conventional manner: If Goethe's three questions can be answered adequately, we shall have laid at least the groundwork for an evaluation of the movement.

1. *What has the Canadian alternative theatre set out to do?*
a. As an alternative to the elitist mainstream establishment, alternative theatre has tried to set up a theatre which is genuinely "popular."
b. As an alternative to the internationalistic, masterpiece-oriented policies of the establishment, alternative theatre has tried to focus on local, regional, and national issues.
c. As an alternative to the fail-safe policy of the establishment, alternative theatre has tried to provide young, untried playwrights with facilities for workshopping, experimentation, and eventually public exposure.
Whereas avant-garde movements must by their very nature limit their appeal to

an intellectual and artistic elite, alternative theatre movements everywhere have always emphasized their essentially "popular" nature. While there is no question about the sincerity of such an attitude, it is also equally obvious that alternative theatre productions are often patronized by a highly elitist group of students and other well-educated lovers of experimental art and eschewed by the popular audiences they seek. Nevertheless, the essentially popular thrust of alternative theatre remains undeniable. This thrust manifests itself on many levels, from admission price and theatre space to aesthetics.

Affordability is the first requirement for a "popular" theatre; a principle which was applied as early as the nineteenth century in the *Freie Volksbuehne* movement in Germany. Canadian alternative companies have experimented with free admission (The Toronto Free Theatre, Juliani's PACET experiment; Quebec Street Theatre). While such a radical policy usually proved impossible to maintain, the basic principle of low cost has always been retained, in contrast to the high cost of admission to establishment theatres.

Popular theatre also means doing away with the conventional theatre space and its connotations of bourgeois exclusiveness. When Jim Garrard called his new theatre "Passe-Muraille," the implications were clear: a going beyond the walls which enclose conventional theatre spaces. George Luscombe emphasized the need to bring theatre into areas where theatre had never been seen before, thus creating a new awareness and new audiences among the people. Both Passe-Muraille and The Mummers' Troupe implemented this principle in their sociological shows, moving into communities and creating their shows with and among the people. Savage God productions have taken place, often unannounced and unexpected, among the people of Vancouver, in parks, cafes, shopping malls and other public gathering places. Jeune théâtre companies in Quebec have been especially active in their experimentation with establishing close links between the people within a certain neighbourhood and a company of actors (for example, Le Théâtre de Quartier); and they have performed on street corners, city squares, parks, cafeterias, and even in city buses (La Gang des autobus).

The popular orientation of alternative theatre is also reflected in its aesthetics. Essentially anti-literary, frequently based on collective creation, it uses a simple contemporary idiom and a production style which emphasizes simplicity and stylization — in other words, "poverty, contemporaneity, democratization," as Juliani states in *The Free Theatre*. Many of the alternative theatre companies stress their popular approach in their choice of a name: Le Grand Cirque Ordinaire, The Mummers' Troupe consciously link up with popular forms; Passe-Muraille, Savage God emphasize their rebellion against convention.

Alternative theatre companies tend to have strong roots in their communities; they also consider themselves an important part of the culture-building process within the nation. This double orientation can be seen in their production of political/sociological shows on the one hand and of historical plays on the other.

Sociological shows may remain simple mirror-images of a community, such as Passe-Muraille's *Farm Show*, they may take a more militant stance, such as the productions of the Grand Cirque Ordinaire, or they may become overtly political, as in the case of the majority of the shows of The Mummers' Troupe. Companies with a definite Marxist orientation will move right into areas riddled with labour disputes or strikes and put their production at the service of the embattled workers: this is the case with the agitprop shows of the Théâtre Euh!, or the Théâtre d'la Shop. All of these represent attempts to make the theatre an organic and dynamic part of the community. Unlike mainstream theatre, which stresses the importance of "universality," the alternative theatre creed firmly affirms the need for theatre to be strongly rooted in the *hic et nunc*.

With their particular approach to Canadian history, alternative theatre companies have attempted to create a basis for what they consider is a much-needed culture-building process. Through the dual technique of demythification and mythopoesis, the events and characters of Canadian history are stripped of the false facades built around them by a colonial view and invested with a new sigificance. Jean-Claude Germain has made this culture-building the central core of his work. Generally speaking, Québec alternative theatre, for obvious reasons, shows a greater concern with the need to re-define and reinterpret its national history than do the alternative theatre companies in English-speaking Canada; English Canada, on the other hand, has probably produced some better individual plays in the genre, such as Passe-Muraille's *1837: The Farmers' Revolt,* and *Buffalo Jump*.

As launching pads for new playwrights, groups like Factory Theatre Lab and Passe-Muraille in English Canada must be particularly emphasized. In general, alternative theatre companies stress the importance of creating a showplace for new writers. They further serve as a stimulating agent in bringing to the fore new talent because of their unwillingness to accept the conventional, rigid differentiation between writer, actor, and director. In a setting where each member of the company is a potential producer of scripts, the transition from actor to playwright often occurs quite naturally (examples in point: Ted Johnson, Linda Griffiths, Paule Baillargeon). In this way, alternative theatre companies have made a very serious effort to contribute to the growth of a truly national theatre in Canada.

2. How well was it done?

In their attempts to create "popular" theatre, alternative companies have been largely, though not fully, successful. Certainly, public reaction to the alternative theatre movement was a far cry from Garrard's Brechtian dream of making theatre "as popular as bowling." The brief lifespan of many of the small groups, both English and French, further attests to their failure to establish the kind of close contact with the people which they had aimed and hoped for. On the other hand, the groups I have singled out for more detailed discussion in this book have all done remarkably well in this respect. Passe-Muraille's sociological shows proved immensely popular both in the communities where they were conceived and outside; several of The Mummers' productions, especially *Gros Mourn* and *Company Town*, appealed enormously to the popular audiences they were aimed at; PACET events in Vancouver drew positive reaction from participants from every walk of life; Germain's Théâtre d'Aujourd'hui caters to an audience which is at least partly popular.

In their concern with local, regional, and national issues, alternative theatre companies have obviously had to contend with the usual difficulties of committed, or political, theatre: and occasionally these difficulties have proven beyond their capacities. Many of the québécois agitprop productions have stressed propaganda at the expense of aesthetic considerations. Other companies have fallen to a level of production below acceptable professional standards as a result of their emphasis on the importance of political commitment, rather than professional training, for the members of the company: this is true, for example, in some cases for The Mummers and also for some Women's theatre. Regardless of their occasional weaknesses, however, these alternative theatre companies did manage to create a very real link between theatrical activity and contemporary social issues. The quality of the scripts developed for the purpose can usually be seen in inverse proportion to the immediacy of the propaganda effect desired. Demythification through satire (such as the many French Canadian attacks on the family) is usually quite successful; Germain has created some particularly effective stage metaphors in this area (the dog family in *Diguidi*; the dining table in *Les Sanssouci*). Mythopoesis is a more difficult undertaking — with cultural conceits as with anything else, the dismantling process presents fewer problems than the task of rebuilding. However, several of the history plays produced by the alternative theatre (especially the Passe-Muraille productions mentioned above) and Germain's recreations of Québec history) have certainly achieved their purpose, adequately, if not brilliantly.

In the area of advancing Canadian dramatic literature by providing a spawning ground for new playwrights who would have found no outlet otherwise, the alternative theatre movement has certainly succeeded in what it set out to do. In view of the short period under consideration, the list is impressive. Some, like David French, David Freeman, Carol Bolt, and Jean Barbeau, have moved on to mainstream theatre; others have remained mostly within the confines of the alternative movement. These include George Walker, Rick Salutin, Hershel Hardin, Ken Gass, Hrant Alianak, and André Simard. The list is by no means exhaustive; with each region, young playwrights are at work, trying out their ideas with the help of small alternative theatre companies.

3. *Was it worth the doing?*

Certainly, the question must be answered in the affirmative, in spite of the fact that a large number of the productions of the alternative theatre have, of necessity, been less than professional. For one thing, it has meant educating Canadian audiences to a whole new concept of theatre. Within the evolution of Canadian theatre, the alternative movement has meant a gigantic step forward into a new area of experimentation, a new concept of theatre in keeping with lines of development internationally.

From the point of view of the development of a body of national drama, the alternative theatre movement, despite its largely anti-literary orientation, has also made very significant contributions. It has provided a broad base for experimentation, and out of this broad base, a number of good plays have emerged. Not "great" plays, perhaps, in Eliot's definition of that term, but plays which exhibit a solid craftsmanship, an understanding of the requirements of the stage, and a thoroughly contemporary approach. One hesitates to make a selection, but among the plays discussed here, I would suggest that George Walker's satires, Ken Gass's *The Boy Bishop*, Hershell Hardin's *Esker Mike and His Wife Agiluk*, Rick Salutin's and Carol Bolt's historical plays with Passe-Muraille, and some sociological scripts such as The Mummers' *Company Town* and Passe-Muraille's *The Farm Show* are most likely to enter a permanent repertoire as "good" Canadian plays of the period.

If we look upon theatre as an important instrument in the process of consciousness-raising for the nation, the alternative theatre movement again has made a significant contribution. Set up in conscious opposition to the concept of a Canadian national theatre situated at Stratford and specializing in Shakespearean performances, the alternative theatre movement has managed to convey through its productions a sense of regional and sometimes, national identity. This is particularly true in Québec (where the two concepts of regional and national are seen as one). Jean-Claude Germain's massive output must be evaluated mainly from this point of view. Individually, his plays certainly do not qualify as "great," hardly even as very "good" plays; *in toto*, his work represents an important contribution to the demythification of his society and its reorientation along lines of national consciousness and national pride.

As a cultural phenomenon of the 1970's, alternative theatre will remain an eloquent expression of an ebullient and dynamic period in Canadian history.

Notes

NOTE TO THE PREFACE

1. These authors, both English and French, are dealt with in the forthcoming study *Towards A Canadian Theatre — Patterns of Evolution In The Two Cultures*, by Renate Usmiani and Geraldine Anthony.

NOTES TO CHAPTER ONE

1. "Das Neue, das Andere, liegt heute im Bewusstwerden des Reziprok-Kommunikativen des Theaters," Ulf Birbaumer, *Maske und Kothurn* 33 (1977): Heft 1, p. 62.
2. Gratien Gélinas, "Pour un théâtre national et populaire," appendix to Renate Usmiani, *Gratien Gélinas* (Toronto: Gage, 1976).
3. Cf. Bertold Brecht, *Der Rundfunk als Kommunikationsapparat*, 1932.
4. H. M. Enzensberger, *The Consciousness Industry* (New York: Seabury Press, 1974), p. 113.
5. Schechner, *Public Domain* (New York: Bobbs-Merrill, 1969), p. 157 ff.
6. The following information about the methods used at Toronto Workshop Productions is based on an interview of George Luscombe by Renate Usmiani, 19 November 1980, Toronto.
7. The terms "introspective" and "committed" are used by Martin Esslin in "From the Avant-Garde of the 50's to the Avant-Garde of the 70's," *English Quarterly* 5 (Spring/Summer 1972).
8. Margaret Croyden, *Lunatics, Lovers and Poets: The Contemporary Experimental Theatre* (New York: Dell, 1974), p. xxv.
9. Quoted in Croyden, *Lunatics, Lovers and Poets*, p. 45.
10. André Breton, "First Surrealist Manifesto," in B. F. Dukore, and D. C. Gerould, *Avant-Garde Drama, 1918-1939* (New York: Crowell, 1976), p. 563.
11. Ibid., p. 566.
12. Ibid., pp. 570, 571.
13. Antonin Artaud, *The Theatre and Its Double* (New York: Grove Press, 1958), preface.
14. Ibid., p. 122.
15. Ibid., pp. 30, 31.
16. Ibid., p. 79.
17. Ibid., p. 37.
18. Ibid.
19. Ibid., p. 48.
20. Ibid., p. 92.
21. "Wirtschaft und Politik sind unser Schicksal, und als Resultat beider die Gesellschaft, das Soziale. Und nur dadurch, dass wir diese drei Faktoren anerkennen . . . bringen wir unser Leben in Verbindung mit dem 'Historischen' des 20. Jahrhunderts" (Erwin Piscator, *Das politische Theater* [Hamburg: Rowohlt, 1963], p. 133).
22. "Es handelte sich direkt darum, die grossen zeitgenoessischen Stoffkomplexe auf die Buehne zu bewaeltigen, die Kaempfe um das Petroleum, den Krieg,

die Revolution, die Justiz, das Rassen-
problem, u.s.w." (ibid., p. 9).

23. "Das historische Drama nicht als
Schicksalstragoedie irgend eines
Helden, sondern als das politische
Dokument einer Epoche" (ibid., p.
161).

24. Walter Gropius, quoted in ibid., p. 128:
"Das Ziel dieses Theaters besteht . . . zu
erreichen, dass der Zuschauer mitten in
das szenische Geschehen hineingerissen
wird, seinem Schauplatz raeumlich
zugehoert und ihm nicht hinter den
Vorhang entrinnen kann. Im uebrigen hat
der Architekt eines Theaters die Auf-
gabe, das Buehneninstrument so unper-
soenlich, so fuegsam, und variabel zu
machen dass es den jeweiligen Spielleiter
nirgends festlegt und die verschieden-
artigen kuenstlerischen Auffassungen
sich entwickeln laesst."

25. Cf. Ernst Toller, *Masse Mensch*, in Dukore and Gerould, *Avant-Garde Drama*.

26. Quoted in Introduction to Walter H.
Sokel, *The Writer in Extremis: Expressionism in 20th Century German Literature* (Stanford: Stanford University
Press, 1959).

27. Quoted in ibid., chapter 2.

28. Ibid., Introduction.

29. V. E. Meyerhold, *La rivoluzione teatrale*
(Roma: Editori Riuniti, 1964), p. 37.

30. Alexander Tairoff, *Das Entfesselte Theater* (Potsdam: G. Kiepenheuer, 1927), p.
69.

31. Max Frisch, in an interview with Peter
Ruedi, *Theater Heute* (Juni 1978): p. 53.

32. Gilles Sandier, *Théâtre et Combat* (Paris:
Editions Stock, 1970), p. 9.

33. M. Croyden, *Lunatics, Lovers and
Poets*, p. 79.

34. Julian Beck, quoted in Renfreu Neff, *The
Living Theatre, U.S.A.* (New York:
Bobbs-Merrill, 1970), p. 234.

35. Richard Schechner, *Environmental Theatre*, (New York: Hawthorne Books,
1973), p. 2.

36. Richard Schechner, *Public Domain*,
(New York: Bobbs-Merrill, 1969), p.
157 ff.

NOTES TO CHAPTER TWO

1. David A. Hogg, quoted in Sandra
Souchotte, "Canada's Workers' Theatre," *Canadian Theatre Review* 9 (Winter 1976): 170.

2. The authors were Oscar Ryan; E. Cecil-
Smith; H. Francis, and Mildred Gold-
berg.

3. Herman Voaden, "What is Wrong with
Canadian Theatre?", Toronto *Globe*, 22
June 1929.

4. Roy Mitchell, *Creative Theatre* (New
York: Kindle Press, 1969), p. 124 ff.

5. Quoted in Gilbert David, "Notes dures
sur un théâtre mou," *Etudes françaises*
11:2 (mai 1975).

6. Don Rubin, "John Juliani's Savage
God," *Theatre Quarterly* 5
(1975–1976): 152.

7. Jean-Claude Germain, "C'est pas
Mozart, c'est le Shakespeare québécois
qu'on assassine," reprinted in *Jeu* 7
(hiver 1978).

8. Ken Gass, *Prelude*, programme notes for
the 1971/72 season of Factory Theatre
Lab.

9. Jim Garrard, quoted in Robert Wallace,
"Growing Pains: Toronto Theatre in the
70's" *Canadian Literature* 85 (summer
1980).

10. John Juliani, *The Free Theatre*, 1972
(unpublished).

11. John Palmer, *Henrik Ibsen: On the Necessity of Producing Norwegian Theatre*
(Toronto: Playwrights Co-op, 1976).

12. George Ryga, "Theatre in Canada: A
Viewpoint on Its Development and Future," *Canadian Theatre Review* 1 (Winter 1974), p. 28 ff.

13. Black Theatre Canada, Creation 2, Fac-
tory Theatre Lab, Global Village The-
atre, Homemade Theatre Company, The
NDWT Company, New Theatre, Open
Circle Theatre, The Performing Theatre
Company, Redlight Theatre (Women's
Theatre), Smile Company, Theatre Foun-
tainhead, Theatre in the Dell, Theatre
Passe-Muraille, Theatre Plus, Theatre
Second Floor, Toronto Free Theatre,
Toronto Workshop Productions, Upstairs
at Old Angelo's.

14. Ken Gass, "Toronto's Alternates: Changing Realities," *Canadian Theatre Review* 21 (Winter 1979): 130.

15. George Luscombe, in an interview with Renate Usmiani, Toronto, 19 November 1980.

16. George Luscombe, Toronto Workshop Productions European Tour Folder, 1976.

17. All quotes in this section are based on the interview, cf. n. 15 above.

18. For example, his use of the famous Goethe lyrics "Ueber allen Gipfeln ist Ruh" in his poem "Das Lied vom Hauch."

19. Connie Brissenden, ed., *The Factory Lab Anthology* (Vancouver: Talonbooks, 1974).

20. Ken Gass, Introduction to *The Factory Lab Anthology*, p. 7.

21. Herschel Hardin, *Esker Mike and His Wife Agiluk* (Vancouver: Talonbooks, 1973), p. 5.

22. Produced at *Factory Theatre Lab* April-

May 1976; published in *Canadian Theatre Review* 11 (summer 1976).

23. *Canadian Theatre Review* 11 (summer 1976): 123ff.

24. *The Boy Bishop*, ibid., p. 85.

25. Gass, Introduction, *Factory Lab Anthology*, p. 8.

26. George Walker, *The Prince of Naples*. First produced at the *Factory Theatre Lab* July 1971; (Toronto: Playwrights Co-op, 1971).

27. Ibid., p. 5.

28. Ibid., p. 11.

29. Ibid., p. 37.

30. Ibid., p. 48.

31. Published by Playwrights Co-op (Toronto, 1972).

32. Bill Greenland, "We Three, You and I," *Factory Lab Anthology*, p. 22.

33. Ken Gass, Introduction to "Strawberry Fields," *Factory Lab Anthology*, p. 10.

34. Sandra Souchotte, "Toronto Free Theatre," *Canadian Theatre Review* 14 (Spring 1977).

35. Quoted in ibid., p. 36.

NOTES TO CHAPTER THREE

1. Jim Garrard, quoted in Robert Wallace, "Growing Pains: Toronto Theatre in the 70's," *Canadian Literature* 85 (Summer 1980): 76.

2. Ibid., p. 77.

3. Roger Planchon, quoted in Michel Corvin, *Le nouveau théâtre en France* (Paris: PUF, 1974).

4. Paul Thompson, quoted in Urjo Kareda, "Theatre Passe-Muraille," 1977 *Stratford Festival Information Brochure*, p. 5.

5. Quoted in Kareda, *Stratford Information Brochure*.

6. Paul Thompson, quoted in Toronto *Globe and Mail*, 6 November 1972.

7. Paul Thompson, quoted in Robert Wallace, "Growing Pains," p. 77.

8. Cf. chapter on Chris Brookes and The Mummers' Troupe.

9. In an interview with Renate Usmiani, 20 November 1980.

10. Ibid.

11. Gary Geddes, in an interview with Renate Usmiani, 27 November 1980, Montreal, referring to his experience

with *Passe-Muraille* and *Les Maudits Anglais*.

12. Rick Salutin, in an interview with Renate Usmiani, 18 November 1980, Toronto.

13. Coach House Press, Toronto.

14. Paul Thompson, Introduction to Theatre Passe-Muraille, *I Love You, Baby Blue* (Toronto: Press Porcépic, 1977), p. 2.

15. Ibid., p. 75.

16. Described in the Introduction to Rudy Wiebe and Passe-Muraille, *Far As The Eye Can See* (Edmonton: NeWest Press, 1977).

17. Rick Salutin and Theatre Passe-Muraille, *1837: The Farmers' Revolt* (Toronto: Lorimer, 1976).

18. Ibid., p. 19ff.

19. Ibid., p. 31ff.

20. Carol Bolt and Passe-Muraille, *Buffalo Jump* (Toronto: Playwrights Co-op, 1976), p. 8.

21. Ibid., p. 42.

22. *Toronto Star*, 17 October 1974.

23. Linda Griffiths with Paul Thompson,

Maggie and Pierre, Vancouver: Talonbooks, 1980.
24. Ibid., p. 19.
25. Ibid.

26. Ibid., p. 66.
27. *Tantrums; Western; The Violinist and the Flower Girl; Brandy; Noah's Kiosk; Christmas; Night; The Blues.*

NOTES TO CHAPTER FOUR

1. Author of three nationwide hits *"Eighteen Wheels," Billy Bishop Goes To War,"* and *"Rock and Roll."*
2. Quoted in Malcolm Page, "Report on the Vancouver Fringe," *Canadian Theatre Review 7* (1975): 125.
3. This and other information not otherwise documented is based on interviews and informal discussion with Ed Astley and other members of the Tamahnous Theatre Company, 27–29 January 1981, Vancouver.
4. Published in *Vancouver Province*, August 1973.
5. James Barber, in *Vancouver Province*, May 1971.
6. Christopher Dafoe, Vancouver *Sun*, June 1971.
7. Christopher Dafoe, Vancouver *Sun*, 2 December 1971.
8. All quotations from Tamahnous productions are based on unpublished typescripts made available to the author by

Tamahnous Theatre and/or Jeremy Long.
9. Quoted by Wayne Edmonstone, *Vancouver Sun*, 9 April 1980.
10. In an interview with Christopher Dafoe, *Vancouver Sun*, 9 January 1970.
11. Views expressed in an interview with the author, 4 February 1981, Edmonton.
12. Cf. the discussion of Schechner's work, chapter 1.
13. Dafoe interview, n. 10 above.
14. Programme Notes to *Arrabalesques*, Simon Fraser University, 1969.
15. E.g., Nathan Cohen, in Toronto *Daily Star.*
16. John Juliani, *The Free Theatre*, unpublished manuscript, 1972; all quotations based on this manuscript, made available to the author by John Juliani.
17. "A Philosophical Blueprint for PEAK," 14 July 1974; made available to the author by John Juliani.
18. Ibid.

NOTES TO CHAPTER FIVE

1. Chris Brookes, quoted in John Fraser, "Those Mummers of Newfoundland Just Won't Keep Their Traps Shut," Toronto *Globe and Mail* 18 October 1975.
2. Chris Brookes, in an interview with Renate Usmiani, 2 January 1981, St. John's.
3. Chris Brookes, *The Newfoundland Herald, T. V. Week*, 14 December 1977.
4. For a detailed, scholarly discussion on the Mummers Play, see E. K. Chambers, *The Medieval Stage* (Oxford: Clarendon Press, 1903), Book II, Chapter 10.
5. CBC Radio review, September 1977; in Mummers' Troupe archives, St. John's, Newfoundland.
6. Quoted in Audrey M. Ashley, "Politics

or Theatre?", *Ottawa Citizen* 1 May 1976.
7. Chris Brookes, "Useful Theatre in Sally's Cove," *This Magazine* 8 (June 1974).
8. John Fraser, quoted in "Critic Says Mummers' Troupe Weakest in Political Humour," *St. John's Evening Telegram* 30 April 1976.
9. Cf. Audrey M. Ashley, n. 6 above.
10. Michael Cook, "Buchans — A Mining Town," *St. John's Evening Telegram* 16 September 1974.
11. These views expressed in an interview with Renate Usmiani, 2 January 1981, St. John's.

12. Brookes, "Useful Theatre in Sally's Cove."
13. Typescript, Research Foundation for the Arts, Petty Harbour, Newfoundland.
14. All quotations from this play based on above.
15. Quotations based on typescript, made available to the author by Chris Brookes.
16. Michael Cook, *St. John's Evening Telegram* 16 January 1975.
17. S. Heindsmann in *Mayday* 1.
18. "Buchans — A Mining Town." Typescript, Research Foundation for the Arts, Petty Harbour, Newfoundland, p. 21ff.
19. Ibid., p. 41ff.
20. Ibid., p. 53.
21. William MacVicar, "Company Town," Toronto *Globe and Mail*, 1975.
22. All quotations from this play based on typescript made available to the author by Chris Brookes.
23. Jamie Portman, "Troupe Bashes Away at Seal Hunt Foes," *The Gazette* 3 March, 1978.

NOTES TO CHAPTER SIX

1. Claude Des Landes, "Remise en cause de l'auteur," *Jeu* 8 (printemps 1978): 3.
2. Jacques Vezina, "Il faut appeller un chat un chat," *Jeune Théâtre* 2 (1974): 1.
3. André Paradis, quoted in "1969–1974: Régionalisation/Identité/Implication," *Jeune Théâtre* 1 (1974): 4.
4. Ibid., p. 10.
5. Claude Gauvreau's 1970 statement is typical: "Moi, j'ai la certitude inébranlable qu'un object de création collective de l'espèce la plus forte possible est tout-à-fait incapable de s'avérer vraiment concurrentiel par rapport à un objet de création personelle de l'espèce la plus forte possible. La plus haute qualité créatrice réside encore dans le cerveau unique." "Réflexions d'un dramaturge débutant," *Jeu* 7 (hiver 1978). ("I am absolutely certain that a product of collective creation, of the best possible kind, cannot be truly competitive with a product of personal creation of the best possible kind. The highest creative power still resides in the individual brain.")
6. Robert Claing, interviewed by Claude Des Landes, *Jeu* 8 (1978): 43.
7. Marc Doré, "Quitter l'improvisation pour l'écriture," *Le Devoir*, 3 novembre 1979.
8. Memorandum addressed to the Minister for Cultural Affairs, M. Jean-Paul L'Allier, September 1976; typescript, made available to the author by the Centre d'essai.
9. *Jeune Théâtre*, 1 (1974).
10. Published in *Jeu* 7 (hiver 1978). Author's translation.
11. "S'organiser ou se faire organiser," *Jeune Théâtre* 1 (1974): 12.
12. In the Montreal daily *Le Devoir*, between July and September 1971.
13. Reprinted in *Jeu* 7 (hiver 1978): 44–50.
14. Quoted in "Manifeste pour un théâtre au service du peuple," *Jeu* 7 (hiver 1978): 83–88.
15. Michel Tremblay's *Les Belles-Soeurs*, 1968; Sauvageau's *Wouf Wouf*, 1969.
16. Jacques Marchand, "Raymond Cloutier du Grand Cirque Ordinaire à Riel," *Le Devoir*, 14 avril 1979, p. 29.
17. Raymond Cloutier, in a letter to Albert Millaire, quoted in *Jeu* 5 (printemps 1977): 34.
18. Paule Baillargeon, "Entretien," *Stratégie* 9 (été 1974).
19. *Jeu* 5 (printemps 1977): 41.
20. Jean-Cléo Godin, "La tragédie américaine de l'enfant prodigue," *Jeu* 5 (printemps 1977): 75.
21. Ibid., p. 77.
22. Ibid., p. 78.
23. Cf. "Orientations et mutations du Théâtre Euh!" *Jeu* 3 (été-automne 1976): 17.
24. Cf. Desrochers, Cazelais, et al., "Théâtre québecois et théâtre au Québec," *Jeune Théâtre* 1 (mai-juin 1972).
25. Ibid., p. 13.
26. Quoted in "Orientations et mutations du Théâtre Euh!", *Jeu* 3 (été-automne 1976).
27. "On se forme et on s'informe," *Jeune Théâtre* (janvier–février 1973): 22.
28. Pol Pelletier, co-founder of the Théâtre Experimental des Femmes "Contre la vi-

olence faite aux femmes," *Le Devoir*, 21
juillet 1979.
29. Editions remue-ménage, Montreal.
30. Published in *Moman travaille pas, a trop*

d'ouvrage (Montreal: Editions remue-
ménage, 1975).
31. Ibid., p. 7.
32. Ibid., p. 78.

NOTES TO CHAPTER SEVEN

1. Jean-Claude Germain, *A Canadian Play/
   Une plaie canadienne*, typescript, made
   available to the author by Jean-Claude
   Germain.
2. Jean-Claude Germain, *Si les Sanssoucis
   . . .* (Montréal: Leméac, 1972), p. 107.
3. In the postscript to *Sarah Ménard*,
   (Montreal: VLB, 1976), p. 143.
4. Pataphysics — a nonsense philosophical
   system proclaimed by Alfred Jarry and
   defined in his posthumous novel, *Gestes
   et opinions du docteur Faustroll* as "the
   science of imaginary solutions, which
   symbolically attributes the properties of
   objects, described by their virtuality, to
   their lineaments." In 1949, a *collège de
   pataphysique* was founded by Jarry ad-
   mirers.
5. Gilbert David, "Jean-Claude Germain
   au Théâtre d'Aujourd'hui," *Jeu* 13 (automne 1979): 6.
6. Cf. Interview in *Voix et Images* 6 (hiver
   1980): 170.
7. Laurent Mailhot, "Jean-Claude Germain, critique," *Jeu* 13 (automne 1979):
   93.
8. Cf. Interview in *Voix et Images 6
   (hiver 1980): 180.*
9. These views expressed in discussion with
   the author, Montreal, November 1980.
10. Jean-Claude Germain, interviewed in
    Voix et Images 6 (hiver 1980): 172.
11. Based on interview with the author,
    November 1980.

12. Ibid.
13. Ibid.
14. Ibid.
15. Jean-Claude Germain, interviewed in
    Jeu 9 (automne 1979): 78.
16. M. Caron, in *A Canadian Play/Une plaie
    canadienne*, typescript, p. 19.
17. Jean-Claude Germain, quoted in *Ar-
    chives des Lettres Canadiennes-fran-
    çaises*, vol. 5; *Le théâtre canadien-
    français* (Montreal: Fides, 1972), p.
    331.
18. Ibid., p. 798.
19. A major problem: Germain's idiosyncra-
    tic transcription of *joual*, difficult to read
    and hard to translate.
20. For complete list of titles, see bibliogra-
    phy.
21. Jean-Claude Germain, *Diguidi, diguidi,
    ha, ha, ha!* (Montreal: Leméac, 1972), p.
    48.
22. Ibid., pp. 91, 92.
23. Postscript to *Les hauts et les bas d'la vie
    d'une diva: Sarah Ménard par eux-
    mêmes* (Montreal: VLB, 1976), p. 143.
24. Jean-Claude Germain, *Un Pays dont la
    devise est je m'oublie* (Montreal: VLB,
    1976).
25. Ibid., p. 22.
26. Ibid., p. 51.
27. 1847-1930.
28. Sarah Ménard, p. 62.
29. Ibid., p. 123.
30. Ibid., p. 133.
31. Ibid., p. 142.

Bibliography

SECONDARY MATERIAL, GENERAL (BOOKS)

Artaud, Antoine. *The Theater and Its Double*. New York: Grove Press, 1958.
Brecht, Bertold *Schriften zum Theater*. Suhrkamp, 1963.
Corvin, Michel. *Le nouveau théâtre en France*. Paris: PUF, 1974.
Croyden, Margaret. *Lunatics, Lovers and Poets*. The Contemporary Experimental Theatre. N.Y.: Dell, 1974.
Davis, R. G. *The San Francisco Mime Troupe*. Palo Alto: Ramparts Press, 1974.
Dort, Bernard. *Théâtre Réel. Essais de critique, 1967–1970*. Paris: Editions Seuil, 1971.
Dukore, B. F., and Gerould, D. C. *Avantgarde Drama, 1918–1939. A Casebook*. New York: Crowell, 1976.
Enzensberger, Hans Magnus. *The Consciousness Industry*. N.Y.: Seabury Press 1974.
———. *Baukasten zu einer Theorie der Medien*. Berlin: Kursbuchverlag, 1971.
Fo, Dario, *Le Commedie di Dario Fo*. Torino: Einaudi, 1966.
Franzen, Erich. *Formen des modernen Dramas*. Muenchen, 1961.
Gerould, Daniel, ed. *20th Century Avant-Garde Drama*. Ithaca: Cornell University Press, 1977.
Melchinger, Siegfried. *Geschichte des politischen Theaters*. Friedrich Verlag, 1971.
Meyerhold, V. E. *La rivoluzione teatrale*. Roma: Editori riuniti, 1962.
Neff, Renfreu. *The Living Theatre, U.S.A.* N.Y.: Bobbs-Merrill, 1970.
Pasolli, Robert, *A Book On The Open Theatre*. N.Y.: Bobbs-Merrill, 1970.
Piscator, Erwin, *Das politische Theater*. Hamburg: Rowohlt, 1963.
Sandier, Gilles. *Théâtre et Combat*. Paris: Editions Stock, 1970.
Schechner, Richard. *Environmental Theatre*. N.Y.: Hawthorne Bks., 1973.
———. *Public Domain*. N.Y.: Bobbs-Merrill, 1969.
Sokel, Walter H. *The Writer in Extremis. Expressionism in 20th Century Germany*. Stanford: Stanford University Press, 1959.
———. *An Anthology of German Expressionist Drama*, New York: Doubleday, 1962.
Tairoff, Alexander. *Das entfesselte Theater*. Potsdam: Kiepenheuer, 1927.
Trotsky, Leon. *Literature and Revolution*. Ann Arbor: University of Michigan Press, 1960.

SECONDARY MATERIAL, GENERAL (Articles)

Billeter, Erika. "The Living Theatre. Paradise Now." *Bentelikunstreport*, Bern, 1968.
Birbaumer, Ulf. "Alternatives Theater — eine kulturpolitische Alternative?" *Maske und Kothurn* 33 (1977): Heft 1.
Demers, Maurice, and Moreau, André. "Théâtre d'environnement." *Jeu* 7 (hiver 1978).
Dérôme, Gilles. "De la sous, de l'infra, et de la contre-culture." *Jeu* 7 (hiver 1978).
Esslin, Martin. "From the Avant-Garde of the 50's to the Avant-Garde of the 70's." *English Quarterly* 5 (Spring/Summer 1972).
Mnouchkine, Ariane. Quoted in "Entretien avec Ariane Mnouchkine: l'itinéraire d'une troupe." *Etudes Françaises* 15 (avril 1978)
Rubin, Don. "Notes on the Avant-Garde." *Canadian Theatre Review* 14 (Spring 1977).
Rubin, Don. "Abroad." CTR I (Winter 1974).

Sang-Kyong, Lee. "Auswirkungen des Noh auf das europaeische Theater." *Maske und Kothurn* 22 (1976): Heft 3-4.
Schechner, Richard. "Postmodern Performance — The End of Humanism." *Performing Arts Journal* 11, IV, vol. 1-2 (1979).
Servin, Micheline. "France; la tradition éclate." *Jeu* 8 (printemps 1978).

SECONDARY MATERIAL, CANADIAN (Books)
ENGLISH CANADA

Mitchell, Roy. *Creative Theatre*. N.Y.: John Day, 1929: N.Y.: Kindle Press, 1969.
Rubin, Don, ed. *Canada On Stage*. 1974, 1975.
———. *Canadian Theatre Yearbook*. 1975–1982.

QUEBEC

Belair, Michel. *Le nouveau théâtre québécois*. Montréal: Leméac, 1973.
———. *Ecrivains québécois de nouvelle culture*. Montréal: Ministère des affaires culturelles, 1975.
Gobin, Pierre. *Le fou et ses doubles*. Montréal: Presses de l'université de Montréal, 1978.
Sigouin, Gérald. *Théâtre en lutte: le Théâtre Euh!* Montréal: VLB, 1982.

SECONDARY MATERIAL, ENGLISH CANADA (Articles)

Ashley, Audrey. "Politics or Theatre?" *Ottawa Citizen*, 1 May 1976.
Bell, Wade. "A Savage God Summer." *Canadian Theatre Review* 17 (Winter 1978).
Bessai, Diane. "For Christians Only: The Horseburgh Scandal." *Canadian Drama* 3 (Fall 1977).
———. "Documentary Theatre in Canada: An Investigation into Questions and Backgrounds." *Canadian Drama* 6 (Spring 1980).
Brookes, Chris. "Useful Theatre in Sally's Cove." *This Magazine* 8 (June 1974).
Cook, Michael. "Company Town." *St. John's Evening Telegram*, 16 January 1975.
Dafoe, Christopher. "New Spark In An Old Drama: Bacchae Presented As Powerful Blast of Ritual Drama." *Vancouver Sun*, 2 December 1971.
Filewood, Alan. "Alberta's Populist Alternative." *Canadian Theatre Review* 20 (Fall 1978).
Fraser, John. "Those Mummers of Newfoundland Just Won't Keep Their Traps Shut." Toronto *Globe and Mail*, 18 October 1975.
Gass, Ken. "Toronto's Alternatives: Changing Realities." *Canadian Theatre Review* 21 (Winter 1979).
Heindsmann, Sandra. "Company Town. The Story of Buchans, Newfoundland." *Mayday* 1.
Johnson, Chris. "The Farm Show." *Canadian Literature* 85 (Summer 1980).
Kareda, Urjo. "Theatre Passe-Muraille," *Stratford Festival 1977 Information Brochure*.
Lamb, Jamie. "Pro-Sealer Troupe Scores More Hits Than Misses." *Vancouver Sun*, 22 March 1978.
Page, Malcolm. "The Vancouver Fringe." *Canadian Theatre Review* 7 (1975).
Plaskin, Robert. "Hitting the High (and Low) Notes of Nfld. Oil." *Maclean's*, 29 October, 1979.
Portman, Jamie. "Troupe Bashes Away at Sealhunt Foes." *The Gazette*, 3 March 1978.
Rubin, Don. "Creeping towards a Culture: The Theatre in English Canada Since 1945." *CTR* 1 (Winter 1974).
———. "John Juliani's Savage God." *Theatre Quarterly* 5 (December 1975/February 1976).
Scott, Andrew. "Tamahnous Theatre Gets Personal with Infectuous New Play." *Georgia Straight*, 6 January 1979.
Souchotte, Sandra. "The Workers' Theatre." *Canadian Theatre Review* 9 and 10 (Winter/Spring 1976).

————. "How Many Newfies Does It Take to Get a Laugh?" *Maclean's*, 17 May 1976.

————. "Toronto Free Theatre." *Canadian Theatre Review* 14 (Spring 1977).

Wallace, Robert. "Growing Pains: Toronto Theatre in the 70's." *Canadian Literature* 85 (Summer 1980).

Wyman, Max. "Clown of God, A Bewildered Pawn." *Vancouver Sun*, 7 July 1972.

————. "Crossland Cuts Deeply in Play Seeking Truth." *The Express*, 6 April 1979.

SECONDARY MATERIAL, CANADIAN — QUEBEC (Articles)

Andres, Bernard, and Lacroix, Yves. "Jean-Claude Germain au Théâtre d'Aujourd'hui." *Voix et Images* 6 (hiver 1980).

Anon. "Le Centre d'essai se porte bien." *Jeune Théâtre* (Janvier-Fevrier 1973).

Anon. "1969–1974: Régionalisation/Identité/Implication." *Jeune Théâtre* 1 (1974).

Anon. "Théâtre populaire et théâtre militant." *Jeune Théâtre* 4 (1974).

Beauchamp, Hélène. "Le Jeune Théâtre." *Jeu* 8 (printemps 1978): 79ff.

Beaudry, Jean. "L'Implication et la création collective." *Jeune Théâtre* 3 (1974).

Bonneville, Lise. "Le Voyage Immobile/Les Enfants du Paradis." *Jeu* 11 (printemps 1979).

Cloutier, Raymond. "Le Grand Cirque Ordinaire: réflexions sur une expérience." *Etudes françaises* 15 (avril 1979).

Cunningham, Joyce, and Lefèbvre, Paul. "Acteurs: La ligue nationale d'improvisation." *Jeu* 11 (printemps 1979).

Dassylva, Martial. "Parminou ou la déconcentration dans la décontraction." *Le Devoir*, 12 février 1977.

————. "Un Théâtre nouveau pour en arriver à une société égalitaire." *La Presse*, 10 février 1977.

David, Gilbert. "Notes dures sur un théâtre mou." *Etudes françaises* 11 (mai 1975).

————. "Jeune Scénographie québécoise: lieux communs?" *Jeu* 10 (hiver 1979).

————. "L'Autre théâtre français au Québec." *Jeu* 12 (été 1979).

————. "Jean-Claude Germain (au Théâtre d') Aujourd'hui." *Jeu* 13 (automne 1979).

————. "Pratique/théorie: petit traité des vases communicants." *Jeu* 7 (hiver 1978).

Des Landes, Claude. "Remise en cause de l'auteur." *Jeu* 8 (printemps 1978).

Doré, Marc. Interviewed by Ginette-Julie Stanton, "Quitter l'improvisation pour l'écriture." *Le Devoir*, 3 novembre 1979.

Dufresne, Michel. "L'Art de masse n'existe pas." *Revue d'Esthétique* 3/4 (1974).

Gauvin, Lise. "Vers une typologie théâtrale." *Etudes françaises* 15 (avril 1979).

Germain, Jean-Claude. "C'est pas Mozart, c'est le Shakespeare québécois qu'on assassine." *Jeu* 7 (hiver 1978).

————. "Un Théâtre d'aujourd'hui." *Jeu* 9 (automne 1978).

Gobin, Pierre. "La Sottie (sic) démultipliée." *Voix et Images* 6 (hiver 1980).

Godin, Jean-Cléo. "Noces: l'Eskabel." *Jeu* 20 (1981).

————. "La tragédie américaine de l'enfant prodigue." *Jeu* 5 (1977).

Gruslin, Adrien. "Le Parminou: de la comédie politique pour un théâtre populaire." *Le Devoir*, 5 novembre 1977.

Gruslin, Adrien. "Le Théâtre de Quartier; informer tout en faisant rire." *Le Devoir*, 3 juin 1978.

————. "La grande Réplique." *Le Devoir*, 21 octobre 1978.

————. "Le Théâtre d'Aujourd'hui: dix ans de création." *Le Devoir*, 11 novembre 1978.

————. "Le Rire contre la bêtise: Jean-Claude Germain." *Le Devoir*, 8 avril 1978.

Larue-Langlois, Jacques. "Le Parminou: le théâtre de la société." *Le Devoir*, 18 octobre 1980.

————. "Gilbert Lepage et les Pichous." *Le Devoir*, 26 avril 1980.

————. "Le Théâtre de la grande réplique." *Le Devoir*, 8 mars 1980.

————. "L'Eskabel, un laboratoire de théâtre loin des modes." *Le Devoir*, 10 mai 1980.

Mailhot, Laurent, "Jean-Claude Germain, critique." *Jeu* 13 (automne 1979).

————. "T'es pas tannée, Jeanne d'Arc." *Jeu* 5 (printemps 1977).

Trudel, Clément, "O Travail: pourquoi s'échiner." *Le Devoir*, 17 février 1979.

Vaïs, Michel. "Un Théâtre qui s'écrit." *Jeu* 21 (1981).

Vézina, Jacques. "Il faut appeller un chat un chat." *Jeune Théâtre* 2 (1974).
Villemaire, Yolande. "Un Prince, mon jour viendra," *Jeu* 5 (printemps 1974).
Villemure, Fernand. "Aspects de la création collective au Québec." *Jeu* 4 (hiver 1977).

ORIGINAL WORKS, ENGLISH-CANADA

Alianak, Hrant. *Western.* Toronto: Playwrights Co-op, 1972.
———. *Brandy.* Toronto: Playwrights Co-op, 1973.
Bolt, Carol, and Theatre Passe-Muraille, *Buffalo Jump.* Toronto: Playwrights Co-op, 1976.
Brissenden, Connie, ed. *The Factory Lab Anthology.* Vancouver: Talonbooks, 1974.
Gass, Ken. *The Boy Bishop. Canadian Theatre Review* 11 (Summer 1976).
Griffiths, Linda (with Paul Thompson). *Maggie and Pierre.* Vancouver: Talonbooks, 1980.
Hardin, Herschel. *Esker Mike and His Wife Agiluk.* Vancouver: Talonbooks, 1973.
Palmer, John. *Henrik Ibsen: On the Importance of Producing Norwegian Drama.* Toronto: Playwrights Co-op, 1976.
Salutin, Rick. *1837: The Farmers' Revolt. Canadian Theatre Review* 6 (Spring 1975).
———. *Les Canadiens.* Vancouver: Talonbooks, 1977.
Theatre Passe-Muraille (script prepared by Ted Johns). *The Farm Show.* Toronto: Coach House Press, 1976.
Theatre Passe-Muraille. *I Love You, Baby Blue.* Toronto: Press Porcépic, 1977.
25th Street House Theatre, Saskatoon. *Paper Wheat. Canadian Theatre Review* 17 (Winter 1978).
Walker, George. *The Prince of Naples.* Toronto: Playwrights Co-op, 1971.
Wiebe, Rudy, and Theatre Passe-Muraille. *Far As the Eye Can See.* Edmonton: NeWest Press, 1977.

ORIGINAL WORKS — QUEBEC

Bissonnette, Danielle, Munger Léo, Vallée Manon. *Le Fleuve au coeur.* Montréal: Leméac, 1982.
Germain, Jean-Claude. *Diguidi, Diguidi, Ha, Ha, Ha!* Montréal: Leméac, 1972.
———. *Le Roi des Mises à bas prix.* Montréal: Leméac, 1972.
———. *Les Hauts et les bas de la vie d'une diva.* Montréal: VLB, 1976.
———. *Un Pays dont la devise est je m'oublie,* Montréal: VLB, 1976.
———. *L'Ecole des rêves.* Montréal: VLB, 1979.
———. *Les faux Brillants.* Montréal: VLB, 1977.
———. *Mamours et conjugat.* Montréal: VLB, 1979.
Les Femmes de Thetford Mines. *Si Cendrillon pouvait mourir!* Ottawa: Editions du remue-ménage, 1980.
Théâtre des Cuisines. *Moman travaille pas, a trop d'ouvrage.* Montréal: Editions du remue-ménage, 1975.

Index